FIRED!

The Outrageously Ridiculous Adventures of Scotty J. Fahrenheit

CAROLANNE PORTO

Fired: The Outrageously Ridiculous Adventures of Scotty J. Fahrenheit
Copyright 2022 by Carolanne Porto

All rights reserved. No part of this book may be reproduced, stored in a retrieval system, or transmitted in any form or by any means-electronic, mechanical, photocopy, recording, or otherwise-without prior written permission of the copyright owner.

This is a work of fiction. Aside from reference to known public figures, places, or resources, all names, characters, places, and incidents have been constructed by the author, and any resemblance to actual persons, places, or events is coincidental.

ISBNs: 979-8-9867816-0-0 (Paperback)
        979-8-9867816-1-7 (Ebook)

Printed in the USA.

To Mom,

Thank you for being there every step of the way.
And yes, mom, America needs Scotty.

Chapter 1

He promised himself 1983 was going to be his year. It was already the end of May and things weren't looking too promising. With no responses from the 201 illegible handwritten resumes he sent out, babbling buffoon Scotty J. Fahrenheit is down in the dumps. Suffering from severe insomnia hasn't helped the thirty-six-year-old's growing waistline or overall emotional stability. His patience has reached its end. Trying to cure his insomnia, he kisses his seventy-three-year-old mother, Mable, before heading to bed at 7:00 p.m. The hours continue to pass as he stares up at the ceiling.

At 6:30 a.m. he finally begins to get sleepy, when he suddenly hears a faint tapping on his window. He tries to drown out the noise by putting a pillow over his head. Unable to get comfortable, he removes the pillow. The faint tapping continues. Desperate to stop it, he jumps from his bed and heads to the window. There he spots the culprit—a huge raven! Scotty taps on the window and scares the bird away and he hurries back to his bed and once again tries to fall asleep. But within a few minutes, he hears the noise again. Frazzled, he picks up his pillow and throws it at the window. This infuriates the bird, causing it to perch on the window ledge and let out loud, croaking calls between pecking the window. Enraged, Scotty opens the window and leans out, trying to get the bird to move. But instead of flying away, the

FIRED!

bird panics and flies into his room, its wings slapping the walls in the enclosed space. Scotty slams the window shut and begins chasing the massive bird around the room.

Startled by all the commotion, Mable rushes to his room and pounds on his door. "Are you alright in there?"

"No," is all he is able to muster out.

Anxious, she swings open the door and asks, "What in God's green earth is going on in here?"

"Help me," he manages as the large bird incessantly pecks at his head.

"Haven't I told you playing games with wildlife can be dangerous?"

By now, Scotty is running around in circles trying to shake the raven off his head.

"Please don't tell me anything happened to the pillow your grandmother made for you. Every feather was taken from one of the chickens on our farm. When I think of all the hard work that went into making that pillow, it brings tears to my eyes looking at your complete disrespect," she says, shaking her head while retrieving the old pillow from the floor.

"For the love of Pete! Get him off of me. Can't you just let him out?"

"If you wanted him out, then why is your window shut?"

"Because you preach over and over not to open a window when the air conditioner is on," Scotty bellows, waving his arm at the pesky bird, which is still attacking his head.

"Okay, okay," Mable rolls her eyes and crosses the room to open the window and then speaks to the huge raven, "Come on,

The Outrageously Ridiculous Adventures of Scotty J. Fahrenheit

you crazy bird. Get out of my house!" She ushers the bird out the window like it's an everyday occurrence. As she shuts the window behind the bird, she continues to reprimand Scotty.

"I must admit, I am really disappointed with your behavior. I have no idea what you were trying to prove. You have no regard for the Lord's creatures. I should also bring up the fact that you have no respect for all the work your grandmother put into making this pillow," She says, waving it in his face.

Scotty hangs his head now and mutters, "Come on, Ma, you're making me feel beyond bad. I know Granny made it for me. All I did was throw it at the window. I promise it never touched that crazy bird."

"Son, get over here," she says, not listening to a word he said.

"What are you going to do, slap me on the butt?"

Mable's head snaps up and she points a finger in Scotty's face, "What have I told you about profanity? It's not your behind you need to be concerned about. It's your head."

"Ha, ha with your jokes," He says, touching his head and smearing blood on his face.

Mable grabs the pillow and exclaims, "Whatever you do, don't you dare put your hands on this!"

"Are you banning me from the pillow?"

"Only until your hands aren't covered in blood."

He goes over to his mirror and hollers, "I'm bleeding to death, and all you can think about is that damn pillow!"

"Sit on the bed so I can assess what that defenseless bird was provoked to do."

FIRED!

"So now the bird attack is somehow my fault?" He asked, exasperated.

"Looks like the scared fella did his best to protect himself. I can't fault the poor thing for digging one heck of a hole in your head. Sit still until I get back," she says before retrieving some unlabeled bottle from the medicine cabinet. With blood still dripping from his head she pours half the bottle in his wound.

He jumps up screaming, "My head is on fire."

"Quiet," she orders while wrapping a large, white towel around his head.

"Now get dressed and meet me in the kitchen. I made your favorite chocolate chip pancakes."

As soon as she leaves, he throws on a pair of striped shorts and a colorful Hawaiian shirt.

Rubbing the towel gingerly over the wounded area, he suddenly realizes that he's been smelling the pancakes all along. "Ma, they smell awesome."

"Food always seems to make you better," she says with a smile as they make their way to the kitchen. "Oh, I was going to ask you how your sleep went, but by the looks of those huge bags and that gaping wound, I guess I don't need to." Mable puts her hands on her hips and continues, "Look, it's more than obvious that your health is on the line. You have got to stop dwelling about this job thing. I know you think cutting coupons means we're broke. Not to worry. Things may be tight but not as bad as you think," she preaches.

By now Scotty is seated at the table with a large pile of pancakes in front of him, syrup drizzling down the sides and onto the plate. He cuts and stabs his fork through several large

The Outrageously Ridiculous Adventures of Scotty J. Fahrenheit

pieces as he replies, "You're only saying that to make me feel better. If we weren't running out of money, then why did you hold onto all of daddy's clothes?"

Tears start falling from her eyes. "Scotty, you know how emotional I get when you bring up your father."

Seeing her tears, Scotty sets down his fork, which had been halfway to his mouth, and says, "Can you forgive me? If only I could be half the man daddy was. You know without a job I am not a man at all."

Swiping at her tears, she says, "Don't you think you should eat before your favorite pancakes gets cold?" successfully diverting the subject. She smiles as he shoves a huge mouthful of food into his mouth.

Suddenly, he clutches his throat.

"What's wrong?" Mable asks, sensing trouble. When Scotty is unable to speak, she rushes over, yelling, "Stand up." She tries to do the Heimlich maneuver but is unable to get her arms around his gargantuan chest. Panicking, she rushes over to the stove and grabs a heavy cast iron frying pan. With full force, she hits him square on the chest. The food flies out of his mouth. She drops the skillet back onto the stove top with a loud clang and turns back to her son, "Oh, my dear Lord, are you alright, Son?"

Now Scotty is rubbing his chest as he replies, "Well, besides having a throbbing head and an aching chest, I still don't have a job."

"All successful people have one thing in common."

"And what, my genius mother, would that be?"

She lifts her chin and points a finger at him as she states, "Every last one of them had a plan. They followed it no matter how hard and painful it was."

FIRED!

Suddenly Scotty's eyes get big and a smile lights up his face. He wraps Mable in his meaty arms as he says, "Ma, your brilliant. I have a great idea."

"Are you going to give me a clue or are you just going to suffocate me?"

He releases her and moves back toward the table as he says, "Well, it's all about your cooking."

"Son, forgive me, but how can my cooking help you with a plan?" she asks, clearly not sure where this is going.

"You're a great cook for one reason."

"And what's that supposed to mean?" She asks, bewildered.

"Come on, Ma, it's about all those old cookbooks. You once said you would be lost without them."

Mable puts one hand on her hip and the other on her forehead, trying to figure out what he could be up to, "Scotty, please tell me what my cookbooks have to do with helping you find a job?"

"You're a great cook cause of books," he replies, beaming.

She looks at him more confused than ever and just shakes her head.

Scotty motions excitedly with his hands, "See, Ma, I just need to go to the bookstore and find the right book."

Now Mable throws her hands in the air in relief, "Oh, I get it. You're going to find a book about how to get a job. Now that makes sense."

"Correctamundo, or however that dang saying goes," he said, looking pleased with himself.

"I think that's a brilliant idea," she replies, picking up his unfinished plate, assuming that he's done eating.

"Hey, where do you think you're going with that plate?"

"I just figured you lost your appetite after almost choking to death."

"Why should I let something as trivial as choking to death stop me from eating? Now, if you don't mind, give me back my plate." He grabs the plate and sits down, licking his lips, and then says, "Oh, one other thing. While you're at it, can you please pass the chocolate syrup?"

Mable shakes her head again as she moves to the fridge to get the syrup, "Do me a favor please, and concentrate on the amount of food you shove in your mouth. Next time you may not be so lucky."

He takes her advice and cuts the remaining pancakes into tiny pieces and polishes the rest of it off in short order.

When he is finished, Mable removes the large makeshift bandage from around his head, satisfied that the bleeding had now stopped.

"Thanks, Ma. I wonder what people would think seeing me wearing that towel around my head."

"They may ask you if you're from another country," She answers with a chuckle before he leaves.

Chapter 2

As Mable is washing the dishes, the phone rings. She picks it up and greets the caller with a clear lack of joy.

"Hello, Mable. How are you feeling?" The cheerful voice of her old friend Lois greeted her.

"Lois, I'm fine, but it's Scotty."

"Is he alright?"

"I am concerned over his obsession with finding a job. Poor boy, I don't know what to do," She says, confiding in her friend.

"How ironic. Would you believe that's the exact reason I am calling. In just a few minutes, some special commercial is going to air. It's supposed to be about finding a job."

"What channel is it on?" Mable anxiously asks.

Lois quickly replies, "Oh, it is on now. Turn on channel nine. I'll let you go."

Mable hangs up the phone and dashes to the living room, adjusts the antenna, and sits down on her husband's old yellow recliner. A well-dressed man with a big smile starts speaking.

"Hello out there. If you are unemployed, I'm here to let you know—yes, I mean *you*—your days of trying to find a job are over! Just think, no more rejection letters. No more worrying

The Outrageously Ridiculous Adventures of Scotty J. Fahrenheit

over call backs that never seem to come. Not to mention all the resumes you sent out in vain. Just think of all the wasted time and energy you spent trying to find a job. It's time you made a stand. Look into your television and repeat after me: 'In just a matter of time, I will no longer be unemployed.' I can't hear you. Say it like you mean it! If you are truly ready to find a job, then you need to jot down the number at the bottom of the screen," He says as the one-eight-hundred number begins to flash on the screen.

The man on the TV continues, "Our breakthrough system guarantees everyone a job. So don't delay! Pick up the phone and make that call today."

Wasting no time, Mable picks up the phone and enrolls Scotty in the program immediately.

Meanwhile, Scotty is at the bookstore, unaware that he is wasting his time. He walks quickly up and down the aisles, feverishly trying to locate a book on how to find a job.

A friendly, young female sales associate notices him fumbling through the aisles and asks, "Is there something I can help you with?"

Scotty turns and sizes up the young lady—from her oversized purple clogs, past her calf-length yellow and green brocade skirt, farther still to her bright red, fuzzy wool cardigan (which makes him start to itch just by looking at it), up to her thick cat glasses that seem to magnify her eyes. The sweater brings out the redness of her cheeks and Scotty can't help but stare.

Suddenly Scotty realizes that he hasn't said anything yet but has been staring at her. Red faced and embarrassed he confesses, "Please forgive me for being so rude. I couldn't help myself from eyeing you up and down."

FIRED!

The young lady begins blushing. She clears her throat and asks, "Is there something in particular you are looking for?"

Looking straight into her eyes he blurts out, "You."

Now she blushes more fiercely and averts her eyes.

He goes on, "You remind me of Adrian from the first Rocky movie. I mean, before she was all fixed up. See, most women wear a lot of makeup, and you don't look like you're wearing any at all." He nods to her clothing, "I do all my shopping at thrift shops, so it's refreshing to see a woman who seems to do the same. And those cat glasses remind me of my grandmother's." Shaking his head, he rambles on, "Gosh, maybe bringing up my grandmother wasn't such a good thing. Sorry."

She looks at him confused while he continues.

"You see, I got in a scuffle with this monster bird this morning that flew in my room and was pecking a hole in my head. And my mother claims grandma is rolling in her grave because I shot a pillow she made me across the room." Realizing that he had chattered on long enough, he tries to change the subject. "But enough about that. What about you? I bet you have thousands of boyfriends."

"Actually, I have never been on a date not even once." She sheepishly admits.

"You've got to be kidding. You're so incredibly beautiful," he blurts.

She smiles shyly and looks up at Scotty, "Um, thank you." Obviously not used to being praised for beauty, she changes the subject away from herself. "So can I help you find anything in particular?"

Scotty explains his situation and the young woman points him in the right direction.

"Charlotte…do you mind if I call you Charlotte? I happened to notice it on your name tag." He awkwardly asks, pointing at the tag on her shirt.

"That's fine."

"I'm sorry, I can barely contain myself," he says and looks around the bookstore, spotting a coffee shop in the far corner. "Can I buy you something in the café, say on your break?"

Charlotte seemed taken back and responded slowly, "Okay… but I just got here, so my break is in three hours."

Scotty smiles and almost jumps for joy, "Perfect! I'll meet you there. I have a lot of research to keep me busy. I'll do my best to get it all done by then." He says, nodding.

Charlotte says, "Sounds good," and gives a small little wave before leaving to help other customers.

Not being able to help himself, Scotty watches her walk away until she disappears around a bookshelf.

***

A little while later, Scotty hustles to the café in hopes of finding a table, his hands overflowing with heavy books. Securing a good spot amongst the other people in the café, he settles his large body into a small chair and begins by opening the largest book. Unable to understand anything on its pages, he slams it shut. Every book seems to pose the same problem. Hopefully, it will give him some answers. Conjuring up a new scheme, he takes out several small pieces of scrap paper. He frantically begins writing gibberish. Every couple of minutes he

FIRED!

goes up to the friendly man behind the counter asking, "Sir, can you please tell me the time?"

The man kindly obliges. About every five minutes, Scotty continues pestering the clerk to get the time. Finally he's had enough and says, "You've come up here over twenty times asking the same question. Can we make this situation a bit easier?"

"Obviously, you have no clue how excited I am to have lunch with the most gorgeous lady ever."

The man taps a finger on his chin and replies, "I bet it's Charlotte."

"How did you figure that out?"

"It's really obvious."

"I bet you wouldn't mind a date with her. I can't believe she agreed to spend her break with me. Talk about being at the right place at the wrong time," Scotty says, confusing the worker.

"You mean the right place at the right...oh, forget it." The café worker realizes it's futile trying to explain anything to Scotty.

Finally, Scotty notices Charlotte walking into the café. He jumps out of his seat flailing his arms screaming out her name. Charlotte smiles and quickly walks over, sitting down in the seat across from Scotty.

Just then a voice comes over the loud speaker, saying, "Charlotte Rattinger, please come to the front desk."

"If I am correct, I just heard someone call out your name. Did you hear it too, or am I just hallucinating?" Scotty worries.

Charlotte shakes her head and says, "I didn't hear it."

The Outrageously Ridiculous Adventures of Scotty J. Fahrenheit

Scotty looks relieved and says, "It's got to be that dang insomnia of mine. I haven't slept in days. I guess I am hearing things now. No big deal. I guess it's only when I start to see things that I need to worry."

One of her coworkers walks over to her and says, "Charlotte, I don't mean to interrupt, but I just heard your name called."

"Thank you," Charlotte replies to her coworker.

"Obviously, I'm not the only person hearing things. That girl must be suffering from insomnia too." Scotty thinks to himself.

"Let's go up to the front desk and see what they want," Charlotte says to Scotty, moving her chair away from the table.

"I thought you said you didn't hear them call your name?" Scotty says as he gets up.

"I didn't."

As the pair begins walking toward the front desk, Scotty says, "Look, you don't have to make me feel better. I guess my mom is right, my health is fading fast. This lack of sleep is putting me at risk."

"No silly, it's just that I can't hear."

"I can't believe how damn good you hear for someone who can't hear. I mean, how can you be talking to me if you can't hear?"

"I am deaf, not dumb," She explains.

"I think that came out wrong...I would never call you dumb. I'm the one people call dumb all the time."

"No don't feel bad. Being called dumb simply means you are unable to speak," Charlotte tries to explain.

17

FIRED!

"Oh, wow, so I'm really not dumb after all," Scotty smiles at this.

"I bet it's my sister. I forgot my hearing aids."

"What good are they if you can't hear?" Now he is really confused.

"They enable me to hear loud sounds. That's really important when I drive and all," She admits.

"I am so lost right now," Scotty says, shaking his head.

"Oh, by the way, wait until you see my sister, Kate. It's easy to see who got all the looks in my family."

As they approach the front desk, Charlotte's gorgeous dark-haired sister waits patiently while all the men in the line gawk at her. As soon as Kate spots Charlotte, she smiles.

As usual, Scotty blurts out what he's thinking with no filter, "Charlotte, you are one thousand percent correct. It is so obvious who was blessed with all the looks," Scotty says, looking directly at Kate.

Kate's eyes widen in surprise at this strange man's statement and tries to make Charlotte feel better by saying, "My sister was blessed with so many talents."

Scotty countered back, "So what were you blessed with? Charlotte seems to have gotten it all—the looks and the talent. Really must suck for you."

Kate looks at Scotty and smiles. "Thank you for such a wonderful compliment about my sister. I agree with you. She is so beautiful."

Charlotte is dumbfounded about what just came out of his mouth.

The Outrageously Ridiculous Adventures of Scotty J. Fahrenheit

After bidding her sister goodbye, the two of them walk back to the café where Charlotte puts in her hearing aids.

After settling back down in their seats, Scotty says, "I've been meaning to ask you where you got that accent from?"

"Oh, no," she replies, shaking her head. "This isn't an accent at all. It's because I am deaf that I sound this way. I hope it doesn't bother you."

"Not at all. I think your accent is absolutely stunning," Scotty looks at her dreamily and then questions, "By the way, what do you think about meeting my mother?"

Charlotte just sits there smiling. Scotty continues doing all the talking. "I need to ask you a question. I don't want to upset you. Please don't think I am rude and all. Do you think it's alright if I ask you something personal?"

"I guess so—" She gets out before being interrupted.

"Here goes. Just how old are you?" he asks nervously.

"Is that all?" She laughs before answering that she's twenty-two.

"I can't believe it. You dress and act much older. I thought you were my age or maybe even older."

"So how old are *you*?" She asks.

Scotty leans forward, as if letting her in on a big secret and says in a lowered voice, "I know you won't believe it, but I am thirty-six. People tell me all the time I am so immature for my age. Let's put it this way, we are sort-of the same age." He leans back and crosses his arms in satisfaction.

Charlotte looks really confused. She glances at her watch and says, "I guess I have to let you go."

FIRED!

"Was it something I said?" he says, jumping up.

"No nothing like that. My break is over and I have to get back to work."

But Scotty pulls her chair away before she is fully out of it, causing her to fall. "I am so sorry. I didn't mean to make you fall."

"Not to worry. It was just a fall," She says with a red face.

"I have to admit you aren't the only one," He adds, making no sense.

"What do you mean by that?" she asks.

"I, too, am falling."

"Now stop thinking you're having hallucinations. You're fine."

"I am falling alright, in love with you," He blurts out.

Stunned and left speechless, Charlotte just smiles and walks away.

Scotty sits back down and once again begins feverishly taking useless notes.

Chapter 3

Two hours pass, and Charlotte finds Scotty still sitting in the café gulping down a soda. "My shift is up. I was hoping I would see you again," she says with a smile as she approaches his table.

Scotty stands up, almost knocking the table over with his wide girth. "Are you kidding with that? I am so ready to ask you to marry me. I don't want any other man to get to you before me. What's your phone number?" he belts out all in one breath.

Completely flabbergasted, Charlotte blushes and replies, "You talk to me so differently than anyone else does. I'm not used to it."

"Look, some people think I'm a lunatic, but I'm actually a loveable, teddy bear kind-of guy."

She stands there awkwardly for a moment and then says, "Well, I have to say bye for now. If I am late getting home, my daddy worries."

"Do you mind if I walk you to your car?" Scotty offers as they walk out of the café, abandoning all the books on the table.

"As long as you really aren't a lunatic," she answers with a chuckle. "My parents are always warning me about staying away from weirdos," she adds as he follows her to her car.

Scotty notices the car she is walking toward and says, "I dig your wheels. This thing must have some serious pickup."

"Actually, it's really kind of slow," She admits.

"Yeah, but you're so lucky to be driving a punch-buggy car. Everyone loves a bug as long as it doesn't bite em," he comes out with another one of his lame jokes.

"See over there? That's my pair of wheels," He says, pointing to an old clunker a row over. "Driving that 1960 Plymouth Valiant is almost as much fun as being with you. Just call me the 'Mopar Man.'"

All Charlotte can think to say in response is, "Okay...well, bye." Then she just starts her car and overcautiously drives away, leaving Scotty staring pathetically after her.

***

At eleven o'clock in the evening, Scotty arrives home and skips to the living room where his mother is getting ready to watch the late night news.

"What's all the skipping about? And where, may I ask, have you been?" she levels him with a stare.

"Ma, are ya kidding?" He says, taking out all the crumpled pages of notes that were stuffed in his pockets.

She eyes the rumpled paper. "That's impressive, but you haven't answered my question."

"Okay, okay. My belly started growling so I had to stop at a burger joint."

"Are you sure that was the only stop? I know the bookstore closed hours ago. You're lucky you walked through that door when you did."

"Why?" he asks, clearly confused.

She mutes the TV and leans forward, her hands on the armrests of her chair. "Because I thought something happened to you. I was seconds from calling the police. Where else did you go?" she questions.

Scotty answers sheepishly, "I made two more stops: the donut shop and the ice cream parlor."

Mable shakes her head, "You love your junk food."

"I got that from Dad."

"Yeah, and we all know where that got him," she replies sarcastically.

"What's that supposed to mean?"

She waves it off, "Forget it. I will never meet such a gentle giant like that man. God rest his soul," she says while nodding solemnly.

Scotty decides it's time to change the subject and says, "Mom, I've got the best news."

Mable takes a good look at her son and states, "You seem so happy. I must admit, I've been concerned about your mental health status. I mean, all you've done before now is mope around this house with the most pathetic look on your face."

"As of today, all of that has changed," he boasts.

"Am I to assume that the bookstore breathed life into you?"

"I don't know what that means, but I got even better news. You see, Ma, I found the girl of my dreams—probably my future wife. She is the most beautiful thing I ever laid eyes on," he finishes with a dreamy look on his face.

FIRED!

Mable scrunches her face up, confused. "I thought you went to get info on finding a job."

"Well, I did go there for that. But there she was, right out of the clear blue." He motioned with both hands, "It was like God Almighty put her there in front of me. Now that is a true miracle."

Not truly convinced, Mable turned back to the TV, "Great, because I was feeling bad about you wasting your entire day at the bookstore."

"What is that supposed to mean?"

"At least it wasn't a complete waste of time," she replied, talking with her hands, still holding the remote.

Scotty took offense at this. Hands on his wide hips, he asks, "Okay, name one time. And I mean *one time* when I actually did something right in your eyes?"

"Why would you accuse me of such a thing?" she pathetically asks.

"Let's get real, Ma. All you do is tell me how wrong I am." Scotty becomes even more animated and starts swinging his arms as he talks, desperately trying to prove his point. "One minute you're yelling at me for leaving the bathroom window open. So I tried to explain the smell from my irritable bowel was making me want to puke. That's why I opened the window. But *no*, you wouldn't even listen. All you did was preach about keeping the windows shut while the AC is on." He takes a breath while she rolls her eyes at him. "Then just today, you yell at me for not having the window open while a lunatic bird was on a kill mission in my room. I am getting really fed up with opposite day, every day of the week!" he finishes by throwing both hands up in the air.

The Outrageously Ridiculous Adventures of Scotty J. Fahrenheit

Mable has heard enough. She barks out, "Stop with all the drama and listen up. After you left, I watched a commercial about getting a job."

"You found me a job? That's wonderful! Is there anything you can't do, Ma?" He says, completely changing his mood.

"No, I didn't get you a job. But don't get all upset again, there's going to be some paperwork coming in the mail for you. It explains all the details about this new concept."

Scotty ambles over to the table where the notes from the bookstore are scattered. "Am I just supposed to throw these out?" he asks.

Not wanting him to get back in the dumps, she offers, "Just think, you did all that in one day."

Scotty picks up all the papers and stuffs them back in his pocket. All the while, he continues badgering his mother about the commercial.

"Now Son," she reprimands, "you're going overboard. Give it a break—I'm positive things will change."

He looks at her, mouthing, "I sure hope so."

"Remember when you turned sixteen? You were so worried that you wouldn't find an afterschool job. Look at how fast you were hired at the zoo," she reminds him.

"Oh, Ma, I *loved* that job. Scrubbing the animal cages was such a thrill. I will never forget the time an elephant charged after me and kicked elephant crap in my face. The people behind the fence watched in terror. One guy thought the big beast was going to squash me. Everyone looked at me as if I was this fearless hero," he states, smiling and nodding, recalling the heroic moment from long ago.

FIRED!

"See, Son, you have nothing to fret over," she replies.

Scotty snaps back out of his reverie and says, "Now that I think about it, Ma, I bet I could always go back to the zoo and get my old job back."

She shakes her head and says, "I wouldn't count on that. Did you forget the reason you were let go?"

His eyes shift from side to side as he remembers the incident and quickly says, "But that was an accident."

She motions with her hands to calm him down, saying, "I understand. But leaving the tiger's cage opened caused such an uproar. Just think if that animal hurt anyone. They would have put the tiger down. Thank goodness animal control found him walking down the main road. That was *after* the entire city was put on lockdown," She reminds him.

Scotty starts to feel very tired thinking of that past event. "Well, I gotta get to bed, Ma. I need to make sure I get a good night's sleep. Goodnight," he says, exiting the room quickly before she can bring up anything else from the past. For an old woman, she had an iron-clad memory!

Chapter 4

The next day Scotty is awakened by the loud blaring of his alarm clock. He can't believe he actually slept through the night. Maybe he beat back his insomnia. He stumbles downstairs, sees his mother stirring something in the kitchen, and continues his rant over the job seminar. "Ma, what do you think?" he starts.

She turns her head to look at him while continuing to stir the contents in the large mixing bowl in front of her and replies, "Son, if this has anything to do with a job, I want you to stop. I spent hours on end praying for the packet to come in the mail right away. But I truly don't think it will. You have to take your mind off it for at least one minute. I will not be troubled with this all day long; it's beginning to wear on my nerves."

Scotty won't be deterred and says, "I remember the last time I badgered you. I didn't stop until you said I could take in that stray fox."

"I should have never agreed. Look where that got you," she says, shaking her head.

"Yeah, an ungrateful fox."

Now Mable turns around to face Scotty, planting one hand on her hip and pointing at him with a mixing spoon still in hand,

FIRED!

dripping the contents on the floor, "That wasn't the worst thing. It was when he attacked you."

"No, you got that wrong, Ma. There's nothing that hurt me more than having those needles driven through my body when you took me to the hospital after he attacked me."

She shook her head, "Poor Dr. Robertson went through a living hell trying to calm you down. Your daddy stepped up and had the courage to contain you."

Scotty smirks and says, "Is that what he was doing? It felt like he was cutting off my circulation."

Turning back to the mixing bowl, she explains, "He had no other choice but to sit on your belly. Do you know how horrible it was listening to your heart-wrenching screams as the doctor drove that long needle through your body?"

"Aw, come on, Ma, now you're exaggerating, I wasn't that loud."

"That's easy for you to say. My ears rang for weeks on end. I bet you didn't know that to this day I suffer from ringing in my ears because of that."

Now Scotty's face lights up as he says, "Oh yeah! Mom, talking about ears reminds me of Charlotte. Thanks for bringing her up."

Mable's forehead wrinkles as she tries hard to make the connection. "What does ringing in the ears have to do with her?"

"I bet she would love hearing ringing in her ears. She needs to wear hearing aids, cause she can't hear. I better give her a call before she thinks I forgot about her," Scotty says while walking over to the yellow phone hanging on the wall.

The Outrageously Ridiculous Adventures of Scotty J. Fahrenheit

A sociable woman answers the phone. Talking in his gaudy voice, Scotty says, "Hello, this is Scotty J. Fahrenheit. It would be my pleasure to talk to the beautiful and lovely Charlotte."

"Hold on and I will see if she is out of bed yet."

After a few moments that seems to last an hour to Scotty, Charlotte's voice comes over the phone. "Hello, Scotty. How are you?"

Scotty's face breaks into a smile, "I'm fine. I want you to know that all I did last night was dream of your pretty face. By the way, you're the miracle worker."

"Actually, that person would be Helen Keller. She was the real miracle worker," she explains.

"Cool. Maybe someday you can introduce me to her," Scotty replies.

"No, that would be impossible."

"Why?"

"Because she's dead."

"Oh…well…I'm sorry to hear there's one less miracle worker around," he says honestly.

Charlotte chuckles and asks, "Why did you call me a miracle worker?"

"Well, it's been a real nightmare trying to get sleep. Remember I told you I was attacked by a bird. And then my mind wouldn't stop thinking about getting a job. Mom calls them racing thoughts. Anyways, it used to keep me up most of the night. But once I met you, all that changed."

"How could I have cured you?" she asks in a disbelieving tone.

FIRED!

"I don't know, but you did. Everything changed the minute I met you. I am back sleeping and now I'm on the road to a guaranteed job. I should also add that I'm crazy in love with you. Now can't you see how you cured me?"

"Um…maybe," Is all she says.

A thought comes into Scotty's head and he hits his palm on his forehead, "Oh gosh. I'm so sorry. How absolutely rude of me not to ask you if you need time to put in your hearing aids."

Charlotte answers quickly, "Oh, don't worry. I have a special phone for the hearing impaired."

Scotty is very confused and says, "But I thought you said you read lips. I didn't know if that's what you were doing."

Charlotte laughs, "You're so silly. You know I can't read lips over the phone."

"Well maybe you should. What do you say I stop by and visit you at the bookstore for a few minutes? I miss you already."

"I think that would be alright with me," she replies. "What time do you think you'll be stopping by?"

Scotty taps his chin with this index finger and thinks hard, "Well, if my mail doesn't arrive today, I will take a little trip to the post office and demand some answers."

"You seem a bit forceful when you speak," she says cautiously.

"Don't you like that in a man?" he replies.

"Um, I guess so," she says, not sounding too convinced.

Scotty is oblivious and continues on, "That's just what I love in a girl, a docile angel who's not only easy on the eyes but just as easy on the ears." He hits his palm on his forehead again, "Oh gee, can you forgive me for talking about ears? Sorry for my rudeness—"

Charlotte interrupts and hurriedly says, "Scotty, I really got to go. Talk to you later." She ends the call before he could even say goodbye.

Scotty stares at the phone and starts screaming into it, "Charlotte! Come back, Charlotte!"

Mable, who has been listening in on the conversation, now pipes up and says, "Enough, Son. She obviously disconnected the phone. All your screaming isn't going to make her hear you. Put down the phone and call her later."

He puts the phone back on the hook and says, "Yeah I will do that. I bet it was just a bad connection. Happens a lot to me." He decides to go up to his room to wait for the mail truck to come.

***

A little while later, Scotty comes back downstairs, walks over to look out the front window, and says to himself, "I have a good feeling that today is going to be my lucky day."

A few minutes later he spots the mail truck and he races outside to stand directly in front of the mailbox in hopes of receiving his packet.

"Hello Scotty," The mailman says with a smile. He hands him two catalogues.

Scotty looks at the catalogs in confusion and then looks back up at the mailman. "Now wait one minute. There must be something for me."

FIRED!

The mailman tips his head and gives Scotty a sympathetic smile, "That's all the mail for this stop."

Scotty stomps his foot. "I can't believe this. I need that, and I need it now."

"Are you alright?" The mailman asks, looking concerned.

"No I'm not." Scotty crosses his arms, still clutching the catalogues, "I was promised mail."

"Well, maybe it will be delivered tomorrow," The mailman says before hopping back into his mail Jeep and pulling away.

Scotty storms angrily back into the house. He discards the catalogs on the table, grabs his car keys, gets in his car, and heads to the post office. He struts in with the biggest chip on his shoulder. A long line of patrons wait patiently for the two postal workers who are trying their best to keep up with the busy day.

"Excuse me, excuse me," Scotty says, budging to the front of the line.

"Stay away from me, you deviant pervert," cries an old woman holding a small white dog.

A postal worker looks up from the person in front of him and speaks up rudely to Scotty, "Sir, there are a lot of people patiently waiting their turn. You have to go to the end of the line."

"Come on, man. I'm at wits end," Scotty yells.

"Look at the desperation he is displaying. Damn drugs make a man do unthinkable things," An old man shouts out.

"I thought drugs made people thin," the old man's wife whispers.

The Outrageously Ridiculous Adventures of Scotty J. Fahrenheit

Scotty looks around at all the people in line and belts out, "I don't care what you people have to say about me. I'm just here to get my package."

"You probably ate it," an angry customer yells out.

Seeing the disruption from his office, the head postmaster makes his way to the counter and addresses Scotty, "Sir, I need for you to calm yourself down. What seems to be your problem?"

"My mom called some company and they said they were sending me out info. It should be here!" He cries out.

The postmaster, obviously used to dealing with people, motions to Scotty to calm down, "All right take a deep breath. How long has it been?"

Scotty thinks, tipping his head back with his mouth open and face scrunched, "Uh, I guess about one day." He looks back at the postmaster and yells, shaking fisted hands, "But that invitation is my life."

"I don't know if you're some kind of a practical joker, but things take longer than a day to be considered missing," The agitated postmaster explains.

Scotty starts getting even more upset as he continues talking.

"If you don't receive your info in a week, have your mother call the company that sent it out."

Scotty now takes both hands and slowly pushes them down in front of him while breathing out slowly, like he is trying his hardest to stay calm, "I am just wondering if my package was stolen?"

The postmaster smiles and explains, "Sir, nothing is stolen from this post office." Seeing Scotty about to explode, he adds,

FIRED!

"Now I need to ask you to please leave the premises before I'm forced to call the police."

"I already called them when he got here," the other postal worker spoke up, not even looking up from what he is doing.

Before Scotty could comment, two police officers barge in the building.

"That's the derelict, yelling at the postmaster," one of the customers in the line points out.

Scotty looks strangely relieved and turns to the officers, saying, "Oh, good. I was just about to call you. It seems to me that the post office is stealing people's stuff," he explains.

"Sir, we would appreciate if you would leave. You're causing a scene, and we don't take kindly to it. We will give you a few seconds to get out of here," one of the officers orders Scotty.

The entire line claps as he is escorted out.

This just isn't Scotty's day.

Chapter 5

After the officers escort him to his car, Scotty races home. Furious at what transpired, he decides he is in no shape to visit Charlotte. Arriving home, he skids into the driveway and hurries into the house.

"Mom!" he screams at the top of his lungs.

Straightening up from where she's been dusting in the living room, she puts her hands over her ears and says, "Geez, Scotty, I'm right here."

"Sorry, Ma I didn't notice you bending down. I'm just so aggravated."

"What happened now?" she asks, rolling her eyes.

"That head post office guy is a real jackass," he says as though that will make total sense.

"What is that all about?" Mable says with hands on her hips.

"I was just very panicked something happened to my paperwork," he tries to explain.

Seeing that it's not a valid emergency, she goes back to dusting while she says, "What is the matter with you? I told you to calm down about this job thing. You are making me and everyone around you crazy."

FIRED!

"That is exactly what the cops said before they walked me out."

She stops cleaning again and turns back to Scotty, "Oh for the love of God, what did you just say?"

"Mom, the cops showed up and made me leave the post office."

"What did you do now?" she asks, throwing her hands in the air.

"All I did was ask about my package," he tried to convince.

"Scotty, please stop. All I need is the cops arresting you."

"How can they do that?"

"Easy, you keep up your craziness and anything is possible." Mable put her duster down and picked up a paper with a list, handing it to Scotty. "I have some chores for you to do. Please, no more talk about your package. Just take a deep breath while you go downstairs to take the wash out of the machine."

Soon she hears an unusually loud thumping and crashing coming from the basement. Apparently, taking that deep breath caused him to get dizzy and fall down the entire flight of cellar stairs. She rushes over as fast as she can to the basement door.

"What happened? Are you okay?" She asks, seeing him lying at the bottom of the steps.

"Nothing to worry about," he says, shaking it off, "Just help me up."

Mable starts hobbling down the steps one at a time to help Scotty, "Son, you're going to give me a heart attack. I'm too old for this," she grunts as she helps him stand up.

The Outrageously Ridiculous Adventures of Scotty J. Fahrenheit

Brushing himself off, he replies, "Don't scare me, Ma. One dead parent is enough. I don't need to live without you too."

With a sigh she says, "Enough of this talk of death. I know, let's take the laundry outside. It's a gorgeous day for that," She says, hoping to get his mind off that subject.

"Okay, that sounds like a good idea," he agrees. Fortunately the plan works and after they finish with the laundry, Scotty heads to the garage to complete more chores.

***

At five o'clock, Mable calls Scotty in for dinner and he dashes to the table.

"Not so fast, Mister. You march to the bathroom and wash your hands. What have I told you about your hygiene?" she preaches

"Yeah, I know. Cleanliness is close to godliness," he mutters while walking to the bathroom.

When he gets back, he heads straight for the kitchen table. Mable bows her head, and Scotty recites his usual prayer. "Thank you, God, for the food me and mom are about to eat."

After the prayer is ended they both look up. Mable smiles and says, "I cooked you a special treat. I know it's your favorite." She says, uncovering a thick pan of lasagna in the middle of the table.

"Mom, words can't describe how cool you are. Dad and me use to fight over who would get the end pieces," he reminisces.

Mable replies sadly, "Don't get me wrong, but when you talk about your father, it opens a huge hole in my heart. I will never stop missing all the goofy things about the man."

FIRED!

Scotty's face gets red and he cries, "How could the plow driver not see him?"

Mable reminds him again, "He claimed he mistakenly thought dad was a large pile of snow. I begged your father time after time not to go outside wearing that all-white snowsuit. Your dad had a bad habit of shoveling the snow off our driveway and directly into the road. I can't tell you how many times I warned him." She says, grabbing her napkin and wiping her tears.

"Gee, give Dad a break. If he knew the plow driver would run him down, I am certain he would have thrown a snowball at the windshield or something." Scotty gets quiet for a minute, cutting a large slice of lasagna and plopping it onto his plate, steam curling as it rises from the hot food. Then he says quietly, "I often wonder what dad's last thought was. I mean, when he saw the plow coming right for him, what was he thinking?"

All emotional, Mable changes the subject. "Okay, let's start to eat before the food gets cold."

Scotty notices how upset his mom is and decides to let it go, "Okay, Ma. This looks and smells great!"

***

After dinner, Scotty cleans up the dishes and then decides to give Charlotte a call. When she picks up and greets him he tries to explain why he never got to the bookstore.

"Hi, Charlotte. Sorry I didn't come by. I was in no mood to visit you today. I didn't want you to see my ugly side. It wouldn't be too good and all. I mean somebody called the cops on me at the post office."

The Outrageously Ridiculous Adventures of Scotty J. Fahrenheit

"Scotty, that doesn't sound very good. Are you sure I'm safe talking to you? I mean, would you ever hurt me?" Charlotte asks with a concerned tone.

"What, me hurt you?" he replied, "I would rather cut out my tongue. And that would be really bad cause I would really be dumb!"

"I am glad you said that," she says, relieved.

Just then Scotty hears his mother calling him and says, "Charlotte, I've got to go. My mom wants me. After dad died, I became the man of the house. I made him a promise that I would be at mom's every beck and call, and I intend to live by my word. I guess you could call me a momma's boy," he says before saying goodbye and ending the call.

"I hope I didn't interrupt anything, but our favorite game show was just about to start."

"No problem, I just hung up on Charlotte," he says, settling down on the couch. I wouldn't miss this show for the whole world."

"You really love this, don't you?" She asks, wishing just once he could solve the puzzle.

"I love watching the wheel spin around. In my head, I guess what it will stop on. One time, Ma—one time I got it right. I guessed it was going to stop on the car, and it did," he said, very excited at the memory.

Mable looks at her son and smiles. "It would be great if you won a car because your old clunker has seen better days. It won't be long before it breaks down."

"Oh, come on, that baby has a lot more miles to go," he thinks as they continue to watch their show.

Chapter 6

Three days later.

Waking up at her usual time, Mable kneels in desperate prayer for over forty-five minutes, ending her pleas with, "Dear God, please give me the strength not to strangle my son." Standing up, she picks up a wooden cross bigger than the size of her hand. Without hesitation, she gets a shoelace and strings it through a hole in the top and puts the cross around her neck. The weight of the cross practically brings her back down to her knees. Holding the wall for support, she looks up at the ceiling and says, "Dear God, does this get your attention?"

The day is already warming up to be a scorcher, and as she gets dressed for the day Mable is grateful for the AC cooling the house and ceiling fans to circulate the nice cool air down to her level.

As soon as she gets downstairs, Scotty starts right back in, not skipping a beat, "Ma, do you think today will be the day?"

"Look, Son, I prayed and begged God."

"Is that why you are wearing that fancy wooden cross necklace, Ma?"

Not wanting to discuss the situation any further she simply shakes her head.

Scotty looks at her with some concern, "Is something seriously wrong with you? What would you beg God for?"

Eyes rolling, Mable replies, "You must be kidding. Let me spell it out for you."

Losing patience, he blurts, "Spit it out mom. It ain't good to hold that kind of stuff in."

"You really want to know?" she asks.

"Yes, Ma, I do. Have at it."

"I begged God for your info to come in the mail today," she says matter-of-factly.

"Why would you beg for that?"

"So I wouldn't have to put up with your incessant pestering. Did I say enough?" she answers finally, exasperated.

"Ma, I really think you are going way overboard with this," Scotty claims.

"Are you for real? The only one going overboard is you. Sometimes Scotty—," she says but then stops herself from saying something she knows she will regret.

Forgetting the high temperature and humidity, she orders Scotty to go outside and mow the lawn with their push mower.

Halfway through, Scotty bangs on the door.

Opening the door, Mable scans her son, whose face is beat red from exertion and heat. "My Lord, Scotty, are you alright?" she asks.

FIRED!

"I feel really hot," he manages in a strained voice, fanning his face with his stubby fingers.

"Do you think it could be heatstroke?" She worries before rushing in the house to get him a large glass of water. When she gets back, he is laying on the ground.

"Scotty, put your head up and drink some water," she orders.

"Not to worry, Ma," he says before gulping the entire pitcher down.

"Now sit on the steps for a few minutes. Actually, forget about finishing the lawn. I'll get that teenage boy from down the street to do it. He'll get it done much quicker with his gas mower."

Scotty props himself on the stairs and replies, "Ma, have you any clue how embarrassing that is?"

"What do you mean?" she asks, confused.

"Come on, Ma, don't you remember? You gave that punk our mower because you said I would cut my toes off. Instead, I had to use that old thing and get heatstroke," he says, pointing to the offensive mower in the yard.

Mable spots the mail truck and panics, worried that if Scotty's packet hasn't arrived today, it may push him over the edge. "Come on, Son," she motions for him to come inside with her hands in a frantic manner, "you better get inside and cool down."

Her plan works until he realizes he left the empty pitcher on the grass. As he turns to retrieve it, he spies the mail truck. "Got anything for me today?" Scotty yells from the front yard.

The mailman smiles and says, "As a matter of fact, I do. This here packet is addressed to a Scotty J. Fahrenheit."

The Outrageously Ridiculous Adventures of Scotty J. Fahrenheit

"I knew this day was gonna be lucky for me even if I got heatstroke. What more can I ask for?" Scotty says with a huge, goofy grin on his face.

"Sanity would be a good start," The mailman says with a laugh before driving away.

Scotty turns back to Mable and waves the large manila envelope in the air, "It worked! You can take off the cross now. God really answered your prayers!" He ambles inside and Mable follows him to the table where he starts ripping the envelope open. They both start reading the contents together.

Mable points to a paragraph in the letter on top and exclaims excitedly, "This is amazing! They said that everyone in the program is guaranteed a job that best utilizes their skills and talents. Doesn't that seem like a good thing?"

"Depends on what kind of job they're talking about. If I don't even know what I am good at, how can they know?"

"Oh, Scotty," Mable reprimands, "This is not the time to start getting negative."

Flipping to the next page, Scotty scans the page, "I'm reading the fees they charge for enrollment, and according to this, it's really expensive. Good thing they give you the choice to pay in installments. But if I pay all at once, I get a discount."

"What kind of country do we live in now?" Mable asks, "when *you* have to pay to get a job? I thought it was supposed to be the other way around."

"Who's being negative now?" Scotty replied with a grin. "Just be happy that I'm gonna get me a job."

Chapter 7

The big day finally arrives and Scotty wakes up before dawn. He rushes down the hall and begins pounding on his mother's bedroom door. "Ma, are you up yet? It's an emergency," he says, busting into her room.

Mable groggily raises her head off the pillow and squints her eyes at the light streaming in from the hallway. "I'm awake now. What's the problem?"

"I don't know what to wear."

She looks at her clock and lets her head fall back on the pillow. "Seriously, Scotty? It's four a.m. Go back to sleep. It's important for you to be well rested today."

"You're right, Ma," he agrees. "I'll set the alarm and get a little more shut-eye." Scotty heads back to his room and lays back down.

Unable to fall back to sleep, Mable heads to the kitchen to make some fresh bread.

Three hours pass before Scotty comes downstairs. "Well, what do you think?" he announces as he enters the kitchen.

Mable looks at him in utter disbelief. "You've got to be kidding. What are you thinking wearing those tight polyester

The Outrageously Ridiculous Adventures of Scotty J. Fahrenheit

animal-print shorts? And, Son, that pink polka-dot shirt doesn't look any better."

"Thanks, Ma, keep coming with the jokes," Scotty says as he walks over to the cupboard and takes out an oversized box of Frosted Flakes. "Tony, I sure could use the help of a tiger today."

"Make sure not to eat the entire box," Mable warns, "you know what happens when you drink too much milk."

Of course, Scotty ends up devouring the entire box of cereal and a gallon of milk.

Scotty finishes getting ready to leave and before leaving the house he comes back in the kitchen where Mable is sitting at the table enjoying a cup of coffee. "Well, Ma, this is it. Take your last look at me."

"What is that supposed to mean?" she says, putting her mug down on the table.

"When I get back you will see a new man," Scotty says, thinking this will explain everything.

Mable looks at the cuckoo clock. "You have two hours before the conference starts. Why don't you wait another hour before you leave?"

"I want to get there bright and early so I can get a front-row seat," he says while walking out the door.

Feeling excited, Scotty gets into his car and rolls down the window. "It doesn't get better than this," he says, running his fat fingers through his receding hairline.

His exhilaration takes a turn for the worse when he looks at the dash and notices the fuel needle going past the red empty mark. "You've got to be kidding." He immediately heads toward the nearest gas station, which happens to be on the way to where he is heading.

Lucky for him, his car sputters in the gas station. But unfortunately the line for the pumps wraps around the building.

Finally it's his turn. "Fill it up," he says to the attendant.

After a few minutes the man walks back to the window and says, "That will be $20.75."

"Just a minute," Scotty says, taking out his wallet. Horrified, he realizes there is no money in it and starts flipping through all the pockets of it over and over, hoping somehow he finds something.

The attendant starts getting impatient and says, "Sir, if you don't mind, there is a line of cars behind you."

"Give me a minute. I'm sure I can find some money," Scotty says, frantically scavenging under the seats.

He discovers a whopping total of seventy-five cents. Panicked, he contemplates driving off. But by that time the manager has come out to see what's holding everything up. "Sir, what seems to be the problem?" he asks.

"There's no problem, I'm just a little short on cash right now."

"Sir, if you think we are in the habit of giving free gas, you would be mistaken. Is there someone you can call?"

"Yeah, I can call my mother," he says before pulling his car to the side and following the manager into the station.

Scotty dials his house, but after fifty rings, he hangs up.

"She's not answering the phone," he says to the manager, "what do you want me to do?"

The Outrageously Ridiculous Adventures of Scotty J. Fahrenheit

"There must be someone else you can call."

Suddenly, he spots an old woman wearing cat glasses, which jogs his memory. "I can call my girlfriend, Charlotte."

When she picks up the phone, he practically yells, "Charlotte, I am desperate! I forgot that I spent all my money and I ran out of gas, and now the gas station manager wants his money."

Charlotte takes a few seconds to respond. When she does, she says, "Oh, Scotty, that's terrible. How did that happen?"

"It's a long story. I really don't have time to explain," he says, watching the gas station manager looking very impatient by now.

"What can I do?" She asks kindly.

"You work in a bookstore, and you can't figure it out?" Scotty asks.

"Please tell me," Charlotte replies.

"Do you think you could come and loan me some money? I need to be at a seminar. If I don't make it there, it's all over for me. I need a damn job. You hold my life in your Hello Kitty Pocketbook."

"How much money do you need?"

"I have a total of seventy-five cents and I owe $20.75. You do the math."

"Hold on, let me ask my Dad if he will lend me a twenty," she says. She sets the phone down and Scotty hears her talking to her dad in the background.

"Daddy, it's Scotty, you know the one I met at the bookstore."

"What does he want?"

FIRED!

"Normally I wouldn't bother you with this, but I haven't cashed my paycheck yet."

"What does your check have to do with him?"

"He doesn't have enough money to pay for his gas."

"How's that your problem?"

"Daddy, if I don't bring him some cash, he might have the police called on him again. What should I do?"

"You should hang up and refuse to talk to him ever again. That guy is nothing but a hooligan. No child of mine will hang around such a bum like that. Do you understand?"

Scotty hears Charlotte start to cry. "But Daddy, he sounds so distraught. Can you please give me twenty dollars so I can bail him out of this mess? I promise to pay you back as soon as I cash my check."

"What did you just ask me?" He says, asking a rhetorical question.

When she begins repeating her request, he chimes in, "My dear daughter, I am a very wealthy man."

"Then will you give me the money?"

"Money isn't the issue. It is the principal of it. I will give you the money on one condition."

"Daddy, anything."

"You must dump the loser."

Scotty gasps as he hears this interchange. He keeps listening.

"Daddy, is there anything else I can do besides that? He's looking for a job and soon he'll have money."

The Outrageously Ridiculous Adventures of Scotty J. Fahrenheit

"Isn't that's what all losers say? Here's the deal. After you give him the money, you are forbidden from seeing him until he finds a job. And when I say job, I mean a full-time position that pays a decent salary," he preaches before handing her the cash.

Charlotte dashes back to the phone. "I'll be there shortly," she says just before the store clerk grabs the phone out of Scotty's hand. "This is a business phone you can't tie it up."

Scotty stands by the door, waiting for her to arrive. When he spots her, he runs outside and flags her down.

The clerk, under the impression that he is going to drive off without paying, opens the door and yells, "You get back here and pay for your gas!"

"You better get inside," she says, handing him the money.

"Hey, Buddy, you need to calm yourself down," Scotty says, irately throwing the cash on the counter.

He runs back outside to Charlotte and gushes, "You're a lifesaver. I don't mean to be rude, but I really can't talk now. I have to get to the seminar, but I will call you later with the details."

"Please don't," she says with tears in her eyes.

"What's that supposed to mean? Why are you crying?"

"My dad gave me the money, but he forbids me from seeing you. Well, at least until you find a good job," she says, sniffling.

"You've got to be kidding. This was supposed to be the best day of my life. Then I almost ran out of gas, and now you spring this on me. Charlotte, I thought we could spend the rest of our lives together. Instead, I will spend the rest of the day wondering what my life will be like without you. I just can't deal with your

FIRED!

abusive father's demands right now," He says while ambling over to his car.

"Good-bye for now, my love," He says sadly before blowing her a kiss.

Chapter 8

Finally on his way to the seminar, Scotty is driving down the highway with the pedal to the medal, when suddenly his car starts overheating. He spies wisps of smoke are billowing from under his hood and he pounds a fist on the steering wheel and screams out, "God, help me!"

With the smoke continuing to worsen, Scotty begins to slow down. Making matters worse, the car begins making a loud knocking noise. Fearfully he takes his foot completely off the gas, slowing the car to a crawl. People are whizzing by, tooting their horns and pointing to the smoking car. Scotty is enraged. A concerned man in an expensive sedan slows down and calls out, "Having car trouble?"

"Idiot!" He yells at the man. The guy just looks at him and shakes his head before speeding away.

Not even a minute later, another man slows down and motions to him, "Pull over."

By now, Scotty is at his wit's end. "Does this reject think I am blind? I can see the damn thing is ready to blow."

The driver keeps motioning to Scotty.

"Buddy, shut up," Scotty yells out.

FIRED!

He manages to pull his car onto the narrow shoulder. Just as he is about to get out, an eighteen-wheeler has a blowout. The tread comes off and smashes into Scotty's door.

"What the heck just happened?" Scotty shouts, getting whiplash from the impact. Realizing his time is limited he tries to open the door. Unfortunately, it won't open. He tries pounding the door, wiggling the handle, and finally kicking the door. All his attempts are futile. With no other recourse, he squeezes his way to the passenger side and gets out, huffing in exertion.

Scotty walks to the front of the car and without thinking he puts his hands on the steaming hood, then immediately retracts them, screaming in pain. He puts his burning hands to his mouth and spits on them, the only way he knows to try to help ease the agony.

Now Scotty turns his attention back to the car and realizes that he must fix whatever is wrong with it. Having no mechanical skills doesn't deter him. A light goes off in that little brain of his. First he strips off his shirt and wraps it around his burned hands. Then he grabs hold of the hood latch to open it, but the built-up pressure blows the hood wide open, sending a huge puff of searing smoke into his face, severely burning his eyes and forehead as well as scorching his very blonde hair.

Startled and in a lot of pain, Scotty jumps back and begins rubbing his blurry eyes.

Just then a family drives by looking at Scotty. A little girl in the back seat points out the window and asks, "Mommy, why is that fat man jumping up and down without a shirt on?"

"Look away," The mother warns her young daughters.

"No, Sweetheart, don't look away," the father chimes in, "take a good, long look and see what a stark raving maniac looks

The Outrageously Ridiculous Adventures of Scotty J. Fahrenheit

like. That's the kind of crazy man I want you to avoid when you get older." He slows down and puts on his blinkers so everyone in the car can get a good look at Scotty.

The mother offers, "And stay away from anyone like that man at any age. Nobody who acts like that is safe," she adds as they slowly drive by.

Meanwhile, another person takes note of the situation. Instead of just staring, she actually pulls over, gets out of her car, and offers to help. "My dear Lord, your face and hair seem to be on fire. Are you okay?"

"Do I look like I'm okay? No! I'm in serious pain," he shrieks out.

"Oh, Mister, you should get away from the car," she says, backing away. "There's some sort of liquid squirting out from a couple of tiny holes. Look right there, do you see it?" She asks, pointing to the spots, but keeping a good distance in case the car should suddenly explode.

Scotty squints his burning, blurry eyes and looks at the car. Seeing what the woman was pointing to, he brightens and says, "Wait a minute, I can fix that," he says as he ducks his head back into the passenger side and rummages through the glove compartment.

"Perfect," he says, grabbing a roll of duct tape.

"What are you going to do?" The woman says, watching him cut the tape with his teeth.

Scotty tears off several strips of the tape and seals off the holes. He stands back and inspects his work, adding another tape strip and steps back again. Satisfied that all the leaks are fixed, he squeezes himself back through the passenger side to get into

FIRED!

the driver's seat and waves to the helpful stranger before peeling out back onto the road.

The woman just shakes her head in utter disbelief and walks to her car.

***

Finally, he arrives at the building where the seminar is to take place. He squeals up to an empty parking spot and parks the still-steaming car, awkwardly maneuvers his massive weight over the center console, and crawls out the passenger-side door. He lifts the hood to let the car cool down while he's in the seminar, being careful this time to lean away from the car when opening it to avoid scorching what's left of his hair. Then he tries in vain to fix his rumpled and scorched appearance using his reflection in the window before going inside.

He starts walking toward a woman at a receptionist's desk when a well-dressed woman standing by the door remarks, "Sir this is a private event."

Fuming, Scotty can barely contain his emotions. He points his finger at her and says, "Don't you dare give me that. You have *no idea* what I've been through. I belong here just as much as you. Do you understand me?" he says through clenched teeth.

"If that is the case, you need to produce some proof. Show me your invitation letter."

"You've got to be joking," Scotty says in frustration.

"Sir, everyone here has paid a lot of money to attend this seminar. I'm just doing my job. You look like a real degenerate, and if I let you in I could lose my job."

"Just because you have a highfalutin' door job, doesn't mean you can treat me like this. People like you find it so easy to judge people like me. It just ain't fair. After all, I'm a human being, no different than you."

"Well sir—" the young lady gets out before he interrupts, again pointing his finger at her.

"Stop calling me 'Sir.' My flipping name is Scotty. You want to know why I look like this? Let me tell you, Lady," he says before she again demands he show proof.

"I'll get the damn invitation, and then you will owe me an apology," he says before walking away.

He rustles through his car with no luck. "My life has become a freaking sci-fi movie. I can't take one more minute of this."

Just then a man comes walking over, saying, "Hey man, are you having car trouble?"

Scotty straightens and says to the kind man, "Not anymore. That happened on my way over here. My biggest problem is that rude female door hop."

"Why is that?"

"I can't find my invitation, so that demanding witch won't let me in," Scotty explains, clearly frustrated.

Thankfully, the man agrees to escort him in, saying that he has the authority to get him into the meeting. "But...I think you should go in the bathroom before you go to the seminar."

"Thank you, but I really don't have to go right now," Scotty says with a blackened smile.

The man chuckles and struggles to explain, "Let me try to say this nicely; you smell worse than horse manure and you look like you haven't showered in years. You really should freshen

FIRED!

up," he says, pointing to the men's room down the hall and patting Scotty's shoulder gingerly before walking away.

In the men's room, Scotty ambles to the sink and splashes water on his face. Looking up, he's panicked by his reflection. He uses some soap to wash his face, patting it with a paper towel. Now his face is clean, but it is clear that his eyebrows have been scorched right off and there are bright red splotches where his face got burned from the hot steam.

Looking up, he spies his burned hair and tries to fix it, which only serves to cause the burned portions to snap off. Now the burned-end blond hair is sticking straight up so he decides to leave it alone.

With nothing more that can be done to his fair hair, he notices how dirty his shirt is. "I can't go in there like that!" he exclaims. He takes off the filthy shirt and tries to clean it in the tiny bathroom sink, which doesn't work out very well. Now it's not only dirty, but it's also soaking wet.

He looks around frantically, hoping for an air dryer, but the bathroom is well-stocked with paper towels—not an air dryer in sight. He tries his best to wring out as much water as possible and uses paper towels to try to dry it without success. With no other option, he shakes out the dirty, wet, and now extremely wrinkled shirt and puts it back on, the wetness causing it to cling to his body in a rather unfashionable, see-through manner.

Looking in the mirror again, Scotty says out loud to himself, "Well, I guess this is the best it's gonna get," before heading out of the bathroom to find the seminar.

Chapter 9

Scotty is in the hallway on the way to the seminar room when he hears someone saying in a microphone, "We will be starting the seminar in just a moment, so we will ask you all to please take your seats now."

Scotty rushes in the room and looks around. The large space has rows of chairs set up, facing a raised platform where a man stands behind a podium with a microphone coming out of it. Windows line the left side of the room, and the right side has posters about jobs tacked to walls. He scans the rows of chairs and realizes that every seat is taken. Craning his head to scope out any possibility, he spots a tiny elderly woman sitting in the front row and makes his way down to the front.

"Excuse me, Lady," Scotty begins, "there's no seats left and you look like you only take up half of your seat. Do you mind if you share your seat with me?"

The aged woman is taken back, not only by Scotty's ragged appearance, but also by his ridiculous suggestion. She reaches for her purse and hits him in the head.

"Ow! I'll take that as a no," he says, rubbing the sore spot on his head.

"Excuse me, Sir," a large-muscled man in a suit says, taking Scotty by the arm, "but you will have to stand. Come over

FIRED!

here," he finishes, leading Scotty to the end of the front row and showing him where to stand next to the wall.

Soon a well-dressed man addresses the crowd. "Good afternoon, folks. I hope you are all having a marvelous day."

"Anything but," Scotty scoffs and mutters loud enough for everyone around him to hear.

The man continues speaking, "I would like to congratulate you on your latest endeavor."

Suddenly a loud bang could be heard coming from the parking lot. A bunch of people run over to the windows and start pointing, their eyes getting wide as one man speaks up to report, "Looks like the hood just blew off that old green clunker."

Knowing it's his green clunker they are talking about, Scotty is poised like a statue and begins sweating profusely.

It's not long before the man in the chair next to him looks concerned and asks, "Hey, man, are you alright? Looks like you're going to pass out."

Too panicked to speak, Scotty just shakes his head.

Everyone is returning to their seats now and the speaker at the podium begins.

"Every person in this room is here for one reason only—to find a job, of course. As you all know, it can be a very tough process. I know you're all sick and tired of the rejections. That's where we come in. We're here to alleviate the pain and suffering involved with your job search."

"Pain and suffering is right," Scotty thinks to himself. "If they only knew."

The Outrageously Ridiculous Adventures of Scotty J. Fahrenheit

The man continues, "By now you're all wondering how this is done. It deals with a concept that guarantees positive results. I know you're probably at the edge of your seat wondering what it is."

"I would be if I had a seat," Scotty mutters. The man next to him just shushes him softly and they go back to listening.

"It all started a few years back with a man named David Weitzman. Getting laid off from his job caused desperation to set in. With mounting bills and no money in his pocket, he headed down to the local unemployment office. There he was surprised to see all the people in the same boat. That night he came up with the brilliant idea of contacting local companies in order to get a list of their job openings. Next, he hired coaches to find people to fill those positions. This program has been so successful. As of today, I can't think of anyone who has been dissatisfied."

Scotty perked up. It certainly sounded like a good idea and he was hopeful that it could help him get a job too.

"I understand you are all wondering if the money you invested was worth it." The man said with a smile, "I can absolutely promise that everyone in this room will get a job. The only thing I can't tell you is how long it will take. Some of you will land jobs sooner than others, but don't get discouraged. Faster isn't always better. If anyone in this room feels the program isn't right for them, by all means, you may leave now and get a full refund. This is an investment in one's future. Never, and I mean never, has anyone walked out."

All of a sudden, Scotty's stomach begins rumbling. His irritable bowel syndrome is acting up—and drinking a gallon of milk for breakfast didn't help his lactose intolerance either. Too bad he didn't heed his mother's warning. With clenched butt cheeks, he has to walk all the way past the front row to the middle aisle to head for the door at the back of the room. His face turns bright red and he worries that he won't make it to the bathroom.

All eyes are on Scotty as the speaker remarks, "Well, I guess there is a first time for everything. There goes a very foolish man with no interest in his future."

With a hand on his butt to try to help hold things in, Scotty bounces a bit as he tries to explain, "No, I don't want to leave, but I'm about to crap my pants if I don't make it to a toilet," he says in a strained voice before running out of the crowded room and down the hall to the bathroom.

Thrown off by the strange exchange, the speaker laughs awkwardly and says to the crowd, "Well, that may be the first man not to get a job. I've never dealt with anyone so vulgar."

He quickly changes the subject, "I'm going to pass out a questionnaire and ask each of you to answer every question. This is not a test, so there is no right or wrong answers. If you have any questions, please feel free to raise your hand."

A few volunteers pass the forms out in short order and it doesn't take long for everyone to finish answering the questions and turn in their sheets. When everyone is done, the speaker again addresses the group. "The next step is easy. We will look at each of your answers and assign a job coach to you. Then you will all come back here next Monday and we will go from there. Have a wonderful week, and I look forward to seeing you all very soon."

Just after everyone has left, Scotty enters the room. The only one left is the speaker, organizing some papers on a table in the back. "Where did everyone go?" he asks.

The speaker recognizes Scotty immediately and replies with a smirk, "Hope everything came out okay. And by the way, you're just a little bit late. I had everyone fill out their questionnaires. There's nothing more I can do for you."

"Sir, haven't you ever had to go to the bathroom so bad that you can't hold it?" Scotty demands.

"What the hell is that rude question supposed to mean?"

"Don't play the dumb act with me, Buddy. You know damn well you're about to throw me out of the program."

The speaker points at Scotty, "Now you listen here, fat boy. If you know what's good for you, you would shut your big pie hole."

"So you're not throwing me out?" Scotty asks, confused.

"Believe me, if I had my way, you'd be history. But it's not up to me," the speaker says with obvious irritation.

"Would you make up your mind?" Scotty asks.

"Are you some kind of an idiot? Listen, I've got a lot to do, and I don't have time for your stupidity. Since you missed filling out the questionnaire, just put your name on the top, and I will fill in the rest. Understand?"

"What are you talking about?" Scotty is very confused now.

"That would be the questionnaire I passed out while you were blowing up the bathroom. I can tell that you're not going to be easy, probably impossible. Unless your coach is Jesus Christ, it would be easier for him to raise Lazarus from the dead than find you a job." He says, handing Scotty the questionnaire and watching him scribble his name and phone number at the top.

FIRED!

"How dare you use the Lord's name in vain," Scotty says as he shoves the paper back in the man's hand, "My Ma would be appalled at you."

"Just show up next Monday at 8 a.m.," the very agitated man says before walking away.

Chapter 10

Scotty rushes out to his car and slams the hood down. At least it appears that the engine has stopped smoking. He puts the key in the ignition and turns. Scotty is not at all surprised when it won't start.

Looking up to the sky he hollers out, "Hey, God, it's me. Can you have a little pity on this poor soul? I am at the end of my rope!"

Just then the speaker walks over from where his car is parked in the next row and says, "You know, I'm not surprised that this pile of junk belongs to you."

Scotty figures maybe he shouldn't have been so rude in the building. Maybe it would help to try to be nice now. "Look, I know we got off on the wrong foot, but I'm really desperate. My car won't start. Ya think you can help me here?"

"Oh sure, I can help you alright," the speaker chides.

"Thank you so much," Scotty says in relief. Maybe being nice was working.

"Don't thank me. Thank yourself," the man says bitterly.

Scotty is confused, he thought the guy was going to help, but his tone of voice sure didn't sound like it. "Look, I'm not very good at figuring things out. Can you please tell me how you can help me?" Scotty asks.

The man just smirks, "By telling you to call for a tow. I have to leave for another appointment," he says before getting in his car and driving away.

Scotty goes back into the building and asks the receptionist to use the phone. He calls 911 and they answer on the first ring.

"911 what's your emergency?"

"Where do I start?"

"Sir, please tell me your emergency."

"My car blew up in the parking lot."

"Are you burned, having trouble breathing, or experiencing chest pains?"

"No, it's nothing like that."

"Sir this is an emergency hotline. What is your emergency?"

"I need a tow truck. I have no idea how to get ahold of a towing service."

"Sir, we are here for emergencies only. Do you understand that you could be fined for this prank? I advise you to hang this phone up and call a towing service," the woman says before hanging up.

Scotty looks around. By this time he's getting upset. This day isn't what he was hoping it would turn out to be at all.

The receptionist has left, but luckily there was a janitor coming down the hallway. The friendly old man walks over to Scotty. "You feeling alright?"

"I just need a tow truck," he manages.

The old man pats him on the shoulder, "Hey, no problem! I drive an old clunker and I've had my fair share of breakdowns. That's why I carry the tow truck number in my wallet at all times," he says before jotting the number down for Scotty.

Scotty calls the number right away. He gives them his location and tells them what happened, and is hopeful for finally getting some help. After three hours, a truck with "Fifth Brothers" written on the side zooms in the lot. Scotty begins raising his arms. "Over here!" he calls.

The tow truck driver speeds over. "Looks like this baby has seen better days. Where do you want me to take this heap?"

"I have no idea. I thought that was your job."

"My job is to take this car to a garage. You a mechanic?"

"No."

"You know a mechanic?" the man asks.

"Nope," Scotty answers.

"I usually suggest my cousin Vinny to people like yourself. He's probably the best mechanic this side of the map. So what do you think? Is it a go?"

"Right now, anything is a go," Scotty says, watching as the guy hops out of the truck and hooks up his car.

After the car is all set and ready to go, Scotty climbs onto the flatbed and attempts to get into his car.

"Hey, what the heck are you doing?" The tow guy yells.

"I am trying to get into my car so I could come along for the ride."

FIRED!

"You can't ride in the car. Do you want me to lose my license?" the man shakes his head, irritated at Scotty's stupidity.

"I'm sorry, I didn't know, Geez." Scotty gets down off the flatbed and walks to the passenger's door of the tow truck. When he opens the door, the driver loses his temper. "What are you trying to do now?"

"I need a ride. Why are you so hostile; what is your problem?"

"It's against company policy to give any person a ride. You have to find your own ride to wherever it is you need to go. I gotta get this heap to Vinny's garage," He says, reaching over and slamming the passenger's side door.

"What am I supposed to do now?" Scotty asks.

"Buddy, I'm a tow truck driver, not a chauffeur. By the looks of you, walking might be a damn good solution. If all fails, call a cab—that's what they're there for."

Scotty asks out of the blue, "Hey, where did you get the name Fifth Brothers towing?"

The driver shrugs, "I'm the fifth boy."

Scotty is amazed, "Your mom must have been a strong woman to have five kids."

"Not really, she died after the eleventh. She always wanted a girl, and she got one, but it came with a steep price."

"I always thought things got cheaper the more you had."

The tow truck driver just looks at Scotty in utter amazement. "May she rest in peace. I can tell you she would be so proud of her only daughter. She turned out to be the prettiest tomboy this side of town."

The Outrageously Ridiculous Adventures of Scotty J. Fahrenheit

Scotty realizes that he doesn't know where in the world Vinny's garage is so he asks for directions. The tow truck driver is kind enough to oblige before leaving Scotty to walk back.

Chapter 11

After walking just over five minutes, Scotty is already so tired that he decides to hitchhike. Cars continue speeding by with nobody stopping.

After another minute a very old, dark blue Mercedes Benz in pristine condition slowly pulls alongside Scotty. An old woman with white hair wearing what looks like a hospital gown over her clothes yells out, "Where you headed?"

Not hearing the woman the first time, he says, "Excuse me?"

"I said, where you headed? Are ya deaf, Son?"

"No that would be the love of my life. The one I just lost."

"Look, you got your finger stuck out for a ride. You want to hop in, or cry over some girl who dumped you?"

"At this point I would take a ride from just about anyone."

"You're in luck then, cause I'm that anyone. Hop in and shut the door," the old woman orders.

Scotty gets in the passenger side and says, "My car just got towed to Vinny's. You know where it is?"

"Do I look like a road map?" she says, shaking her head. She pulls back onto the road. Tell me where it is and I can take you there. He gives her the directions just the way the tow truck

The Outrageously Ridiculous Adventures of Scotty J. Fahrenheit

driver told him. Changing the subject, she asks, "What do you think of my husband's dream car?"

"It looks brand new. How many miles you got on this baby?"

"Don't have the faintest."

Scotty looks at the odometer shocked at it registering only 100 miles. "Wow! this is what you call an old new car. She is in showroom condition. Why aren't there any miles on her?"

"My husband always wanted a Benz. So one day he went out and picked this one from the showroom. He drove it home and when he pulled her into the garage, he dropped dead just as he was taking the key out of the ignition."

"Sounds a lot like a horror movie."

"How's that?" the old woman asks.

"There was a car in a very scary movie that went crazy and killed people."

"You're making me nervous. How do I know this car isn't the one you're talking about?"

"Your car is a blue German car. That one was a red Chevy. By the way, why haven't you driven this very much?"

"Way before my husband, Jed, died I got my license revoked."

"Why?"

"I suffer from this problem called narcolepsy. Ever hear of it?"

"No, what is it?"

"I can fall asleep at any time," the woman said as she took a turn.

FIRED!

"You mean anytime?"

"Yeah, it can happen right now."

"Do you get any warning signs?" Scotty asks.

"No, I just pass out. But that pales in comparison to my latest blow," she nods her head slowly as she remembers.

"What can be worse than that Narc thing?"

"I got something called dementia, which they are blaming on my paranoia schizophrenia."

"What's the big deal with that?" Scotty wonders.

"It's only the damn doctors in the loony bin who seem to have a problem with it."

"How would you know about that place?"

"Please don't tell me a big guy like you frets over an old woman like me?"

"I don't fret over anything," Scotty replies.

"So it won't bother you to know that I just escaped from the mental hospital today. I don't know what was worse; the crazies, or all the pills they forced down my throat!" she exclaims.

"I thought pills were supposed to be a good thing?"

"Not unless you like having constipation," the woman replies sarcastically.

"Gee, I wish I had that problem during the seminar today," Scotty remarks. He leans over and says to the old woman, "And by the way, I think it's okay that you left the hospital."

"It's beyond okay that I escaped the nut house. Actually, it's so freeing. The only problem with it is that I no longer have protection."

"What do you need protection from?" Scotty asks, now concerned.

"Move close while I say this very softly" she says in a low voice. Scotty leans in again as she continues, "The government is after me. Notice that while I am speaking to you I have my hand over the door lock?"

Scotty peers over to her door, confirming what she said. "No I didn't notice," he replies, "but now that you mention it, I see what you're talking about."

"The government went into this car and bugged every inch of it. Same with my house," she whispers.

"How did you find that out?" Scotty whispers back, his eyes shifting around looking for the hidden devices.

"I noticed an unusual speck on the bathroom floor. It definitely was some sort of a bugging device," she nods as she continues to drive.

"That is some real sick stuff!" Scotty says, appalled.

"I can understand them bugging my house, but, damn, you would think the bathroom would be off limits!" The woman's paranoia begins kicking in, her voice raising a few notches.

"Bastards are perverts bugging your bathroom and all," Scotty can't believe what he's hearing.

"You got that right," she agrees.

"Why did they bug you in the first place?" he questions.

FIRED!

"They're trying to find out about the planet I come from," she says matter-of-factly.

"What planet might that be?" Scotty lifts an eyebrow and unconsciously inches away from the lady.

"It's a secret planet called Norwood," she replies.

"You're the first ET person I've ever met," Scotty says, now enthralled. "I've been stuck here all my life. I would love to take a trip to your planet. Wow, you're so lucky!"

"Thanks, I think so too. See, unlike your kind, I have everyone and everything figured out. The only problem is convincing others about the danger they're in," She says.

Scotty suddenly realizes that for the past few minutes they've just been driving aimlessly around, especially when they pass the same tree for the fourth time.

"Is that why you are driving in circles?" he asks.

"I have to do this to throw them off track," she explains.

Scotty thinks for a moment and an idea pops in his head. "Maybe I should drive. They aren't looking for me."

She agrees and Scotty takes the wheel. When they finally arrive at the auto repair shop, he jumps out of the car and thanks the old woman. "Hey, if you ever go back to your planet, promise you'll look me up."

"You got it, Sonny-boy," she says as she begins to pull away.

Scotty watches her drive off for a moment, saying, "Wow. A true blue alien, you can never tell about people. I never even got her—its—name."

Chapter 12

"Anybody here?" Scotty calls out as he enters the garage.

"Can I help you?" asks a guy who's changing oil in a truck.

"My car was brought in a little bit ago."

"Which car would that be? As you can see, we get a lot of cars brought in."

"It would be the green Valiant over there," he says, pointing to his car.

"Hold on a minute. I'll get Vinny." The man says, grabbing a work towel and wiping the oil off his hands before walking into another room.

A few moments later a very irate Italian man hurries into the room. "So you're the jerk that owns that once-wonderful piece of machinery. I can't believe she hung on as long as she did, seeing all the abuse she's endured. And duct tape? Really? People like you make me sick," The man says, spitting on the ground.

Scotty didn't know what to say. "Look, I had a very important place I had to get to. If I didn't put the duct tape on the hose, I never would've made it."

"You know what this car reminds me of?" Vinny asks.

FIRED!

"No," Scotty replies nervously.

"Let me spell it out for you. This car resembles a person who has been beaten beyond recognition; a person just clinging to life," he says, pinching his fingers close together to illustrate as he talks. He gives Scotty a once-over and adds, "by the looks of things, you don't give two damns."

"Actually, I give three damns," Scotty remarks.

"There's so many rules in this state, you'd think there would be one to keep abusers like yourself from owning cars." The man is getting really upset by now and is practically yelling at Scotty. "So you drop her off—beyond life support—and expect me to revive her. Are you seriously crazy?"

I don't think so," Scotty replies, "crazy is what the hospital called that old woman who dropped me off. She's probably in a narc state as we speak."

Vinny is taken back by the directional shift of the conversation. He scrunches his face in confusion and throws his hands up as he asks, "What gives you the right to call an old woman crazy?"

"Oh, she told me the doctors called her crazy, but I thought she sounded perfectly sane," Scotty says, thinking that he makes total sense.

"There you go, calling someone out for something you say but may not be true. Shut it, buddy," Vinny says, obviously ticked off.

Scotty realizes now that the conversation has drifted away from his car getting fixed. "Anyway, back to my car, can you please have it fixed before Monday?"

Now Vinny looks at Scotty with eyes wide, "What? You're the crazy one, asking me such an insane question."

"I am not trying to aggravate you," Scotty says, "how can I show you how sorry I am for what happened to my car?"

"Let's get this right, jerk boy. What happened to your car is your complete abuse and neglect. Now you expect me to perform a miracle on her? Last I knew, there is only one God—and it certainly ain't me," he adds with a sarcastic laugh.

Scotty takes a step forward and clasps his hands together in front of him, "Please, I am begging you. I desperately need my wheels for Monday."

Vinny thinks a moment. He shifts his weight and puts a hand out, "Okay, listen up; I have a deal for you—" Vinny offers before Scotty interrupts.

"Sure, anything."

Vinny nods "I'll take that as a yes." He walks over and puts a hand carefully on the hood of Scotty's car. "Here is the deal. Since this car was destined for greatness, I'm going to bring her back to life. I mean, the works. She's going to look better than the day she drove off the factory floor. You understand what I'm saying?"

"I do…but when can I pick her up? Remember, I need her by Monday."

Vinny looks down and shakes his head. He looks back up and says, "You're a real derelict. Let me refresh that dense memory of yours: I am not God, Jesus Christ, or the Holy Spirit. That means you've got to give me enough time to restore her to her full potential. Any questions?"

"What do I do to get around?" Scotty asks, now getting irritated.

FIRED!

Vinny looks him up and down and says, "Seems to me that taking up jogging would do you some good."

"You sound just like the Fifth Brothers tow guy."

"Everyone who sees you is gonna be thinking the same thing. But don't you worry, I've got a loaner in the yard. I can let you use it until she's all done," Vinny says before directing Scotty and one of his workers to the back lot.

There in the yard is an old, yellow rusted-out van. "Here's the wheels the boss is letting you use."

Scotty looks at the junker. "Looks good to me," he remarks. "How does she run?"

"I really don't know, but you'll find out soon enough," The man says, tossing Scotty the keys.

Chapter 13

As the worker walks back to the garage, Scotty opens the driver side door to the van, which opens with a loud, metallic creak. He crams his massive belly into the too-small space between the seat and the steering wheel and feels around for the lever to adjust the seat to move back. Finding it, he turns it and it falls off in his hand. Refusing to let that deter him, he decides to drive with his belly wedged up against the steering wheel.

He sticks the keys in the ignition and cringes as he turns the key, half expecting it not to start. Miraculously it starts up, although it doesn't sound the greatest.

Happy to have transportation again, Scotty heads for the highway and races onto the ramp. Just as he begins merging into the traffic it starts to downpour. Because he didn't take time to learn the controls, he's unable to discern what button goes to what, so he just begins pressing buttons, trying to find the windshield wipers. "Wrong one," he yells as the radio begins to blare.

Lucky for him, he finds the wiper switch. He presses the button and the wipers make one swipe before shutting off.

"What the heck is this?" He screams. By this time the rain is beating down hard and the only way to keep the wipers going is to keep pressing the button. Soon the windshield begins fogging up, but he can't stop pressing the wiper button or he won't be able to see. Being in a pickle, he decides he has no choice but to turn the defrost button on. He keeps one hand on the wiper button and takes the other hand off the wheel to find the defrost switch. In desperate need of an alignment, the van veers off the road. Scotty abandons the buttons and grabs the wheel with both hands and slams on the brakes. When the van stops he takes a deep breath and peers out the windshield. One more inch and he would have gone off a steep embankment.

While he's stopped he turns the defrost on and cranks the air vents, hoping the windshield will defrost quickly so he can get back on his way. With the radio still blaring, a puff of dust—carrying dead insects and cobwebs—comes through the vents, directly into his face.

"Ahhh," Scotty yells, spitting the filth out of his mouth. He tries to wipe the junk off, but his skin begins peeling from the burn he received earlier.

He has no choice but to turn the defrost off. Within just a few seconds the windshield fogs up. With one hand, he clears a small spot so he can see. He looks totally ridiculous so close to the steering wheel looking through a spot no bigger than a peep hole.

"Well, this is the best it's gonna get," he says, putting the car in Reverse and backing away from the steep embankment to get back on the road. He can't even see out of the back window at all, and a car blares its horn at him, swerving around him as he backs up.

He drives down the road going very slow, not even trying to keep track of how many cars went around him or people who

The Outrageously Ridiculous Adventures of Scotty J. Fahrenheit

gave him angry stares—or worse—while getting home. It had to be divine providence that got him back safely.

***

After parking the ancient van in the driveway, Scotty does his best to extract his body out of the seat. His belly hits the horn, blaring it loud and long enough to get the whole neighborhood's attention.

Mable has been sitting in the front room and looks out the window, watching as he tries to get out of the van.

She opens the door and stands on the porch, calling, "Who's van is that?"

"Ma, just help pull me out of this thing, would you?"

Muttering to herself, she climbs down the porch steps and plods over to help her son. After taking one look at him she starts in with the questions, "What in the world happened to you? Where is your car? And what happened to your face?"

"Please, Ma, can you wait until we're in the house before you badger me. I'm losing feeling in my legs. Believe me when I say that my day could not get any worse," he says too loudly, his ears ringing from the radio blasting loudly in his ears for so long. He is still struggling to free his massive bulk from the seat.

"The day is not over yet," she says, trying to encourage him.

"Gee, thanks for that, Ma. You're right, something worse may be following me, just waiting to strike me down even more!" he yells, in no mood for niceness.

"Oh, stop with the drama," she lectures.

"There you go again, saying things and calling my reaction to it drama," he says back, yelling even louder.

FIRED!

"Why you are screaming at the top of your lungs?" She says, motioning for him to lower his voice.

"Unlike Charlotte, I can't read lips. You gotta wait until my hearing comes back," he yells as he follows her into the house.

She gives him a motherly once-over and tears up, "Scotty, looking at you makes me cry. This was supposed to be a great day for you, but I can see it didn't turn out that way."

"You're just wasting your time, Ma. Not only can I not hear you, but my eyes are very blurry."

Mable motions for him to lie down on the couch. Then she goes to the medicine cabinet where she finds an old bottle of valium. She is unable to remember when the medication was prescribed to her husband, she just knew that the pills had long expired. "I never thought I would see the day when I would administer drugs to you," she says, filling a glass with water from the sink before handing him the outdated pill and the water.

"What good is this going to do for me?" he asks.

"Honestly, Son, I really haven't a clue. The pill is so old it may not do anything at all."

Scotty asks, "Then what's the use?"

"At this point, anything is worth a try. Please stop running your mouth and swallow the dang pill."

After taking the medicine, Scotty asks, "So what was that, and what it's supposed to do to me?"

"It's Valium. They belonged to your father. I am not sure of the potency, but right now it's my only option. As for what I hope the outcome will be, let's just put it this way: I can't stand one more second of you and your chaotic problems."

The Outrageously Ridiculous Adventures of Scotty J. Fahrenheit

"Wow, Ma, why didn't you just give me the whole bottle and hope they still work. Then you'd never have to worry about me again," Scotty said, irritated.

She stops and turns to her son, pointing at him as she says, "First of all, I never said I wanted anything to happen to you. Second of all, the only medicine your father took on a daily basis was a laxative. So if I were to give you a dose of that, you'd be running to the bathroom."

"Yeah," Scotty agrees, "with my irritable bowel problem, taking those meds would surely be the death of me."

Mable just looks at her son and smiles. Oddly enough, his head droops down and soon he begins snoring. Mable tiptoes out of the living the room.

Unfortunately, her peace and quiet doesn't last very long.

Chapter 14

After just two hours, Scotty wakes up with a stiff neck. "Ma," he calls from the couch.

She walks in the room and sits next to him.

"Let me tell you, Ma, this day was the absolute worst ever."

"What about that rusted out, hideous yellow van parked in my driveway? Just what happened to your car?"

"Where do I begin?" he mutters.

"Try starting with your car."

"The car is the least of my worries. Did you get a good look at my face and hair?"

"I just thought that went along with the whole van thing," she replied, shrugging.

"Oh no, that van was in no way responsible for this. My damn car blew up on the way to the seminar."

"Wasn't it you who told me your car had a lot more miles to go? Please don't tell me you forgot?"

"I have every degree burn known to man, and all you care about is proving me wrong," he says, shaking his head.

The Outrageously Ridiculous Adventures of Scotty J. Fahrenheit

"Please tell me you made it to the seminar," Mable says, clutching her hands together.

"Let me tell you, because of my fast thinking I actually did make it to that stupid seminar. And the guy who was in charge was a first-class—now take the "CL" off the word *class,* and that's what he is."

Mable gasps, "Hush your mouth, Son. What would your father think of your filthy talk?"

"My daddy probably never had a day like this in his whole life. Well, except his last day on earth, of course. I should be asking *you* the same thing."

"Son, we are not here to discuss me," she says pointedly at him.

"Really, Ma? It's not what you said, it's what you did to me."

"I am so lost. What are you talking about?"

"How about giving me some sort of drug that was responsible for knocking me out and giving me the worst stiff neck ever. Now what would my daddy think about that?"

"I'm asking for an apology for your behavior. Do you understand me?"

"I'm sorry, but really, Ma. It all started out good. You know I left early."

"I thought you left much too early," she replied.

"Well, for once you were wrong. Good thing I didn't take your advice. The darn car had no gas, and all I found was seventy-five cents under the seat that probably fell out of your purse. I tried to call you to get money for gas, but you didn't answer the phone."

FIRED!

"I must have had my Richard Simmons exercise tape in," she explains.

"Ma, Richard Simmons must have all the seventy-three-year-old women like you sweating to the oldies."

"Enough about Richard Simmons," she quips, "so who did you end up calling?"

"I called Charlotte. Thank God, she was so kind."

"I find that a positive thing."

"Yeah right, so far. The only problem is that she's forbidden from seeing me."

"Why is that?"

"Because she came to the station with the money to bail me out," he says, as if that explains everything.

"Did you tell her you would pay her back? I'll go in my purse and you can bring her the money right now."

"No, it's not like that. Her father lent her the money and told her she can't see me unless I get a good job," Scotty says, dejected.

"Chin up, Son," Mable responds. "Maybe she's not the one for you. So continue," she says, rotating her finger in a circle.

"Well, when I realized I was going to be late for the seminar, I put the petal to the metal."

"So what's that supposed to mean?"

"Oh, sorry Ma, I forget you're an old lady who's not familiar with my 'jive' talking."

"Please continue," she says again, anxious to hear the rest of the story.

The Outrageously Ridiculous Adventures of Scotty J. Fahrenheit

"Then the car starts smoking."

"I guess she didn't like your petal to the metal," she replies, laughing at her own joke.

"Real funny, Ma," he forced a chuckle.

"I thought it was," she says with a smile then sobers, "Now, for the hundredth time, continue."

"So then the car starts making all kinds of weird noises. You wouldn't believe the creeps who were tooting their horns at me."

"Son, they were probably trying to alert you about your car overheating," she says, peering at him over her glasses.

"Really, Ma? Did they think I didn't notice the smoke coming from the hood?"

"Maybe they were just worried about you," she shrugs.

"So I get to the side of the road and rush to the hood. I put my hands on it to feel how hot it was."

"That explains the burns on your hands," she nods, "I just can't understand what burned your face."

"If you would ever let me finish, you would find out," he raises his voice, upset with all the interruptions to his story.

Putting her hands on her hips, Mable declares, "Scotty James Fahrenheit, I do not know what has gotten into you, but I don't like it. If you can't talk to me in a civil manner, this conversation is over."

Scotty goes from angry to whiney all at once, "Come on, Ma, I just want you to know what I went through. If burning my hands on the hood wasn't bad enough, when I got the hood opened, a big steam bomb practically blew my face off."

FIRED!

"So that's where the burnt hair comes in. You know, Son, it really looks atrocious. Remind me tonight to put some cold cream on it. That stuff does wonders."

"No, Ma, that's only what happened before I got to the seminar, he says before settling in to continue.

"When I got to the seminar, I went into the bathroom to clean up a bit. My shirt had dirt all over it. I tried to spot clean it, but it only made it worse."

"So what did you do about it?"

"Nothing, I just went into the seminar with a dirty, wet shirt on. And by the time I got there, there weren't any seats."

"Please don't tell me you left," she said, slumping.

"Are you for real? Do you think after all I went through, I would have left? I mean, you must think I'm crazy."

"Sometimes I wonder," she replies.

"I can tell you, I stayed and ended up standing at the end of the first row."

"Makes sense," she said, knowing it didn't make much sense at all.

"It feels good to hear you say that, Ma," he says with a smile before continuing. "So the speaker guy went on and on about the importance of the seminar. He said nobody ever walked out of the room."

"I sure hope you didn't."

"Well, I had no choice."

Mable sat up straighter and said, "Not two seconds ago, you told me you didn't leave. Now you are saying the complete opposite. What in God's name would possess you to walk out?"

"You know what happens when I get that stomach cramp?" he asks sheepishly.

"Of course, you refused to listen to me this morning," she says, shaking her head. "Just tell me you made it to the bathroom."

"Yes, I did. I was hoping it was only a false alarm, but I knew it wasn't. I mean, Ma, what a terrible explosion. Every time I tried to get up from the toilet, more kept coming out of my butt—"

Mable closed her eyes and interrupted, holding a hand up, "Okay, you can stop with the graphic description already."

"—By the time I was finished, everyone was gone except Mr. Rude man," Scotty continued.

"Did you miss a lot?"

Scotty shrugged, "How would I know? I was in the bathroom."

"Of course you were. So tell me, are you still in the program?" Mable asks, eagerly waiting for her son's response.

He breaks into a grin, "Yeah, I've got to be there Monday morning at eight."

Visibly relieved, she replies, "That's good. But I still don't know how you got that rusted out run-down van out there," she points out toward the driveway.

Not wanting to get into the rest of the crazy story, Scotty closes his eyes and says, "Please, Ma, my head is pounding

FIRED!

right now. Just know my car is getting fixed by a really great mechanic."

Satisfied for now, she says, "Okay, well at least you made it to the seminar."

"That's true. But let me tell you that this day is up there with one of the worst days of my life," Scotty says, holding a hand way up above his head to illustrate.

Mable sighs and says, "I thought things would get better the older you got."

Scotty takes his mom's hand and says, "Ma, we have to believe that things will turn around for me soon."

"From your lips to the Lord's ears," she rolls her eyes and says, stressed from his never-ending drama.

Chapter 15

Saturday morning arrives and the job coaches have gathered in the conference center. The loud buzzing of conversation abates as Justin James addresses them over the microphone.

"I'm happy to see that you are all doing a great job. I would like to congratulate Stanton Ryan and Stanley Rogers. They have superseded all expectations, and they are currently in a dead heat. If nobody surpasses their numbers, one of them will receive the Job Coach of the Year award. The winner will be awarded a trophy and three thousand dollars. Just remember, in order for an applicant to be considered employed, he must meet the qualifications. First, he must have a job. Secondly, he must maintain the position for at least a week; otherwise, he or she cannot be counted."

"What if the candidate gets a job and keeps it only for a week and then gets another job. Does the job they only kept for a week still count?" one of the new coaches asks.

"Yes, they can be counted," Justin explains.

Stanton, a prestigious university graduate, looks over at Stanley with a gleaming smile and says, "Does it really matter what the rules are? You know as well as I do that I've got this competition in the bag."

"May the best man win," Stanley responds back.

FIRED!

He shakes his head and sizes up the scrawny middle-aged man next to him. He scoffs, "What a lame response. Look at me then look at you. Is there any doubt who the best man is?" Stanton remarks arrogantly.

Justin comes back over the loudspeakers. "As usual, I trust that all you coaches will do your best to help these desperate, unemployed individuals. Remember these people paid a lot of money to be in this program. Due to our overwhelming success, we have more candidates than usual enrolled in the program," he brags.

"Let's just wish one another the best." Stanley says, extending his hand out to Stanton.

Stanton leans away from Stanley's hand, "I don't think so, Loser," he says, crossing his arms and refusing to shake his hand.

"Everyone, please take your seats. I will be handing each of you a packet. Inside you will find the paperwork that your assigned candidates filled out."

One by one each coach is called. They get their packets and return to their seats. Stanley is the last one called up. As soon as he sits back down, he opens his packet and notices the top questionnaire has nothing but a poorly scribbled name and number. He pops back up and returns to where Justin is still standing at the podium, talking with someone.

"Mr. James," he interrupts. Justin gives Stanley his attention. Stanley holds up the card and says, "One of my candidates only filled out his name and phone number." He squints at the scrawled card and says, "To be honest, I'm having trouble making it out."

"That's a good sign. At least he wrote his name and number. I have the utmost faith that you will do a fine job," Justin says, dismissing Stanley's concerns.

Justin then talks again in the microphone and says, "If any of you have questions concerning your candidates, I urge you to get a jumpstart by giving them a call. Stanley, that would definitely be a good thing for you," Justin advises before dismissing the job coaches for the day.

Just as Stanton is about to leave the room, Justin motions him over.

"Once again it looks like you have the advantage. As for Stanley, let's put it this way, never and I mean ever has a worse candidate walked through these doors," Justin confides in a low voice.

"That's great, because in every competition, us Ryans always win, just like my dad, the senator."

Justin chuckles and then points to Stanton's packet. "Looks like one of your candidates is PhD. William A. Dyer. That man has more degrees than a thermometer," he jokes.

"Speaking of a thermometer, I guarantee Dyer is one hot commodity," Stanton brags before walking away.

After finishing his paperwork, Justin gets up to leave. He is startled by Bryant Ryan, Stanton's father, walking into the room. "Hello, Senator, is there something I can help you with?"

Bryant flashes his million-dollar smile and shakes Justin's hand, saying, "Justin, I want to start by telling you how much my son enjoys this interim job. Sometimes you just can't understand your own children. I thought he would've landed a really good job after graduating from one of the most prestigious universities. But for whatever reason, he says he enjoys what he is doing, and when he finally feels like it he will look for a professional job. No offense to this job," Bryant explains.

FIRED!

Justin pats Bryant on the shoulder, "No offense taken. All I can say is that your son is a real go-getter. He's highly competitive, and that's one of the reasons I know he'll go far in life. So what can I do for you?"

Bryant steps closer and lowers his voice, "Well, my son has been obsessing over this contest. I know he can act very self-assured, but believe me, he suffers in silence."

"What do you mean by that?" Justin asks.

"Poor kid has a real problem with anxiety. He grew up with the proverbial 'silver spoon.' Everything he ever wanted was handed to him. When confronted by the slightest bit of stress, he goes off the rails. I don't want him to have to worry about winning this contest, it may send him over the edge," Senator Ryan explains.

"Senator, believe me when I tell you that your son has nothing to worry about. He was given a great group of candidates. One is a Harvard PhD. As for his biggest competitor, he was given a candidate who is practically unemployable." Justin cups his hand over his mouth as though he is telling a secret, "He may be the first person enrolled in the program who won't find a job, he's that bad," he laughs.

"I'm glad to hear that. We Ryans have an image to uphold. My son knows there is no room for second best." The senator keeps his voice low, "I'm sure you'll keep this conversation between us. My son can't know anything about this. When he wins, you will be rewarded," he bribes.

***

Later that evening, Stanton heads to the family mansion. He speeds up the long driveway and parks his new Porsche in front of the magnificent entry way, and rushes into the grand library where his father is seated at a large mahogany desk.

The Outrageously Ridiculous Adventures of Scotty J. Fahrenheit

"Father, I am just on time," he says while pointing to his expensive watch.

"Lucky for you, because you know how I feel about being prompt," his father says, not even looking up from his paperwork.

"What do you want to talk to me about?"

Now Bryant puts his pen down and looks up at his son, "I have this great idea. You see, Stanton it's all about marketing yourself. I've been in politics long enough to know that you have to take every opportunity and make them count."

Stanton is not quite sure where his dad is going with this so he says, "Dad just spell it out. What are you getting at?"

"It's all about making the public love you. It is always a necessity to bring in your constituents. I want this job coach thing to be publicized. I want people to know that the Ryans are all about helping the unemployed find jobs. See how great that looks? The senator's son is concerned with the welfare of others."

"Father, that's my job; I get paid for what I do. It's not like I do it for free."

"Let me tell you what you will be doing. The day they award you the trophy and the bonus, I am going to have the press there. The more exposure the better," Bryant says with a smile.

"What's the big deal about that?" Stanton asks.

"Don't you see? This will be an opportunity for you to shine—"

"Dad it's only a contest," he insists.

"If you could listen without interrupting maybe you'll understand," Bryant says, his winning smile now strained.

FIRED!

Stanton sits back in his seat and mutters, "Sorry, Father."

"Anyway, you will give this elaborate speech prepared by my speech writer. And there in front of everyone you will donate your bonus check to the local homeless shelter."

Now Stanton crosses his arms and says sarcastically, "Thank you, Father, for telling me what I have to do with my money."

Bryant is immune to his son's sarcasm and continues on, "I knew you would see it my way. If you're going to walk in my footsteps, you're going to have to start playing the game—and I'm a pro when it comes to that. With your looks and education, you'll go far in life. Your mother and I have high aspirations for you."

"Thank you for believing in me," is Stanton's cynical response.

"Your granddaddy and his daddy didn't make it to be owners of one of the largest brake companies by being pansies. They knew how to play the game, and they bent the rules as much as they could. All of us Ryans are cut from the same cloth. There is no reason for you to break from the mold. Understand?"

"Yes, Father, I think I do," Stanton replied, resolving that he should go along with his father's plan.

Bryant stands and Stanton follows suit. "Start preparing to stand in front of the cameras and show this town what you're made of," the senator gladly declares.

"You got it," Stanton's shiny smile returns as he walks out of the room.

Chapter 16

Meanwhile, on the opposite part of town, Stanley is sitting at the kitchen table with his wife and five children. Unlike the Ryans, the Rogers are anything but wealthy. Instead of a mansion, their living quarters are old and cramped. Barely able to pay the bills, they don't have the money to relocate or even add on to the house for some extra breathing room.

Stanley was no stranger to such conditions. After his disabled father passed away from a lung disease, he was raised by his mother. Lacking an education, she was forced to work a menial job cleaning rooms at the local hotel, which she did without complaint. At the young age of twelve, Stanley walked downtown and asked a company if they would hire him. In spite of him being too young, the manager had pity on his situation and hired him anyway. Every night he would go home and gladly hand over the little money he earned to his mother. Eventually he accepted that his dream of attending the local community college would never become a reality, and he stayed home to help his mother support the family.

Just before Cindy puts the food on the table, Stanley speaks out, "I have some news that may be positive. I am in a dead heat with another man. The winner gets a pretty big bonus," he adds excitedly.

FIRED!

"Oh, Stanley, we really could use the money," Cindy replies with a smile. "There's so many things that need to be fixed. This house needs some serious renovating. Like that sink in the bathroom that's ready to fall off the wall. Honey, I hope and pray you win that money."

"Dad, do you think I could get new sneakers if you win?" Tommy Jake pipes up.

"If I win, I will do all I can with the money," Stanley promises his wife and children.

After dinner the family crowds into the tiny living room. "I just wish I was competing against someone else," Stanley says, "The guy I'm up against, Stanton, is from a really rich family—and the last thing he needs is more money. I rack my brains out to find these people jobs. Day in and day out, I work, and I work, yet we never seem to get ahead."

"Stanley John Rogers, don't you ever talk like that! You are already a winner. Look at all you were blessed with," She says holding each of her one-year-old twin girls on a hip and looking around the room at the other children.

"I know, Cindy, it's just that I've been feeling guilty," he admits, slumping.

"Guilty for what?"

"The accident that happened while you were giving birth to the twins," he says.

"What in the world are you talking about?" Cindy asked, baffled.

"The doctor claimed that you pulled a nerve, and that's what is causing your eye problem."

"If you're referring to the constant twitching in my eye, let it go. Honestly, I've gotten used to it. For heaven's sake, why would you blame yourself?" She says, exasperated.

"You have my word; if I win the competition, that eye of yours will get fixed," Stanley states while his three-year-old daughter, Ella, jumps on his lap.

Cindy smiles and tilts her head, "You are such a thoughtful man. But if you want to pay for an operation, I would prefer you start with my hemorrhoids. Those things are much more bothersome than a twitchy eye."

"I am going to pray to God. After mass, I am going to ask Father Cliff to say a special prayer for me," Stanley tells her.

"If God is going to listen to anyone, it's definitely going to be Father Cliff. I think that man's a saint," she says with a nod.

Stanley picks up his tattered work bag next to him and flips through the papers in the packet again. After a few moments he says, "So there's just one person in my group of clients who I know nothing about. His name is Scotty. I think I should give him a call. Maybe he and I can meet tomorrow so I can get a jump on things."

"Anything you can do to better your chances makes sense," Cindy remarks.

"I'm trying to come up with something I can do with Scotty to get to know him better. Got any ideas?" He asks Cindy.

Cindy, who just put the twin girls down on the floor to play, taps her chin with her index finger and thinks hard. Suddenly she brightens and says, "Remember last Christmas when my brother gave you two gift certificates for the golf course?"

FIRED!

"Oh yeah, I completely forgot about them, probably because I'm not good at golf," Stanley says with a chuckle.

"You only played once in your life. What do you expect?"

"One time is enough to know," he adds.

"Hush with such negative thinking," she says before going into the kitchen to try to find the certificates.

After a few minutes of riffling through a storage drawer, she finds the certificates and returns to the living room to give them to her husband.

Grateful, Stanley says, "Cindy, you are the most thoughtful wife anyone could ever wish for. I think you're right, going golfing sounds good. I think I'll give Scotty a call right now!"

***

A few moments later, Stanley walks back into the kitchen and calls Scotty.

"Hello," Mable says after picking up the phone.

"Hello. This is Stanley Rogers. I'm Scotty's job coach. I was wondering if he's available?"

"Yes, he is, even if he isn't," She says before putting the phone down and yelling, "Scotty! Pick up the phone!"

Scotty picks up the upstairs phone and practically yells, "Yeah, Ma, what do you want?"

"There is a friendly man named Stanley on the line."

"What does he want?" He continues yelling into the receiver.

"Stanley, I am going to hang up so you can explain whatever it is to my son," Mable says.

Scotty hurries, "Hey, Ma, I found an old, smelly shirt that I thought I lost under my bed. You think you could wash it for me?"

But Mable had already put the receiver down so she didn't hear his question.

"Ma?" Scotty was getting ready to ask his question again when Stanly cleared his voice and spoke.

"Scotty, my name is Stanley Rogers. I am your assigned job coach."

"Well hello, Stanley. I'm so happy you called me. I will see you on Monday," he says and gets ready to hang up the phone.

"Wait a minute," Stanley says urgently, "don't hang up!"

"I thought you called just to say hello," Scotty wonders.

"Well, yes, but I was hoping to meet you before Monday. What do you say we play a round of golf at the Links?"

Having never played golf, Scotty responds, "Uh, sure…I would love to."

"How about I meet you at two o'clock tomorrow?" Stanley asks.

"Sounds like a plan," Scotty agrees gladly.

Chapter 17

The next morning, Stanley and his wife get up early to start their day.

"Stanley, I know you are anxious about winning this contest," Cindy says, "I want you to know that I won't love you any less if you don't win."

Stanley stops to give her a quick peck on the check, "You're just too good for me. Maybe I'm just being selfish about wanting to get the money. It's just that the way your eye always twitches bugs the heck out of me. Can you ever forgive me?" He begs.

Cindy stops what she is doing and puts her hands on her hips, "Gee, I guess I never realized how much I repulse you. I'm so used to it. It must be horrible to be married to such an ugly woman like me."

Stanley tried to take back what he just said, "Cindy, that came out all wrong. If I was repulsed by you, I wouldn't be able to have children with you."

Now she is miffed, "I think you forgot that I had our children before my eye started twitching. If it's alright with you, me and my repulsive eye are going to leave the room now."

"Cindy please forgive me. It didn't come out the way I wanted it to," he continues to beg.

"Please, enough about my eye already," she says, holding a hand up and walking away to get the children ready for church.

The rest of the time while Stanley is getting ready for church, he feels so bad about opening up his mouth. When Cindy comes downstairs with the kids in tow, Stanley remarks, "Can I tell you how beautiful you look today? All eyes will be on you in church," he says with a smile.

Cindy's jaw drops and she says, "Is that supposed to be a joke? All eyes will be on me?"

After apologizing again profusely, Stanley stays quiet the whole way to church. When they enter the building, their three-year-old daughter, Ella, runs toward the front of the sanctuary. Cindy takes off after her, holding the twins on each hip.

She catches up to Ella and reins her in to the front pew. By that time, Stanley and the rest of the children meet up with them. "Good job, Honey," he praises her efforts.

Still reeling over his earlier insult, she refuses to acknowledge his compliment.

During the homily, Father Cliff talks about miracles. He explains how they happen in many of our lives. "Sometimes we think there is nothing bigger than ourselves. We misconstrue what is positive for what seems to be anything but. Do we have such little faith that we are unable to see God working in our lives? God knows what is good, and He rewards us. We should all strive to be disciples of the Lord and hold no hard feelings, instead forgiving and loving one another," he preaches.

Cindy begins tearing up and looks over at Stanley, mouthing, "I am so sorry. I forgive you."

FIRED!

He smiles back and says quietly, "Thank you."

After mass, Stanley and the rest of his family walk over to greet Father Cliff. "Thank you for another wonderful mass. You always give such inspirational sermons. I try my hardest to follow your lead. I have to admit, I am in a tough spot and I really need the Lord's help."

"What's troubling you, Stanley?"

"I'm trying to win this competition, but I don't think I have such a great chance at it. Do you think God can help me?"

"God knows what's best for us. He will never condone anything that is evil," Father Cliff explains.

"This is something that will help my family. Father, there is a monetary award and we could desperately use the money."

"Stanley, I'm sure God will be with you during your competition. It may not be easy, but just remember that when we struggle, God is right beside us. Have faith that God will never abandon you," Father preaches.

"I will, Father," Stanley says and shakes his hand before he and his family walk over to their fifteen-year-old van.

Cindy gushes, "I'm so sure that you're going to win the contest. Like I said, Father Cliff is such a holy man. I really believe he has a direct line to God. I appreciate what he said about the competition. You're going to win. I just feel it!" She exclaims excitedly as they work on getting all the kids in their car seats.

Stanley smiles at his supportive wife, "I have to think positive. I'm not going to let anything get me down. Now I'm really looking forward to meeting with Scotty this afternoon."

After the family gets home, Cindy gets working on fixing a light lunch for the family. While she is busy in the kitchen, Stanley heads to their small bedroom to change out of his only suit. He hurries back to the kitchen and practically inhales his food.

"Hey, slow down there," Cindy says, watching him wolf his food down, "it's not going anywhere!"

"I'm sorry," he manages between large bites, "my nerves are getting the best of me."

"You still have some time before you have to leave. Why don't you lay down and relax a bit? Cindy advises him.

Taking her advice, Stanley lays down on the worn-out plaid couch in the living room. It helps a little bit, even though he can't fall asleep.

When it's time to get ready to leave, Stanley hugs each of his children, kisses his wife, and tells her how much he loves her.

"Go get em', Champ," Cindy says, giving him a big kiss on the lips in response.

He winks as he closes the door. That's exactly what he plans to do.

Chapter 18

Thankfully, the golf course isn't too far away. When Stanley gets there, the parking lot is crowded. While searching for a space, he spots a man wearing checkered pants, a bright yellow shirt, and a purple beanie on his head. Stanley starts smiling uncontrollably as he remembers watching an old sitcom episode. He laughs thinking how much the man resembles Ralph Cramden played by Jackie Gleason.

Finally parking the car, Stanley takes out his borrowed golf clubs and makes his way into the club and looks around, hoping to find Scotty. That poses a bit of a problem because he has no idea what Scotty looks like.

Suddenly Stanley hears someone yell out, "Is someone in this room looking for Scotty Fahrenheit?"

Stanley looks up and thinks to himself, "Oh, dear God, not him."

Hesitantly Stanley raises his hand before the crazily-dressed man, he saw walking through the parking lot, enthusiastically jogs over to him carrying his golf clubs. He introduces himself as Scotty and asks, "You ready to play ball?"

Stanley forces a smile and just shakes his head before saying, "Let's tee off." They get a golf cart and Stanley makes sure to drive the cart straight to the starting place for hole number one.

The Outrageously Ridiculous Adventures of Scotty J. Fahrenheit

Once they arrive, Stanley lets Scotty go first. Not paying attention, Scotty just stands there picking up one club after another, inspecting it and then throwing it down on the ground before grabbing the next club. Stanley just watches Scotty's actions in disbelief, getting madder and madder as it continues. "Um, how many times have you played golf?" he asks the awkward man.

"None, this is my first time. Don't you think I look like a pro?" Scotty brags with a big grin.

Scratching his head, Stanly replies, "Look…um…Scotty. I think this may be a mistake. Maybe we should scrap this idea."

"No way. I will never be considered a quitter," Scotty says, pointing a meaty thumb to his own chest. Abandoning the clubs, Scotty looks at the cart and asks, "Hey, what do you say we take a spin around in the golf cart?"

"I'm a job coach, not a tour guide," Stanley says, trying to change Scotty's mind. "Do you want me to go first?" he asks, grabbing his wood driver from his bag.

"Naw, I don't really want to golf. I want to go for the ride in the cart!" he says enthusiastically.

When it doesn't appear that Scotty will be swayed, Stanley gets in, ready to drive when Scotty says, "Would you mind if I drive it for a while?"

Stanley hesitates, not sure if he should. The guy obviously has his license, he drove to the meeting and he drove here today. "Oh, what the hell," he says under his breath.

Just as Stanley gets out, Scotty scoots over quickly into the driver's seat and drives away laughing and hooting with joy.

FIRED!

Worried over what Scotty might do, Stanley finds the nearest cart and takes off after him.

Golfers start jumping out of the way trying to avoid Scotty. Unfortunately, it's too late.

"There's a lunatic on the course. He just hit that old man lying on the green," the hysterical golfer yells out.

One of the managers grabs a cart and catches up with Stanley. "Pull your cart over immediately," he says, ordering Stanley to drive back with him.

When they get to the clubhouse, Scotty is nowhere to be found. However, there are two police officers waiting to speak with Stanley. "Sir I am asking you to get out of that cart," one of them barks.

"I'm sorry, I should never have taken it, I was just trying to catch—" Stanley tries to explain as one of the officers interrupts.

"Sir, an elderly man was rushed to the hospital because of your reckless joyride. Please turn around and put your hands behind your back. You're under arrest for endangering the public and maiming a golfer," he explains before reading Stanley his Miranda rights.

***

"How did I get myself into this mess?" Stanley wonders as he is sitting in the back of the police car, being taken to the police station. After a few hours of questioning and pleading his innocence, a few witnesses from the golf course explain that Stanley wasn't driving the cart that mowed the old man down and he is released.

Unable to get a ride from the police station, he is forced to walk the five miles back to the course.

The Outrageously Ridiculous Adventures of Scotty J. Fahrenheit

He finally makes it to his car with blisters on his feet and sweat dripping off his brow. Not having a hat or even sunglasses, any exposed skin is sunburned. He staggers to his car and begins pounding on the door.

Another golfer walks over. "Are you alright?"

"No...I mean, yes," Stanley says, trying to calm himself down.

Realizing how frazzled Stanley is and not wanting to fuel any more fire, the friendly man remarks, "Sorry, I didn't mean to get in your business. I just wanted to help." He walks away when Stanley doesn't reply.

Usually Stanley is such a docile man, but today all that changed.

Stanley eventually calms down enough to get in his car and head home. When he arrives, Cindy is waiting near the door. Filled with anger, he blurts out through clenched teeth, "Please give me a minute. I need to get myself a cold glass of water."

Cindy just stares after him without saying a word as he limps to the kitchen, grabs the largest tumbler he can find out of the cabinet, and starts filling it with water from the tap.

"Well, I can't believe it, but it's true," He says finally before gulping down the entire forty ounces of water.

Totally confused, she asks, "What are you talking about?"

"I don't know how to tell you this," He says, hesitating.

"For heaven's sake, Stanley, what is it?" she asks, her hands on her hips.

He sets the empty tumbler down hard. "Father Cliff was wrong. I have no chance of winning that contest."

FIRED!

"Oh Stanley, don't you think you might be exaggerating just a bit?" she scolds.

He puts a hand up and has an incredulous look on his face as he says, "I can honestly say that even the guy who started this whole job coach concept wouldn't be able to find this misfit a job."

"Stanley, you need to have faith."

"Cindy, I'm shot down. I have no chance—and I mean, *no* chance—of ever winning the contest," he says, talking with his hands as he speaks.

"You can't lose hope before you even start, Stanley. Wasn't it you who said from Father Cliff's lips to God's ears?" she reminds him of his own words.

He scoffs, "Maybe God is wearing earplugs because he sure as heck can't hear what Father Cliff said."

"Why are you talking so crazy? It's like you're doubting Father Cliff while mocking the Lord," she says, puzzled by his reaction.

"First of all, I said nothing about Father's righteousness. You're accusing me of talking crazy," he replies. He shakes his head and mutters, "You've got to be kidding."

Now Cindy is getting her dander up, "Oh no, Stanley," she counters, pointing her finger in his face, "You're the one who's been acting so strange since this competition started. You mocked me for my twitching eye. And now you are throwing digs at Father Cliff. What has gotten into you? Maybe we need to make an appointment with Father Amodeo," She worries.

"Father Amodeo, isn't he the exorcism Priest?" he says with his face scrunched up.

Cindy sighs, "That would be him. I think evil has entered your soul."

"You've got no clue what you're talking about. I am in no way possessed by the Devil," Stanley replies.

"Then what's got you acting so strange? I don't even recognize you," Cindy replies, looking at her husband with concern.

He slams his fist down on the kitchen counter and says, "I bust my behind all week and grab up all the overtime I can. Why do you think I'm tied with Stanton?"

"You did say you were tied with another man. He must be working just as hard as you," She concludes.

"No, he's not. He is the son of a rich senator. Life comes easy for him. Every candidate he gets is hand-picked for him," Stanley shakes his head and hits the counter again, "I bet the owner of the company is getting a kick back for helping that prissy-boy out."

His twin daughters, practically attached to Cindy's hip, begin crying and Cindy whines, "Now look what you've done. You're scaring your daughters half to death." She stamps her foot down and declares, "I will not have this in our home." Tipping her chin up she says, "Maybe you better leave."

"You can't make me leave my own house!" He says, then shuffles over to the kitchen table and puts his head down.

Cindy, still trying to console the wailing children, asks again, "Please, Stanley, I am asking you in a nice way to leave until you can be civil again."

He lifts his head up and pleads, "Just give me just five minutes to explain what happened to me. If you would even look at me,

FIRED!

you would have noticed the horrible sunburn I have on my face, and if you cared at all, the blisters on my feet are killing me."

She looks confused, "I thought your face was just red because you're so mad."

"That too, but it's mainly from walking all the way from the police station back to the golf course."

"What in the world were you doing downtown at the police station? And why would you be walking back to the van? Your behavior is scaring me. I really think a call to Father Amodeo is necessary," she moves toward the phone in the kitchen.

He stands up and says, "Cindy, don't call him. I had to go back to the golf course," as if that would help anything.

Cindy shakes her head and scrunches her face, "I'm lost. How many times did you go to the course? And why were you at the police station, you never answered my question."

"Forget about the police station. Let me just start from the beginning."

"Forget about the police station? You throw something like that at me, and I'm supposed to just 'forget' it?" She is getting upset now. "Stanley, you're making matters worse!"

"Okay," Stanley says, his hands out to try to calm her down, "Listen, I'm talking calmly now. Like I said, I'm gonna start from the beginning."

"Finally!" she exclaims, hands back on her hips.

"So I get to the golf course and there's this goofy man who I can only describe as a bumbling fool. He was dressed in the most ridiculous outfit. Every article from his hat to the shoes on his feet were something straight out of a comedy skit," he

The Outrageously Ridiculous Adventures of Scotty J. Fahrenheit

said, pointing to the different places on his body as he spoke, " Anyway, it was funny until I found out that the imbecile was Scotty."

Cindy didn't seem to be getting it, "Why are you judging this man for the clothes he wears?" she asks.

"Please stop sticking up for him before you hear the rest of the story," Stanley insists. "So we go to the first hole and I tell him he can go first. I kid you not when I tell you that he took every one of his clubs out and just threw them on the ground. I just watched in utter amazement. I was pretty sure he had never played golf in his life, which he confirmed." Stanley looked at Cindy in the eyes, and continued, "You know I'm a pretty patient man, but my patience had reached its end."

"Then what did you do?"

"Well, here's where the trouble started. Scotty asked me if he could have a ride in the golf cart. I told him it would be fine. So I got in the driver's seat, and he asks if he could drive. 'What's the harm,' I thought?" then he shook his head, "If I only knew—" he lamented.

"What happened?" She interrupts.

"Could you please wait until I finish the story?" He said, annoyed. He paused and then continues, "He slides over and I start walking over to the passenger's side. Then he just took off, leaving me behind. I didn't worry until another golfer came over screaming—"

"Oh my gosh, what happened?" Again, she interrupts.

"You just can't help yourself, can you?" He remarks with hostility before he continues his story.

FIRED!

"Apparently, Scotty hit another golfer on his little joyride. I got another cart to go find him, but that was the worst thing I could do. The manager ended up yelling at me to pull over. He banned me from the golf course and told me never to show my face there again. I asked him what I did. He told me to ask the man who was just about killed when I dashed by."

Now his face was redder from anger than it was before with just the sunburn, "Can you believe it, Cindy? He thought I hit that old man! I tried to explain that he had mistaken me for someone else, but that fell on deaf ears. When I got back, Scotty was gone and two police officers were there waiting for me."

Cindy just stares at him in disbelief. Stanley continues. "I was read my Miranda rights, then they arrested me."

She put her hand over her mouth in shock, "Oh, my dear! that sounds awful."

"I was handcuffed in front of all the other golfers. Can you imagine the humiliation I was put through?" Stanley says, totally deflated now.

Cindy just shakes her head.

"They actually put me in a jail cell. I guess there were a few guys from the golf course who came forward and told them it wasn't me."

"Thank God. That was a miracle," Cindy said, relieved.

"You call being arrested a miracle?" Stanley asks, incredulously. "Don't you get it? I've got a criminal record now. What if I get fired? Who else would hire someone who was arrested? I was fingerprinted and the whole nine yards. How do you think I felt when the cops wouldn't even give me a ride back?"

The Outrageously Ridiculous Adventures of Scotty J. Fahrenheit

Cindy saw this as an opportunity for Stanley to see what the other side of the fence was like and said, "I bet you felt violated. Now you can understand what women go through when they're violated. They, too, are left to find their way back. It's sad you went through that, but maybe it taught you a lesson—one you'll never forget," She preaches.

Stanley throws his hands up and asks, "What does that have to do with my situation? For heaven's sake, you women always turn everything around. Will you and every other woman out there just know that all men are not evil, vicious monsters. As a matter of fact, most guys out there are probably just like me: Hard working fools just trying to make their way."

Cindy shakes her head slowly and says, "Now you've stooped so low that you're mocking women who have been violated. I really feel I need to call Father Amodeo immediately before it's too late," she says, making her way to the other room to get the phone.

Stanley follows her, "Too late for what? What, do you think I'm gonna start levitating off the ground? Or are you fearful I will do vulgar things with a cross? Or I might start talking in some unrecognizable language," He says, all worked up to a frenzy now.

Cindy gets out her notebook containing all her important numbers. She reaches for the phone, but Stanley grabs it away from her. "Just who do you think you are calling?" he asks.

"Stanley, please step away. I am doing this for your own good. When a person is possessed, he is unable to understand the depth of it." She says, dialing Father Amodeo's number.

Seeing he wasn't going to win this one, Stanley just backs down. "Geez, what is the world coming to?" he wonders.

Chapter 19

After two rings the priest answers the phone, "Father Amodeo here, may I help you?"

"Hello, Father. This is Cindy Rogers."

"Cindy, yes, I remember meeting you at the healing mass. You're the one with all the children. May God bless you and your beautiful family. How can I help you?" she can hear his smile through the phone.

"Oh, Father, it's my husband. I think you need to come over and give him an exorcism."

He pauses, "Well…do you…have you any idea how a person who is possessed acts?"

Stanley is yelling in the background for Cindy to hang up the phone and she knows the priest can hear it. "Can you hear the resistance I'm getting, Father?"

"Please give me a reason you think your husband is possessed," Father Amodeo asks before Stanley grabs the phone out of her hand.

"Father, this is Stanley, Cindy's husband. I haven't the slightest idea why my wife called you," he tries to explain.

The Outrageously Ridiculous Adventures of Scotty J. Fahrenheit

"Stanley, it seems to me that your wife is very concerned about you. Do you feel as though an entity has entered your body?"

Stanley sighs forcefully, "I say one thing about my wife's twitching eye, and that's the end. I tell her what a horrible day I had, and she starts downplaying my awful situation." Stanley gets louder and more animated as he continues, "I mean, then she brings up this 'women's violation' card!"

There is a bit of a pause before the priest replies, "Stanley... are you saying that you raped your wife?"

Stanley pulls the receiver away from his ear and looks at it, baffled, before saying in the phone, "What? Did I rape my wife? You must be just as nuts as she is."

Father Amodeo's voice grows cold after that comment from Stanley and he says, "Can you please put your wife back on the phone?"

"Sure, here she is," Stanley says, shaking his head as he hands the phone back to Cindy.

"Father, do you think you can help him?" she desperately asks.

"Look, I'm not sensing any demon possession going on. I think your husband may be under a tremendous amount of pressure. It would make sense for you to call a good psychiatrist. Left untreated, this behavior could lead your husband to a nervous breakdown. In the meantime, do what you can to calm his nerves," he advises.

"Thank you, Father. One last question: How can you be sure this is just stress and not demonic possession?"

"I've dealt with many people who have actually been possessed. They take on a very evil persona. They actually morph into the demon they are possessed by. I can tell you that

Stanley has not been taken over by a demon. If he was, he would start spewing horrific language over the phone at me. Trust me, it wouldn't be anything of this earth. Go relax, and both of you just calm down." He says before hanging up.

After putting the phone down, Cindy suddenly bursts out in tears. "Honey, I am so sorry," she says, sniffling.

"There's no reason to cry. You have nothing to be sorry for," Stanley says, hugging her.

"When Father Amodeo explained that you were not possessed, I just got so emotional."

"I thought you'd be happy to hear that," Stanley wondered, "Why the tears?"

Dabbing at her eyes with a tissue, she replied, "He told me you're suffering from severe pressure. He said if not treated, you could have a nervous breakdown."

"Losing my mind wouldn't be all that bad. Just think, I would have a bed and three square meals a day—all without working. So be positive; it's not as bad as it sounds," he says, trying to lighten her mood.

Cindy just glares at him from behind the tissue, "That's not funny, Stanley. My aunt had a nervous breakdown when she fell prey to a scammer who stole her life savings. It was so tragic. My poor mother; that was her only sister. When we were young we use to go to the insane asylum to visit her. Mom would cry her eyes out. Her sister's mind was completely gone. The doctor said not everyone who has a nervous breakdown recovers," she explains starting to cry again. "My aunt was one of the unlucky ones. I mean, all she did was sit in a chair and stare out the window. I felt as if our visits never made much of a difference.

The nurse told us not to give up hope," she finishes by taking a choppy breath.

He puts his arm around Cindy to console her, "Don't worry, honey. I'm not about to lose my mind or become possessed by some demon. I just need to calm down. Let's make a pact that we will stop arguing. I love you to the moon, and I hope you know it," He says, giving her a peck on the cheek.

She gives him a watery smile and whispers, "I know you do. I love you too."

***

Meanwhile at the Fahrenheit residence, Scotty is in the dining room, working on a puzzle with his mother.

"Would it be alright for me to ask you how your golf game went today?" she says cautiously, eyeing Scotty.

Scotty shakes his head aggressively, "Ma, it didn't go good at all. My job coach is a rather nasty man. I've got no faith in him," He says, finding and end piece and setting it into place.

Mable decides she'd better change the subject before Scotty blows another gasket and says, "Oh, good! I've been trying to find that piece this whole time. You're so good at this!"

But he ignores the compliment and looks up from the puzzle. "Ma," he starts, "I'm so beaten down about this whole thing. I just want to get a job." He says, talking more with his hands than his mouth, "plain and simple. Ya know, at this point, I aint too fussy. I don't care what it pays," he says, dejected.

She straightens and says, "Son, you must think positively that you will get a great job. A job that accentuates your skills."

FIRED!

They go back to the puzzle, hunting down more edge pieces for a moment before Scotty says, "You're right, Ma. I'm going to think positive—even if I have no skills."

Mable smiles proudly at her son. "That's the spirit. In the meantime, can you try to find this piece?" she says, pointing to a spot where an edge piece is missing. It doesn't take long for him to locate it.

"Too bad there isn't a job doing puzzles," She remarks with a chuckle.

Chapter 20

Scotty spent the entire weekend looking forward to Monday, which was very odd. Most working people can't wait for Friday afternoon to arrive. They look forward to the weekend and dread the thought of Mondays. And most don't think about Monday until Sunday night. Of course, this wasn't the case for Scotty. The only thing was that he was obsessing over what he would wear to work.

Monday morning arrives and once again Scotty is up before dawn. After all, it is his big day. He ravages through his entire wardrobe before getting disgusted. Jumping on his bed, he has a revelation. "Yes, that is it!" he exclaims.

Trying not to wake up his mother, he tiptoes down the hall and into the spare bedroom. Very quietly, he opens the door to his father's closet. Everything was left exactly the way it was before his father passed away because Mable refused to get rid of anything that belonged to her dearest husband. As Scotty peruses through his dead father's clothes, his eyes widen in awe and wonder—like a kid who just got let loose in a candy store.

He has picked out several different articles of clothing before he hits the jackpot. Hidden between two sweaters he discovers an extremely outdated polyester shirt with ducks and ponds on it. As he takes it out, the old material snags on a broken wire hanger. Not realizing what it is stuck on, Scotty tugs on the shirt,

FIRED!

causing it to tear. Of course, that doesn't stop him from trying it on. He wrestles the vintage material over his obese form and the shirt is so tight that the buttons are ready to pop straight off.

Scotty looks in the mirror and reverently rubs his hands over the too-tight sweater, marveling at how good he looks. His next quest is to find a pair of pants. He spots a pair of crème colored polyester pants that have been discolored from age. "Perfect," he says, smiling, "I just hope they fit as good as this sweater," He says, squeezing his massive legs into them.

It's no surprise that once he gets the pants over the bulk of his bottom, he can't get them to close because they are so tight. Looking around for a belt or something, he spots one of his mother's hat boxes and gets an idea to use the pin from the hat to keep his pants from falling down. The plan puts a grin on his face. "I'm sure ma won't mind," he mumbles, opening the hat box and trying to remove the flowered pin from the brim of the hat.

He ends up ripping the hat while pulling the pin off, but continues on with his plan.

The large, multicolored flower pin looks ridiculous holding his pants closed, but not to Scotty. With a proud look on his face, he walks over to the mirror again. "Perfect," he says, posing in the mirror.

Overly excited about his new work attire, he rushes downstairs to show his mother. Mable looks up from the stove where she is cooking and is flabbergasted.

"I'm ready, Ma. What do ya think?" he asks, clearly proud of his appearance.

Not having the heart to criticize, Mable responds, "I thought your dad got rid of those pants."

The Outrageously Ridiculous Adventures of Scotty J. Fahrenheit

"We can thank God he didn't. How do I look?" he repeats, looking for affirmation.

"How do you think you look?" She asks, looking at him over the top of her glasses.

He rubs his hands down the rounded tightness of the shirt covering his massive stomach, saying, "Where do I start? I think I look like a real professional."

"Well, today's society is all about the way one feels and believes," she concludes, answering the only way she knows how to without hurting her son's feelings.

"Thanks, Ma. I knew you would agree with my style," he says. "By the way, what you got cookin'? I don't want to leave on an empty stomach."

"I don't think you or your father ever had an empty stomach," she says, shaking her head as she dishes up some breakfast on a plate for Scotty and set it at his place at the table.

After shoveling down way too much food, Scotty gives his mother a hug and a kiss. Mable chuckles as she watches him skip out of the kitchen.

Stepping outside he takes a look at the hideous van and begins to smile. *It's going to be a great day*, he thinks to himself.

***

Scotty arrives at the parking lot where the seminar will be and notices a parking spot right up front. He puts his blinker on and begins to turn, but as he starts pulling into the spot, Stanton whips his Porsche in the spot and cuts him off. Startled, Scotty starts blaring his horn. Stanton looks at him and rolls down his window, yelling, "Loser! Is that your newest set of wheels? That looks just as bad as your old, hood-blowing green machine."

FIRED!

Scotty blows out a breath and calms himself down, trying to ignore Stanton as he backs up and continues around the parking lot to look for a spot. He winds up driving around the entire parking lot with no luck. with nowhere else to park, Scotty decides to park on the street directly in front of a no-parking sign.

He hurries in, hoping to find a good seat. Lucky for him, he finds one pretty close to the front. Looking over he spies a man next to him, who looks anything but personable, and decides to strike up a conversation.

"How are you doing today?" he asks the man excitedly.

"Not good," the man answers honestly.

"Yeah, I know the feeling," Scotty agrees.

The man gives Scotty a once over and nods at him, saying, "Looks like you've got it much worse than me," he says with a huff.

"Why do you say that?" Scotty asks.

"Have you looked in the mirror lately?" The man looks totally disgusted as he continues, "That outfit is hideous. Dude, the 70's are so over. Not even John Tavolta could revive those clothes," he insults.

Scotty is unfazed, "Hey, he's one of my mother's favorite actors!"

Seeing that Scotty was being nice back to his rude comments, he changes his tone and says, "Hey man, I'm sorry. Things must be tough for you too. I really hope you find a job soon. Then you can afford yourself some new clothes," he adds, nodding.

Scotty smiles and says, "Thanks for that."

The Outrageously Ridiculous Adventures of Scotty J. Fahrenheit

In just a few moments Justin James walks in the room. He heads to the podium and says, "Good to see you all back here. I hope you had a great week! Today you will be assigned a job coach. I am sure you will all connect. Some of you may have already met your coach, and since I have heard nothing negative, I suspect that everyone is happy."

Scotty nudges the guy next to him and whispers, "That's not true, my coach is a real arse—"

"You mean—" The guy just about gets out before Scotty interrupts.

"My mother told me I had to watch my tongue. She said my dead daddy would roll over in his grave if he heard my foul mouth," Scotty nodded.

As they tune back in to the seminar, the guy says with a smirk under his breath, "Well, now we know who the former owner of his outfit is."

Chapter 21

Soon all the coaches walk in and take their spot at the front of the room. Stanley is not excited at all to be here today. In fact, he's been dreading it.

Justin swings an arm out toward the coaches and says, "Let's give a round of applause to these wonderful men and women who will be your job coaches."

Everyone starts clapping and Scotty waves feverishly and yells, "Way to go, Stanley!"

The coach next to Stanley laughs and leans over to him, "I take it that loser is yours?"

"Why, do you want him?" he asks, joking but not really.

"Sorry man, I'm here to hopefully get my commissions up. You've got your work cut out with that one," he scoffs.

"Gee, thanks for the encouragement," Stanley replies flatly, eyeing Scotty who is now bouncing up and down while waving at him. He gives a small wave and a tight-lipped smile, hoping Scotty would stop.

One by one, Justin begins calling the job coaches and pairs them with their clients. For whatever reason, he makes sure to pair Stanley with Scotty last before addressing everyone.

"Alright, now the hard work begins. It's up to your job coach to find job opportunities that best fit your needs as well as skills. These job coaches are trained professionals. I am sure you will treat them with the utmost respect. It's their job to set you up with interviews, and it's your job to be well prepared the day you walk through the doors of a perspective employer."

Justin continues, "Thank you all for coming in. You are to meet here every Monday unless you find gainful employment. In that case, you are to call and let your job coach know. Remember, our job coaches can only do their best. It is up to you to both act and dress appropriately," Justin says while looking directly at Scotty.

He goes on to give more instruction to the prospective employees. "Remember, when you're in an interview, flattery gets you everywhere. Your coach will teach you all the tricks of the trade. Okay, that's all from me. Now if you would all follow Mary Perry," he says, gesturing to where Mary is standing. She waves as he continues, "She will lead you to the conference room. All of the tables have the name of a job coach so look for the name of your coach and take a seat at that table," Justin finishes.

All the attendees get up and head in Mary's direction, following her to the conference room.

Stanley goes straight to his table and stands next to it. As Scotty comes in the room, he is in disbelief over Scotty's behavior. Instead of looking at the card on each table, he continues to ask other job seekers where Stanley's table is. In spite of everyone telling him he has to look at the cards on the tables, he keeps asking people. Within a few minutes, everyone except for Scotty makes it to their table while he is left at the front of the room looking like a lost puppy.

FIRED!

Not able to take it any longer, Stanley walks up and retrieves his lost candidate.

"Thanks boss, I was having a bit of trouble finding ya," Scotty says, patting Stanley on the back.

An irate man who can't take any more of Scotty's behavior, calls out, "Dude, it might come as a surprise to you, but everyone here is trying to land a job. This might be a joke to you, but nobody here finds you or your antics very amusing. So just sit down and shut up, or get the heck out!"

Feeling pressured to defuse the situation, Stanley says, "I can guarantee you everything will be fine. Let's just all calm down," he says, leading Scotty to his table where a few other job seekers are patiently waiting.

As they sit down, a petite blond woman who is sitting at the table too, gets Stanley's attention and says, "Excuse me, I'm wondering if you only work on a one-to-one basis? Because, if that's the case, it looks like all your time will be spent on him," she worries, pointing at Scotty.

Stanley smiles at the woman and replies while looking at each candidate, "I promise I will give you all a fair amount of time. As for Scotty, it will take a heck of a lot of overtime to find him a job. I know these times can pose extra stress and anxiety, but we must stay positive and focused. Hostility and negativity will only work against us—"

"Anything you say, Boss," Scotty interrupts.

"Please, call my Stanley," he says. Then he clears his throat and says, " Let's go around the table and explain a little about ourselves."

The Outrageously Ridiculous Adventures of Scotty J. Fahrenheit

At that, Scotty gets up and starts walking around the table, introducing himself to each of the other candidates.

"Sit down!" One of the guys at the table reprimands.

Scotty withdraws his hand from the person he was introducing himself to and replies, "Excuse me. I was only following the boss's instructions. I just thought I would go first. Why are you yelling at me for following directions?" he says while returning to his seat, looking confused.

The petite woman just looks down and shakes her head while the man sitting to Stanley's right asks, "Is there any chance I can switch groups?" he pleads.

Stanley responds as kindly as possible, "No. But you should all know that I have never been unsuccessful at finding anyone a job. Can we please move on?"

The man looks satisfied and starts, "Well in that case, my name is John Taylor. I do research about history and antiques, and would love a job in that field," he finishes and they all look at the next person.

"My name is Mark Webster. I love outdoor activities. I am looking forward to getting a job dealing with anything that keeps me in the fresh air," Mark says with a smile.

The woman next to mark sees it's her turn and she sits up straighter and says, "I'm Carrie Sanders. I enjoy knitting and taking long walks with my dog. I am hoping to get a job in an office."

They all look at the woman next to Carrie and she clears her throat before saying, "My name is Sherry Cameron. I like reading books written by the old masters, and I hope to get a job in the construction industry."

FIRED!

Finally it's Scotty's turn and they all turn to him. "Hi, I'm Scotty J. Fahrenheit. I enjoy eating junk food, drinking soda pop, and doing puzzles. I just want to get a job—any job—so I can get my hard-of-hearing girlfriend, Charlotte, back. Her father forbids her from dating me because I don't have a job or any money. But I really like her and want her back. For me, any job will do."

Everyone stares at Scotty in disbelief.

Stanley gets their attention back by saying, "Thank you all for sharing. Now that we've all met one another, the tough stuff begins. I have a list of places that are hiring. What you need to understand is that all the other coaches are working from the same list."

"Is that good?" Scotty asks loudly.

"That just makes it more competitive," Stanley replies, "Anyway, what you have to be concerned about is you landing the job. So now I want to go over skills that are an absolute necessity."

"Skills," Scotty pipes up, "I'm a pro at doing puzzles."

"Thank you, Scotty," Stanley says awkwardly.

"Sure thing, Boss," Scotty beams.

Everyone at the table begins to chuckle.

Stanley continues and gives them his office location and then says, "The building is very easy to find, and it's right next to the House of Donuts. Right now I am going to set up individual appointments with each of you. On Mondays, those who are still unemployed are to meet me here. Justin James keeps up with all the progress. I promise I will do my best, like I told you earlier." He says before going around the table and setting up appointments.

Scotty's appointment is made the first thing on Tuesday morning. Stanley has strategically planned it this way, knowing Scotty would be the most problematic.

"I look forward to seeing you all tomorrow," he says before dismissing all the job seekers at his table. "I'm going to give you some homework. It deals with looking in the mirror while talking to yourself. That gives you an idea of what a person who is interviewing you sees. I find this makes for a useful activity to hone in on your stance and speech."

They disband and Stanley stays at the table after all of them have left, watching Scotty as he bumbles his way out the door of the conference center. *I've really got my work cut out for me*, Stanley says to himself as he closes his eyes and takes a deep breath, determined to get Scotty Fahrenheit a job.

Chapter 22

When Stanley gets home he walks in, feeling rather chipper.

"Hello, is anyone home?" He asks as all his children pile in the living room to greet him.

Cindy follows the kids and says, "Stanley, you seem to be in a great mood. You must have had a good day."

"You know, my group seems to be pretty good," he remarks.

"What happened to Scotty? Did he drop out of the program?"

"No, sweetheart, he's still in my group. But he's the only deadbeat. Not to worry though, I am going to get him started first. I will concentrate on him, but I will also make sure my other candidates don't get left out. If I can get Scotty employed, I may stand a good chance of winning. The rest of the group will be a breeze to get hired."

"Oh, Stanley, I am so happy for you. Keep yourself as positive as you are right now," she gushes.

***

Meanwhile, Scotty is also in good spirits. He eagerly gets out of the old van, walks to the front door, and reaches for his keys. In a panic, he realizes he doesn't have them and begins relentlessly ringing the doorbell. Mable swings open the door and wonders why her son is standing there. "Is there something wrong with your key?" she questions.

"How should I know? I don't even know where they are," he says, pushing his bulk past her into the house.

"You obviously have your keys, Son," she says.

Scotty turns around and looks at her dumbly, "If I did, I wouldn't have been ringing the doorbell."

"Son you drove home," she says matter-of-factly.

"What does that have to do with the keys?" he asks.

"Really Scotty?" She motions to the van outside, "you needed your keys to drive home."

Scotty looks as though a light bulb went off in his head, "Oh yeah, you're so brilliant, Ma. I would have never figured that out."

He skips back to the van, whistling a tune. But that happiness ends the minute he spots a ticket on his windshield. "This has to be a mistake," he yells out to his mother.

"Concentrate on finding your keys," she calls from the front door.

"But I got a ticket, Ma!" he says, waving it in the air.

"Bring it in the house and show it to me," she offers.

Thankfully, he notices the keys on the driveway. "Oh here they are!" he exclaims.

When he gets in the house he hands his mother the ticket. After inspecting it for a moment she asks, "Do you remember parking in a no-parking zone?"

"If I did, I don't. Let's just forget about it." He says, shrugging. Then he grabs the ticket out of her hands and rips it up into tiny pieces.

"Why did you do that?" Mable asks.

"Because if I can't remember breaking the law, then what have I got to worry about?"

"I fear a lot," is all she can say while crossing herself in true Catholic fashion.

"Nothing to fret over," he arrogantly replies.

"Son, I want to tell you how proud I am of you. Just think, very soon you'll have a job. Enjoy the rest of the time you have because soon your free time will be limited."

"Ma, I don't mean to cut you short, but I've got homework to do," he says before making his way to the bathroom to practice talking in the mirror as they were instructed.

He closes the door and smiles at himself in the mirror. Noticing an errant piece of hair sticking straight up, he leans forward and licks his hand, patting it on the rebellious hair to get it to lay flat while straightening, pulling on the too-tight sweater before sticking his hand out to an imaginary potential employer. "Hello, I'm Scotty J. Fahrenheit, nice to meet you. I'm here to get a job. What do you have for me?...no," He shakes his head before starting over. "Hello, Sir. I am referred to as Scotty J. Fahrenheit. Have a job for a guy like me?" Not pleased with that either, he starts again, "Look here, Sir, I'm Scotty, and I need a job," he says.

Hearing Scotty talking in the bathroom, Mable comes over to the door and puts her ear up to it, trying to figure out what in the world he is doing. "What are you doing in there, talking to yourself?" she asks, knocking on the door.

"Ma, please, I'm doing my homework. Give me a break," he says in a stern voice.

"Whatever you say, Son," she mumbles, shaking her head as she retreats to her chair in the living room to watch some TV.

Scotty spends the rest of the night practicing in front of the mirror. He is determined to get this job.

Chapter 23

Before long, Tuesday arrives and Scotty makes his way to Stanley's office building. A friendly woman sitting at the front desk asks, "May I help you?"

"I have an appointment with Stanley," he replies happily.

She buzzes Stanley's office and instructs Scotty to have a seat until Stanley comes out.

Just a minute or two later, Stanley appears. Scotty stands and shakes his hand, a little too forcefully. "Hello, Scotty, how are you?" Stanley says, retracting his hand and leading him to his small cubical.

"I'm great. Nice to see you, Boss. I spent the entire night doing my homework. I think my mirror got sick of seeing me," he chuckles.

"Good. Have a seat," he says, motioning to a small chair in his cubicle.

Trying to maneuver his massive body in the small cubical, Scotty hits the divider and almost knocks it down. He grabs the divider to steady it and says, "Gee, your office is sure small on space!"

Stanley laughs nervously then clears his throat and says, "Okay, let's try to get serious." He sits down and sifts through some papers on his desk. Looking up he says, "Scotty, you never answered the questionnaire, so I really have no history on you. What do you say we go over that now?"

"No problemo, Boss," Scotty responds.

Stanley looks at the questionnaire and reads the first question, "What do you consider a dream job?"

Scotty looks up as he thinks hard, then says, "Uh…I would describe that as any job that's not a nightmare." Satisfied with his answer he says, "Next question."

Stanley rolls his eyes before moving on. "Okay, what do you expect to get out of a job?"

"That one's easy: a paycheck," he replies quickly. "How am I doing so far?"

Stanley is starting to get a bit annoyed so he answers Scotty question sarcastically, "You're doing so good that I am going to skip the questionnaire altogether." He pretends to throw the paper in the air. Just kidding. Have you ever had a job?" he continues.

"Duh, I had a great job at the zoo. My job was cleaning the animal's cages."

"Great, now I have something to go on. I can assume you like animals?"

"I don't like animals, I flippin love 'em!" he says enthusiastically.

Stanley puts the paper down and turns to his computer, looking through the lists of job openings. "Hey, look what I have here!" he says with a smile.

"What do you see?" Scotty anxiously asks.

FIRED!

"Dr. Spinelli is looking for a dog groomer. Let me see what the qualifications are." He scans through the listing and says, "They are looking for someone who has previous experiences with animals. However, they do specify that they will train the employee."

Scotty gets excited and says, "That job is perfect for me! I even have experience with a dog. Her name was Sally. My neighbors, the Smith family, owned her. I used to pretend she was Lassie. We would go on all kinds of adventures." Scotty says, reminiscing. He gets a sad look and says, "Was I ever broken up when the Smiths moved. That left such a scar on my heart," he says, now crying.

Stanley sighs, "Please calm yourself down, Scotty. I'm going to call Dr. Spinelli's office," he says as he picks up the phone.

When they respond he says, "Hi, my name is Stanley Rogers, I'm a job coach and I would like to set up an interview for the dog grooming position; I have the perfect candidate for the job. A few moments later Stanley says goodbye and turns to Scotty. "It's all set up!" he declares with a big smile.

"Great, thanks, Boss," Scotty says loudly.

"You're welcome. Now you need to be at Dr. Spinelli's office tomorrow for an interview at 10:00 a.m. He gives him a card with the address and information.

Scotty starts jumping up and down but then stops, "Does this mean I won't see you again, Stanley?" he asks sadly.

"I certainly hope so," he says too quickly before correcting himself, "I mean, for your sake," he offers with a smile. Then he stands to let Scotty know that it's time to go.

"I have one question for you. It has been bugging the heck out of me," Scotty asks as he stands too. The receptionist rings Stanley, alerting him that his next candidate is waiting in the lobby.

Stanley, eager to get Scotty going, says, "Let's just save it for another time." Before they leave his cubicle he says, "There are a few things you need to know." He counts these out on his fingers, "First and foremost, you need to dress the part. You're going for a job working with animals, so you should wear something suitable for that of a dog groomer. Make sure you stand out. It is important for you to leave Dr. Spinelli with the belief that you are the best candidate for the job."

"I get the drift, Boss."

"And please, whatever you do, don't call him 'Boss.' You need to refer to him by his name. Also, it is necessary for you to answer his questions with short answers. Don't go on and on. Nobody likes a long-winded man. You must stress the point that you've worked with animals before. If he asks you something you don't understand, don't lie. Just try to bluff your way through." He ticks off another finger while looking right at Scotty, "And the worst thing you can do is to bring up money. That's a real no no. You need to act very professional. Now do you get all that?"

"You said those things so fast," Scotty says feverishly trying to write down what Stanley just stated on the back of the small business card he handed him.

"If you make a good impression, you'll get the job."

"You have no idea how much I hope I do." Scotty replies with tears in his eyes.

FIRED!

"Trust me, it's you who has no idea." Stanley says with a forced smile, making the sign of the cross.

Stanley advises Scotty that his next candidate is waiting so he must end the session. Scotty enthusiastically shakes his hand saying, "Thanks, Boss."

"What have I told you about that?" He once again reminds him.

"Oh yeah, thanks Stanley."

***

When Stanley is all through for the day, he runs into Stanton in the hall. "Well, how is it going with that loser candidate you've been plagued with?" Stanton chides.

"You mean the candidate that I've already landed a job interview for? That loser?" Stanley proudly boasts with his chest puffed out.

"Whippy-do," Stanton mocks, rolling his eyes, "so you got the loser an interview. Let's see if he can score the job. Even if he does, do you really believe he can keep it?"

"He has a chance," Stanley fires back.

"I have a PhD candidate that employers are lining up to hire," Stanton brags.

"I'm confused," Stanley quips, "if you're so sure you are going to win, why are you trying to convince me?" he adds as he budges around Stanton and heads out of the building.

Chapter 24

Back at the Fahrenheit residence, Scotty is in the kitchen, calling out to his mother because he doesn't know where she is. She takes a mop and begins hitting the ceiling with it. Scotty hears the noise and opens the basement door. "Ma, are you down there?"

"Yes, I will be up soon," she replies.

When she finally makes it to the kitchen, Scotty is sitting at the table with the biggest grin on his face.

"Okay, what's up with you? I haven't seen you this happy in a long time."

"Happy can't even describe it, Ma. It looks like my days are about to get better!" he exclaims.

"Oh, Son, I am so happy for you. Did you get a job?"

"Something better, I got an interview."

"With who?"

"Well," he starts eagerly, "ya know how I love animals and all?"

"Yes," she nods.

"Stanley hooked me up with an interview at Dr. Spinelli's—the vet."

FIRED!

"That's great news. Did Stanley go over things you should and shouldn't do on your interview?"

"Oh, yeah. He gave me all the info I need to know," Scotty says, ticking things off on his fingers. "He talked about dressing the part and bluffing my way through. Ma, excuse the language when I say he said I have to kiss Dr. Spinelli's butt. That part I think I might have to skip. I mean, I need a job and all, but that is one thing I refuse to do," he says as his mother begins laughing hysterically.

"If only everyone was as innocent as you. This world would be a much better place," she admits between laughs.

"I'm going to get that job, and after a week I'm going to give Charlotte a call. Then I will waltz into her house and tell her father what a great job I got, and he'll have to let me date her."

"Sounds like you've got it all worked out. In the meantime, I'll get dinner ready, so clean up and change into your comfortable clothes," she says, opening to refrigerator to see what she can make.

"I'll be in Dad's closet, looking for the perfect dog-grooming outfit. I need to find clothes that fit the part," he says before running upstairs.

Within an hour, Mable calls him down for dinner. He hurries into the kitchen with an anxious look on his face. "I'm sensing something is wrong," she says hesitantly.

"Ma, I can't find a thing to wear for tomorrow's interview," Scotty replied in a panicked tone.

"Sit down and have some dinner. Maybe it will be easier to find something on a full stomach."

Scotty eats his food in record timing.

"What's your hurry?" Mable asks.

"I'm so nervous about not dressing the part."

"Please, you need to calm down. You don't want to be a nervous wreck for your interview," she reprimands.

"Do you mind if I spend the rest of the night trying on outfits for tomorrow?" he pleads.

"You go ahead, Son. It will just give me a chance to watch my shows in peace," she says with a smile.

For over two hours Scotty continues trying on one outfit after another. Then he notices a box at the top of his father's closet. He opens it to discover an old leather jacket. He spots the fur lining and notices he can unzip it from the jacket. Thinking that he found the jackpot, he puts on the too-tight, sleeveless furry liner. Posing in front of the floor-length mirror, he remarks, "This is perfect!"

While he has a mirror in front of him, Scotty decides it's a good time to prepare what he is going to say during his interview, so for the next hour he talks to the mirror before calling it quits for the night.

***

When the next morning arrives, Scotty immediately puts on his pathetic outfit. He looks for his mother, only to find that she's taking a bath. He knocks on the bathroom door. "Ma, I don't want to disturb you, but I'm going to be leaving for the interview."

"I'm sorry I can't see you off, Son. I hope you are dressed appropriately. Just be your cheerful self and you'll do fine. Good luck!" she calls from the other side of the bathroom door.

FIRED!

Unfortunately, she is unable to see the ridiculous outfit he is wearing. When she is through with her bath she gets dressed and decides she is going to wash the bedding. She gathers the sheets from her bed before going into her son's room to short-sheet his bed also. There she spots her husband's old leather coat with the fur liner missing. "Oh, God, please tell me he's not wearing that. He is going to look like a fool for his interview," she says to herself.

Chapter 25

When Scotty spots the large statue of a German Shepard along the road, he's sure he is at the right place, so he pulls in and walks into the building.

The friendly receptionist asks his name as he points to his watch alerting her that he is fifteen minutes early for the interview.

"That's great. Have a seat in the lobby and someone will be with you very shortly," she says, examining his outrageous outfit.

Suddenly, a young man with jet-black-dyed hair that has been spiked up on his head walks by. "Hey man, where'd you get that vest?"

"Ya like it?" Scotty says, rubbing his hands down the tight furry front.

"Like it? Dude, I absolutely love it!" the young man exclaims, stepping closer to pet the furry vest.

"It feels good, doesn't it?" Scotty asks, giving permission to touch the fuzzy liner. "I really want to dress the part. You see, I've got an interview with the doc for the dog groomer's job."

"Look the part—you're a dead ringer for it. I can tell you've got the job in the bag," the punk rocker kid says with a nod. "Oh, one more thing—when you get the job, can I borrow the vest?" he asks while petting the vest.

FIRED!

"Sure, man, you can borrow it. It's just you're a lot smaller than me. It might be really big on you."

"I think it might fit me cause it's really too small for you. Look the zipper is ready to bust out," the punk says with a chuckle.

The secretary gets Scotty's attention and he says, "Hey I have to go to my interview now. Nice to meet you."

"Yeah. Good luck!" the spikey-haired kid says as he walks away.

Scotty is led to Dr. Spinelli's office by one of his workers. "Have a seat. The doctor will be in shortly."

Soon the young man who looks like a punk rocker walks in the room. "Hey," he says, startling Scotty who is in the process of picking up an expensive paper-weight on the doctor's desk. It slips out of his hand and drops on the floor—shattering into a million pieces.

"Was that the glass paper weight?" the young man asks.

"I'm sorry. You startled me; I didn't mean to drop it." Scotty explains, embarrassed.

"I just came in to tell you my name."

"Okay. So what's your name?" Scotty replies, picking up the pieces of glass from the floor.

"It's Jarod. Look, I better help you pick that up." He says, bending down.

Suddenly, blood starts gushing out of Scotty's hand, having been sliced by a sharp piece of glass. "Uh oh, do you think you can help me out here?" he says, getting woozy from seeing the blood.

The Outrageously Ridiculous Adventures of Scotty J. Fahrenheit

"Oh, yeah I will go and get something to stop the bleeding." He says rushing out of the room.

Jarod leaves while Scotty continues picking up the glass. Jarod comes back with gauze. "Give me your hand."

"Thank you, Man," Scotty says thankfully as Jarod starts bandaging his hand up.

"No problem," Jarod remarks with a smile.

Soon Dr. Spinelli walks in the room. "Jarod, what is going on?" he asks.

"Dr. Spin, take a look at all the blood on the floor. Can't you see I am here to help the man?"

"Oh my. How did you hurt your hand, Sir?" he asks, looking at Scotty.

"He was trying to pick up the glass from your broken paperweight," Jarod says as Scotty starts having an anxiety attack.

Scotty's face grows pale. He starts sweating immensely. He picks up a magazine on Dr. Spinelli's desk and begins fanning his face. "Are you alright?" The doctor worries.

"My heart is racing out of my chest," Scotty says, all shook up.

"Do you suffer from heart issues? Could this be a heart attack?" The doctor looks very concerned now.

"Doc, do you think I should bring in some ketamine?" Jarod asks.

"No, no," he shakes his head with a frown. I will take care of him from here, you can go now, Jarod. Close the door behind you," he says with a scowl.

FIRED!

Dr. Spinelli dumps his lunch on his desk and hands Scotty the paper bag.

"What am I supposed to do with this?" Scotty asks, holding the bag out.

"Hold it to your mouth and breath."

"Is that supposed to stop my hand from bleeding?"

"No, it is supposed to help alleviate your anxiety."

Scotty starts breathing heavily in the bag for several seconds.

"Are you feeling a little better now?" the doctor asks.

Scotty shakes his head and the doctor tells him to put the paper bag down.

"I don't want to ask you what happened to my expensive paperweight. However, I would like to check your hand. Would you let me look at it?"

Scotty nods and holds his hand out. The doctor carefully removes the gauze and inspects the wound. Then he declares with a smile, "Scotty, looks like you're in luck. The wounds are superficial, but you must keep them clean."

"Please Doc can we get down to business about the dog grooming job? See, I've never been so desperate about getting a job."

"Oh," the doctor says, "You're the candidate here for the interview." He picks up a folder that he had put down when he came in the room, and perused its contents. Still looking at the files, he says, "Scotty Fahrenheit. I understand you have experience with animals." He looks up at Scotty and says, "Your job coach explained you previously worked at the local zoo. I'm sure you were exposed to many vicious animals. I say that because many of the animals that come in this office are trained guard dogs. You must be able to subdue them. The animal groomer I hire must be able to think fast, because these animals sure do."

"As for pay—" Dr. Spinelli says before Scotty interrupts.

"I'm sorry, Doc, but I am not supposed to talk about pay," he says proudly that he remembered.

"You are not talking about pay; I am. What I was about to say was that the rate of pay depends on one's job experience."

Suddenly, Jarod comes busting back into the room. "Hey, Dude, how's that hand feeling?"

Dr. Spinelli starts to reprimand Jarod. "Can't you see I am in the middle of something? How many times do I have to tell you to knock before you barge in?"

"I knocked and you obviously didn't hear it," Jarod says with a shrug.

"I didn't hear you knock," the doctor says, ticked off.

"I must admit I did hear a faint tap on the door," Scotty interjects.

"Thanks for sticking up for me, Dude," Jarod says to Scotty.

"Can you tell me what's so important this time, Jarod?" the doc huffs.

"Mrs. Martin is in the hallway screaming that her precious Missy is not responding to the Prozac you prescribed."

"Please let her know I will be with her in a few minutes. She's not aware that her poor Missy is not allowed to be a dog. You know she's always bringing her dog in for one problem or another, even though the dog doesn't have a problem," Dr. Spinelli complains as Jarod leaves the room.

Scotty is racking his brain, wanting to find a way to help the doctor with this problem. Maybe that will help him look good on his interview. "Doc," he spits out, "I must admit, without you thinking I'm gay, you're a good-looking guy. Maybe that lady is just finding an excuse to come in to see you," Scotty offers.

"I appreciate the sentiment, but I personally think she's just crazy," the doctor remarks, shaking his head. He asks Scotty a few more questions, and once again Jarod busts in the room.

"Do you mind?" The doctor asks in a nasty tone.

"Sorry, Dad, I forgot to ask you one last question."

"You mean he's your son?" Scotty asks, confused.

"Yes, he's the black sheep of the family," the doctor mumbles.

"Um, I'm right here," Jarod says flatly.

"Now that you mention it, you two look like twins," Scotty notes.

The doctor looks at Scotty with surprised expression and says, "Well, you would be the first person to ever say that." He turns to his son, "As for you, Jarod, what is it now?"

"I want you to hire Scotty. We'd make a great team. I mean, instead of me hating this job, I might actually like it if he's here. Don't you think he would be good for this place?"

Put on the spot, the doctor clears his throat and leans closer to his son, whispering, "I don't think so. One of you is enough for me to handle. Let me have a little time to think about it."

"Oh, no you don't. I know what that means," Jarod replies.

"Son, please let's not get into this now," he says, offering Scotty a strained smile.

"Hey, I'll make a deal with you," Jarod tries to negotiate with his father.

"Spell it out, man!" Scotty shouts out, having eavesdropped on the conversation.

The doctor just crosses his arms, waiting to hear the "deal."

"So, you know how you're always telling me to stop being such a loner and mingle with people."

"Son, I meant with *normal* people. No offense to you, Scotty," the doctor turns to Scotty with another strained smile.

"Okay…none taken," Scotty replies awkwardly.

"Come on, Dad. For once, I might actually have a real friend in this world."

"Yeah, that would go for me too. I haven't a friend either," Scotty admits.

The doctor throws his hands up and shakes his head, "For the love of Pete, I'm a veterinarian!" he cries.

Jarod pipes up, "Dad, we all know that. What's the big deal?"

"A veterinarian's job is to take care of sick animals. Not to be confused with mentally deranged imbeciles like you two."

Jarod jumps up and starts getting excited and says, "Hey, it sounds like you're going to take me up on my offer?"

The doctor rolls his eyes and says, "Do I have a choice? If I say no, you'll just go home and cry to your mother. And I don't want to listen to her nagging at me all night. So yes, Scotty is hired."

FIRED!

"So…does this mean I got the job?" Scotty asks, confused.

"Dude, that's what the Boss just said," Jarod says with a big grin, clapping Scotty on the shoulder.

"Did you say Boss?"

"Yeah, why? That is what he is: the big Boss," Jarod replies.

Scotty looks anxious, "I promised my job coach I would never refer to anyone as 'Boss.' He told me it was a 'no, no.'"

Before Jarod could answer, Dr. Spinelli interjects, "Scotty, we open very early so make sure to be here by seven a.m."

"No problem," Scotty agrees heartily.

The doctor shakes his hand before leaving the room mumbling something under his breath about not believing what he got himself into.

"Hey, man, let me show you around," Jarod says happily.

It takes just a few minutes to get the tour of the office and as they are concluding, one of the receptionists tells Jarod that a dog is waiting in room number 2. "Well, that concludes our tour," Jarod says, giving Scotty the peace sign. "I'll see you tomorrow!"

"I can't wait!" Scotty remarks.

Chapter 26

Later that day, Stanley shows up at Dr. Spinelli's office and asks to speak to the doctor. Within a few minutes the doctor comes out to the waiting room. Stanley stands up and shakes hands with the doctor as he approaches. "Hello, I'm Stanley Rogers, Scotty Fahrenheit's job coach."

"What can I help you with?" Doctor Spinelli asks.

"Well, I stopped by to see how Scotty's interview went this morning."

A look of disgust crosses the doctor's face as he asks, "How are you involved with that character?"

Instantly feeling defeated, Stanley replies, "I'm so sorry to have inconvenienced you. I realize your time is valuable. My company was hired to find him a job. I can tell this is definitely going to pose a problem," Stanley explains.

"Not to worry, because your problem has just become mine," the doctor sighs.

"I lost you, Doctor," Stanley says, confused.

"Leave it up to my derelict, spoiled rotten son to get me into all these terrible situations. You've got him to thank for getting Scotty off your back."

FIRED!

"Am I getting this right? You hired Scotty?" Stanley asks, completely surprised.

"Unfortunately, yes. My son is one of those loners into punk rock. He's been looking for a friend and for whatever reason he's taken a liking to Scotty. What else could I do?" the doctor shakes his head, "Let me tell you, there would have been war at home if I didn't hire the guy."

"I don't know what to say," Stanley replies, trying to hide his enthusiasm.

"God be with you. Would be a good start," Dr. Spinelli says before both men burst out in laughter.

"True, true. Well, if you run into any problems, don't hesitate to give me a call," Stanley says, handing the doctor his card.

"I can foresee an awful lot of problems. I won't bother you with the trivial stuff. However, I can assure you that I'll give you a call if things get out of hand," he says before the two men shake hands.

Stanley walks out of the place in complete disbelief. He keeps his cool until he makes it to his car. Then he jumps around, yelling, "Yes! Yes! Yes!" He is on cloud nine, still not comprehending what exactly transpired.

***

When Stanley gets home he calls Scotty to congratulate him on his new job. "Please, whatever you do don't screw it up. You getting this job means the world to me. My whole family is counting on you."

Scotty's voice sounds annoyed coming through the phone, "You're putting so much stress on me. I don't think it's fair for you come down on me like this. It would have been nice if you wished me good luck. Instead, you put pressure on me. I mean, about your family and all. I haven't even been able to tell my mother my great news, and I got you on the other end of this phone giving me crap. Thanks a lot," he says before hanging up on him.

"Stanley who was that on the phone?" His wife asks as Stanley is putting the phone down.

"You'll never believe who went on his first interview and got hired right there on the spot."

"Don't even tell me it was Scotty?" she says shocked.

"Bingo!" he says with a giggle.

"I must admit, Father Cliff was right," she reminds Stanley.

"My dearest wife, Cindy, I just witnessed a miracle today," he sits back into his chair, still amazed.

"You better fall on your knees and thank the dear Lord for what he has done for you," she quips.

"We both should do that, seeing you'll be benefiting from this as well," he remarks.

"Please stop bringing me into everything. I am really sick of it," Cindy says with her hands on her hips.

"Geez, everything I say offends you. I really wasn't trying to be mean," Stanly replies as kindly as possible.

"I guess it's me. I am just a bit sensitive, that's all," she apologizes.

***

FIRED!

Back at the Fahrenheit house, Mable is just coming in the door. Scotty runs over to her and before she can even close the door Scotty yells, "Where the heck have you been, Ma?"

"Settle down, Son. I was at my monthly book club meeting. What's gotten you in such an uproar?"

"This has got to be the best day of my life. I guess you forgot all about my job interview today," he replies.

"Actually, I didn't. I was so nervous about the outcome."

"Have you no faith in me, Mother?" he says with arms crossed.

"I can't lie, sometimes it's questionable," she replies honestly.

"What is that supposed to mean?" Scotty asks dejectedly.

Curious about the interview, Mable motions with her hands, "Stop with the third degree, Scotty. Just tell me how it went."

"You're looking at your son, the dog groomer," Scotty says proudly.

"Oh, Scotty, that's great news!" she exclaims before wrapping her arms as far as they can go around her son, which isn't too far. She steps back and says, "And to think I was worried about it all day long," she adds with a sigh of relief.

"Never doubt such a dynamo like me. Never fear when Scotty J. Fahrenheit is near," Scotty says, standing tall. If he was wearing a cape, it would be flying behind him in the wind like some sort of superhero.

Mable gives him another hug and says, "I am so happy. I hope your run of good luck continues."

Chapter 27

At 6 a.m. Scotty arrives at his new job. Pulling his car into the parking lot, he spies an empty parking space and pulls into it—the spot that is clearly marked that it's reserved for injured animals only. He heads for the front door and tries to open it. It's locked, but he notices a man inside vacuuming the floors. Scotty starts banging on the door. He does his best to get the guy's attention. "Buddy, answer the door," he says, continuing to pound on the door.

Soon Scotty spots a canary yellow jeep racing in the parking lot with music blaring, top down and doors off. He immediately notices that it's Jarod.

Jarod parks right beside Scotty. "Hey, man, are those your wheels?" Jarod asks, looking over the ancient van.

"Yes, but no," Scotty replies. "My real car is in the shop. I have this one on loan."

"Cool," Jarod says, "that's great, but you can't park there. Better move your car unless you're an injured animal."

Scotty gets in the van and parks very close to Jarod.

"Did you spend the night in that thing?" Jarod asks.

"Why would you think that?"

FIRED!

"How else could you make it here before the crack of dawn?" Jarod wonders.

"I didn't want to be late. No sir, I wanted to be early. Weirdest thing going on in there right now. The guy vacuuming the floor is doing his best to ignore me."

"You mean Martinez?"

"Yeah, that must be the guy."

"He just came from another country and doesn't speak English, so he just avoids everyone."

Soon Jarod spots his father pulling up in his old Cadillac. "Here he comes, the Boss man."

"Check out those wheels. That car is awesome," Scotty says in awe.

"I call that the boat from the past. One of his customers traded that for this show dog dad had." Jarod shakes his head, "I curse the day my dad made such a trade."

"What I would give to be seen driving that," Scotty admits, still ogling the car in wonder.

"Dude, you're not Italian. Why would you want an old, stand-out car like that?" Jarod asks, schooling him.

Before Scotty could reply, the doctor gets out of his car and calls over to the two guys, "Nice job, you two. Jarod, I see you're on time for once in your life."

Jarod ignores the criticism and grinned, "See, Dad, I told you what a good move it was for you to hire Scotty. You're already seeing positive things happening."

The Outrageously Ridiculous Adventures of Scotty J. Fahrenheit

Dr. Spinelli opens the front door and they all file in. "Hey Jarod, why don't you find Scotty a uniform?"

"Coming right up!" Jarod says before going to the back. A few minutes later he comes back wearing a white coat. He hands another one to Scotty. "Here, Dude, try this on."

"Fits great," Scotty says, struggling to pin the top of the jacket shut.

"When you two are done playing dress-up, could you please take Scotty to one of the grooming rooms and familiarize him with the products we use?"

"Yes sir, Boss. We will march right to it," his son says, saluting him.

They head to a grooming room and Jarod opens the cupboards and familiarizes Scotty with the supplies. "Why are there so many different shampoos?" Scotty asks.

"Because there are so many different skin and allergy issues."

"I didn't know shampooing an animal could be so difficult."

"Trust me, depending on the animal, it could be real difficult. One screw-up can be a big problem. Make sure to read the chart for each patient, understand?"

Scotty nods his head as if he is comprehending everything Jarod just told him, in spite of the fact that he didn't really understand a word of what he just heard.

"What's all the nail polish for?" Scotty asks while picking up a bottle of florescent pink polish.

"Yeah, that's a favorite used on poodles," Jarod explains.

FIRED!

"I'll make sure to remember that," Scotty says, gingerly replacing the bottle of polish.

Jarod leads him back out front to the work desk and picks up the clipboard. "These are our assignments for the day," he says, showing the contents to Scotty. "Sometimes some of the patients are difficult, so would you object to flipping a coin to determine who gets the tough assignment?" Jarod offers.

"Sounds great to me," Scotty says, shrugging.

"I knew you were the right person for the job. Unlike the last bum dad hired," Jarod mumbles.

"Why? What did he do?" Scotty asks.

"It's not what he did, it's that he didn't want to do anything. I mean, he made a slave out of me, and I told Daddy that he either fire him or I was quitting."

"How did that play out," Scotty asks.

Jarod laughed, "I can tell you're a real jokester. Anyway, my dad really doesn't have much of a choice about things when I complain. See, this business was financed by my mother's family. Mom calls all the shots. My dad doesn't want to do anything to tick her off. So if I have a problem, I just have to tell my mom and she goes after my dad; I mean, worse than any dog I've ever had a run in with. It's always more entertaining than a movie," Jarod spills out.

"Then what does your dad do?" Scotty wonders.

"You sure like to joke. You know he's a doctor. He owes that to grandma and grandpa too. They paid for him to go to Veterinarian school," Jarod explains.

"Can your dad do anything around here?" Scotty asks.

The Outrageously Ridiculous Adventures of Scotty J. Fahrenheit

"Yeah, I guess he can fire someone who's really screwing up." Jarod leans closer and says in a low voice so his dad doesn't overhear them, "Here's a private joke between me and my grandparents about my dad; Grandpa always says, 'Do you know why your dad chose to be a vet? Because he doesn't like to be the only one led around on a leash,'" Jarod continues telling the family gossip.

Scotty laughs and then looks around and asks, "So what do we do after we groom the animals?"

Jarod shrugs, "We take the dogs that are boarded for a walk. You have to give each dog enough time to do their business. Some go really fast and others have to find the perfect spot to go." He thinks a minute and says, "Oh, and if you see poop and pee in the cages, you have to clean them out. Whatever you do, make sure to spray the cage with the disinfectant after you clean it. That stuff is amazing. It takes the stink right away."

"Got it," Scotty says, hoping he can remember everything.

"Now that I showed you the ropes let's get to work," Jarod says.

"Sounds good to me," Scotty replies confidently. *It's going to be a good day*, he thinks to himself.

Chapter 28

Soon one of the vet techs comes in to let the guys know about the first grooming patient. "Mrs. Randal is here with her sweet cat, Peaches."

"You want to take her?" Jarod asks.

"I certainly will. Just bring her in," he replies as if he is a pro.

Jarod puts a finger up and says, "One thing about Peaches, she always has a bunch of dingle berries hanging down."

Scotty scrunches up his face and says, "Hmm, I've never really heard of that kind of berry."

Jarod tilts his head and remarks, "Seriously? Everyone knows it means there's poop hanging from the hair on the cat's butt."

"How am I supposed to get that crap off?" Scotty asks, looking disgusted.

Jarod shrugs, "Everyone has their preference. Hopefully you'll come up with something good."

In just a few moments the tech comes in with Peaches and sets her on the black-topped grooming table, motioning for Scotty to take hold of her so she doesn't jump down.

"See the dingle berries?" Jarod laughs, pointing to the cat's backside.

"Holy cow! How does that cat walk around?" Scotty exclaims, "She's got mounds of dingles hanging off her butt!"

"Told ya so," Jarod says just before exiting the room.

Now Scotty and Peaches are left alone. Peaches eyes him suspiciously and meows.

Scotty has no idea how to securely hold a cat down with a scruff hold, or that he could sedate it safely for grooming so he tries to be confident. "Okay, Cat, I'm going to tell you once, and only once, that you are certainly full of crap," he chuckles at his own joke then gets serious again. "This can go easy if you just relax and let me take over. Do you understand me?" he says as if the cat knows what he's saying.

He looks around to come up with a way to clean the cat's butt. He reaches over with his free hand to a counter and gets a dry cloth.

"Okay, looks like this just might work," he says with a smile. He spots the sink nearby and takes the cloth and runs it under warm water. When he gets the cloth close to the cat, she begins hissing and raises her back, her fur standing straight up. "How can I calm you down?" he says, looking around the room.

"Maybe I need to speak your language," he says to Peaches and starts making cat noises. Peaches doesn't seem impressed. Having let go of her, the fat cat jumps off the table and goes over to the door where she begins clawing at it. "Get over here, you," he says, reaching down trying to pick her up. Peaches turns around and claws him in the face.

"Ahh! Nice kitty," Scotty yells, ignoring the shooting pain in his face as he tries to calm her down. "I have to get you cleaned. But how?" He wonders before spotting a jar filled with cat treats. He takes the glass jar down and tries to pry the lid off, but it's stuck. Scotty bangs the top of it against the grooming table. Suddenly it opens and some of the food drops on the floor. The cat notices the food and makes her way over before lapping it all up.

"Wonderful, you relate to food. I should have figured that."

He goes back to the sink and gets the towel wet and soapy. He hurries back to the cat and notices she is almost out of food. He scatters more on the floor and abandons the grooming table to start washing her there. The cat seems oblivious while she's eating. Scotty is in his glory, except the cat's butt isn't getting any cleaner.

Looking back to the counter, he notices an electric shaver and comes up with an outrageous idea. He puts more food down and takes the shaver to the cat's backside. The powerful, professional-grade shaver does the trick and in seconds the cat's entire backside is shaved clean. Scotty looks in disbelief at the dingle berries on the floor. "Now take that, you pieces of dingles," he says with pride.

Peaches is still eating, oblivious to what's happening on the other end so Scotty bends down close to her butt to inspect the perfection of his work. Suddenly cat diarrhea spews out of Peaches and directly into Scotty's face. He jumps up and runs over to the sink, dipping his entire head under the faucet. There's no soap left in the dispenser so he can't wash it all off. Realizing he can't stand the smell, he goes into the cabinet and takes out the disinfectant that Jarod bragged about and starts spraying it all over his hair and coat. He shakes his head like a dog to get the excess water off his hair, sending poop-and-disinfectant smelling water all over the cabinets. Then he walks over to Peaches and does the same to her.

The Outrageously Ridiculous Adventures of Scotty J. Fahrenheit

"You have cat crap all over your fresh-shaved butt. Couldn't you at least have waited until you got home?" he says. She hisses back at him in response.

Scotty knows he has no other choice but to get the cat in the sink. He finds a stopper and fills it up with warm water and makes a trail of food. His plan works perfectly. The cat follows it right to the base of the counter. Now he has to come up with a way to pick up the cat. He strategizes by putting food on the counter.

He picks the cat up and the problem starts all over again. She puts her tail up and hisses, followed by clawing. This time she gets him in the eye. He screams but quickly contains himself as he tries to get her in the sink. "Please, Cat, I hate this as much as you." He takes the cat and drops her in the water, holding her down while enduring an onslaught of scratches.

Now for the tricky part. How is he supposed to get the cat's behind cleaned? He grabs the nearest towel and scrubs her backside, but Peaches will have none of it. She jumps out of the sink, looking like a drowned, fat rat. However, his strategy worked the cat's behind is finally cleaned.

The next step is to get the cat dried. Scotty goes back in the cabinet and finds a blow dryer. He plugs the dryer in and the cat goes ballistic. He turns it on high heat and starts chasing the cat around the room. Peaches jumps on everything in the room. Scotty keeps running around to catch up to her and barely hitting her with the warm heat. By the time the cat is mostly dry, Scotty is exhausted.

There's a knock on the door and the tech walks in. "Hey, it's been a while—What is that smell?" She asks walking over to Peaches and picking her up easily. Peaches nuzzles her and starts purring. "Aww, she's so fuzzy. Isn't she so loving?" The

FIRED!

tech asks, not even noticing that Scotty is covered with scratches. She just seems to be interested in petting the cat. "You're such a good girl. Mommy is waiting for you in the waiting room. You're so—" she stops as she notices the cat's shaved backside.

"What in the world did you do to her?" The tech yells at Scotty, only now looking at him. "What happened to you?" she asks, not in a caring way either.

"I…couldn't free the dingles. I mean, they were really bad. She just scratched me a bit," he chuckles nervously and shrugs, trying to make light of it.

The tech waves her hand in front of her nose. "Oh my God, you stink so bad. I mean you smell like a can of Lysol poured over a fresh pile of cat poop. I can't take one more minute in this smelly room," She says before running out, still holding Peaches.

Soon Jarod comes running into the room, saying, "Oh, Dude, what's smells so bad? Did you crap your pants?" As Scotty is about to say something, Jarod adds, "Oh, Mrs. Randal is in the waiting room, demanding to see you."

Scotty's shoulders slump as he follows Jarod out to the waiting room, knowing he's about to really get reamed out. Mrs. Randle walks up to him with Peaches resting contently in her arms and says, "Are you the man who did this to my precious Peaches?" Then she holds up a hand and says, "Before you answer, I would like the doctor present to hear what I have to say," she states.

In just a few moments the doctor arrives, looking worried. "Is there something wrong?" he asks.

Mrs. Randal holds up the cat and exposes the cat's shaven backside. "What do you think about this?"

The Outrageously Ridiculous Adventures of Scotty J. Fahrenheit

Dr. Spinelli just looks over at his son in horror. "Jarod, what happened here?"

Jarod points a thumb at Scotty and says, "That would be the work of your new hire, Scotty."

"I want to tell you something—" Mrs. Randal begins to say before the doctor interrupts.

"You can have any service you want for no charge," he offers nervously.

"—I have been coming here since I adopted Peaches—" she continues before Dr. Spinelli interrupts her again.

"I really appreciate your business, and I will do whatever it takes to keep you as a customer," he adds quickly.

She points at Scotty and says, "Is this the person responsible for grooming Peaches today?"

"That would be me. I really did the best I could. I hope you are pleased," he says happily.

Dr. Spinelli turns to Scotty and opens his mouth to reprimand him when Mrs. Randal takes out a twenty-dollar bill from her pocketbook and hands it to Scotty.

Everyone in the room is in complete disbelief. "Scotty, you're brilliant! I've been dealing with those damn poop balls forever. I could tell how embarrassed my poor Peaches was. Not anymore. What a bright idea to shave her rear end. What a clever thought. Well, whenever I bring her back the only person I want to groom her is you. And I've never seen her fur so fluffy! What did you do?"

"A groomer never gives away his secrets," he says with a smile, relieved.

FIRED!

"Thank you for treating my dear Peaches so wonderfully," she says to Scotty. Turning to the doctor she adds, "What a great worker you have there!" before exiting the building.

In complete disbelief, Doctor Spinelli walks over to Scotty and clears his throat, "Nice job, Scotty…um…why don't you go to the bathroom and clean up?"

"Thank you. Yes, I will do that," he replies with a smile, thankful for the chance to do that. By now there was sweat pouring down his face, causing the scratches to burn.

As Scotty retreats to the bathroom, the doctor just stares after him, confused and amazed by what just happened.

Chapter 29

Jarod meets up with Scotty in the bathroom, handing him a clean coat. "Man, you really smell bad," he remarks.

"Oh, Peaches pooped on my face, that's all. No big deal," he says as though it happens every day.

"Mrs. Randal just about pissed herself bragging about the butt-shaving you gave her precious cat. You might stink, but in Mrs. Randal's mind, you came out smelling like a rose," he says with a laugh as they exit the bathroom together.

The vet tech sees them in the hallway and comes over, looking down at a chart. "Hey, Scotty, Stone is here ready to be groomed." She looks up and recoils, "Your eye is swollen shut. What's up with that?" she asks, grossed out.

"Yeah, it's really starting to burn," he admits. "What do you think I should do?"

"I think you should go see the doctor," she advises. "I'll have Jarod groom Stone so you can see the doc."

"Thanks," Scotty replies. He turns and goes down the hall and into the doctor's office. Dr. Spinelli looks up from his computer as Scotty enters.

"What happened to your eye?" he asks, looking concerned.

FIRED!

"Oh, just doing my job," Scotty answers proudly.

The doctor gets up and crosses the room to inspect Scotty's face more closely. "Seriously, between your hand and your eye, you're looking at a possible severe blood poisoning. Come with me in the operating room," he says, leaving the room.

Scotty follows him to the operating room. The doctor pulls a chair next to the table and motions for him to sit down because the table can't handle his weight. Scotty sits in the chair and the doctor points the bright operation light in his direction before administering a solution to sterilize his hand and eye. It stings badly, but Scotty tries to hold as still as he can.

"Now, I want you to go into the recovery room and lay down on the floor for a bit. There some blankets you can put down to make it softer. When you feel better, come back and see me. Do you know where the recovery room is?"

"Yeah, Jarod showed me earlier," he says, getting up and making his way to the recovery room. It's early in the day so there aren't any animals in recovery yet. He takes some folded up blankets and places them on the floor to the side of the room and lays down.

Fearing his job, Scotty doesn't spend more than two minutes lying down. He gets up and finds the doctor.

"Didn't I tell you to lay down and relax?" The doctor scolds.

"Look, Doc, this job means the world to me. I'm taking it so serious. Please let me to go back to work," Scotty begs.

"Are you sure you're able to work in your condition?" he asks.

"I'll be fine," he swipes his hand in the air. "Please, I beg you to let me to go back to work."

The Outrageously Ridiculous Adventures of Scotty J. Fahrenheit

"Well...okay...but I want you to come back the minute you experience any problems," the doctor demands.

Scotty heads into the room where Jarod is just about ready to start grooming Stone. Scotty takes one look at the dog and asks, "What's up with him?"

"Oh, he's got one of those skin allergies. It causes severe hair loss because the dog keeps itching his skin raw," Jarod explains.

"I hope Stone's pain 'aint as bad as mine. I feel like someone's actually sticking needles in my eye," He says.

Jarod seems to ignore Scotty's dilemma and continues about the dog, "We have to wash him with a certain shampoo that's supposed to calm the itching down. Can you get it out of the cabinet for me?" Jarod asks.

"Yeah, but right now I'm blind in one eye, and to be quite honest, the vision in my other eye seems to be blurry at best. It would be so helpful if you could guide me to the shampoo."

"You might need of one of those seeing eye dogs," Jarod jokes before telling him exactly where to locate the shampoo.

After the dog is done getting washed, Scotty comes up with another lame-brain idea. "I've a great way to patch up the bald spots on Stone."

"Scotty, what's up your sleeve now?" Jarod asks in bewilderment.

Scotty rushes back into the other room and comes back with a handful of cat fur.

"What is that, and where did you get it?" Jarod asks.

"Just be quiet and tell me where I can get some glue," Scotty asks.

FIRED!

Jarod thinks a moment and then brightens, "Dad uses this special glue in surgery. Give me a minute and I will bring some back," He says while running out the door.

In just a few moments, Jarod returns with the glue. Scotty tells Jarod to start putting glue on the bald spots.

After applying a liberal coating of glue all over the poor animal, Jarod steps back and says, "Okay, that's done. Now what?"

"Here's the tricky part. Now you have to carefully place the fur on the glue," Scotty explains.

"But some of this fur is still wet?" Jarod worries after grabbing a fistful of fur.

"That's because I got it out of the sink. We have Peaches to thank for that. Hopefully, we will have enough."

"I can't believe you're actually making me put cat fur on a dog," Jarod says while applying a bunch of fur to a glue spot. "Don't you have a bit of an issue with that, Scotty?"

Scotty looks at Stone and shakes his head. "No not at all." Then he steps back and says, "Well, maybe just that Stone's going around with female fur on his body. It's kind of like the pooch is cross-dressing without even knowing it."

Jarod cocks his head to give Scotty a bewildered look, "You're really are whack job. What happens when Mrs. Dashner notices that the fur doesn't match Stone's?"

"What do you mean by that?"

"Really? Peaches is a flipping calico cat. Stone is a jet-black dog. That's what I mean."

The Outrageously Ridiculous Adventures of Scotty J. Fahrenheit

"I guess I didn't really think about that. I think it's fine," Scotty says, happily applying the calico fur on the black dog.

After a few minutes the vet tech shows up and asks. "Jarod how are you doing with Stone? Mrs. Dashner called and said she has to come back early. I told her you would have Stone ready before she arrived," she finishes before leaving the room.

"Oh man, we better get this done quick," Scotty says. The guys hurry and get the fur put on Stone as quickly as they possibly can.

Soon Mrs. Dashner arrives and the vet tech comes back to retrieve her dog. She looks confused for a second as she looks at Stone. "What happened to the bald spots? What happened to his fur?" She says grabbing the dog by the leash and walking him out.

By this time, Dr. Spinelli is in the waiting room talking with Mrs. Dashner. She is busy explaining how the dog continues to scratch his skin raw.

"Hopefully, the constant prescription shampoo will eventually do the trick," He says as Stone is brought in.

The dog runs over to her. "My big boy, how are you feeling?" she says, then does a second-take in shock before looking back at Dr. Spinelli. "It's amazing! Stone doesn't have his bald spots anymore! I didn't know you were doing that hair transplant thing."

Dr. Spinelli doesn't know what to say so he just asks, "Are you satisfied with the job?"

The woman is clearly overjoyed and gushes, "Yes, he looks great!" Then she sobers a bit and asks timidly, "But how much is this procedure going to cost me?"

FIRED!

"Nothing at all," Doctor Spinelli replies with a forced smile, "it's on the house."

She claps her hands and asks excitedly, "Thank you so much. I just have one question."

"What's that?"

"How long will this hair transplant last?"

"I would have you ask either Jarod or Scotty, but unfortunately they aren't available at the moment," Dr. Spinelli says.

"That's alright, I am just so happy they could help him!" she says, leaving with a bounce in her step.

Chapter 30

Once Mrs. Dashner is gone, the doctor tracks down Scotty and his son. "I have no idea what you two think you are doing. Is it my imagination, or are you both trying to put me out of business?" he demands.

"You really need to seek medical attention for your paranoia problem," Jarod responds rudely.

"I'm beginning to think you and Scotty are one in the same."

"What's your deal? So far the customers have been in awe over our work. Stop your complaining, would you?" Jarod chastises.

"I'm letting you know now that if that Scotty does one more crazy thing like that, he is out of here. No questions asked," He warns as he points at Scotty's red face.

"Dad, you seriously need to chill. Maybe some ketamine would help."

"What's that supposed to do?" Scotty unknowingly asks.

"It's horse tranquilizer. My son is being his usual condescending self." He answers.

"Well, if it can help a horse, I'm sure it can help you," Scotty concludes.

FIRED!

"Please, I am ordering you two to get out of my sight."

Jarod makes a rude gesture to his father as they walk away.

After they are out of earshot from the doctor, Scotty says, "Man, I'm feeling really bad cause all I want to do is make your father happy. What more can I do?"

"Nothing. The guy is one of the most ungrateful men to walk the earth. I think he's jealous of your accomplishments. He can't stand anyone outshining him. I think he suffers from that Napoleon complex."

Scotty stops walking and his face gets sober. "Is he terminal? How long's he got?"

"I hear ya; that crap is terminal. Those types of guys die with their nasty attitudes."

"Maybe we can teach him a thing or two." Scotty innocently adds.

"Haven't you ever heard the old saying, you can't teach an old dog new tricks?" Jarod scoffs.

"It doesn't hurt to try."

As they continue walking, Jarod peeks over at Scotty before saying, "Gee man, your eye doesn't seem to be getting any better. How's it feeling?"

"Oh, it probably looks better than it feels."

"If that's the case, then you are in some serious trouble," he says with a whistle.

"Why do you say that?" Scotty worries.

They stop walking and Jarod faces him. He motions to Scotty's face as he says, "I just noticed a large red line running down your face. I don't think that's a good thing. You'd better get it checked out," he advises.

"Your father already took care of me. No worries."

"You're trusting that hack? The same man who is jealous of you? Jealousy makes a man do crazy things," Jarod says, scaring Scotty.

"What could he do to hurt me?" Scotty wonders.

"He could blind you."

"Would he really do that to me?"

"You have no clue. You know the connections that man has?" Jarod says to a very nervous Scotty, as they arrive in the grooming room to clean it up.

Just then Dr. Spinelli comes into the room. "Oh, my God, Scotty, I really think I should take another look at your eye. It looks infected."

"No thanks to you," Jarod shouts out.

"What do you mean by that?" The doctor angrily asks his son.

"Dad, you hang around with a bunch of shady guys. I have no clue what any of you are capable of. For all me and Scotty know, you could be out to kill him!"

Riled, the doctor shakes a fist at Jarod, "You better get out of here before I kill *you*."

Jarod throws his hands up and says, "What did I tell you Scotty? You heard that threat with your own ears. If I wind up dead, make sure you tell the authorities that my dad is responsible for it!" Jarod yells before his father forces him out of the room.

FIRED!

The doctor settles himself a bit before looking over at Scotty and saying, "Scotty, clearly your eye is infected and causing problems. I think I need to give you a shot of antibiotics. Otherwise, you may lose your eye," He looks worried.

Just then Jarod peeks his head back in the door. "Scotty, don't let him touch you. Run!" Jarod yells before his father practically slams the door on him. Every veterinarian has to go through so much schooling. Actually, we have more schooling than any other doctor. In order to be a veterinarian, you have to be very smart," He admits.

"But Jarod told me you weren't very smart. He said something about his grandparents paying for your degree."

Dr. Spinelli refuses to reduce himself to justify insults from his spoiled-rotten son, turning the attention back to Scotty's eye. "Keep an eye on the line on your face. If it gets worse, you *must* go to the hospital. I'm going to write you a prescription for an antibiotic. Make sure you fill it and take it as directed."

When Jarod returns to the grooming room he asks, "Hey, buddy, what did the quack have to say?"

"He told me to keep an eye on the line on my face."

"So your one eye is swollen shut, and your other eye isn't far behind. How the heck does he expect you to check for blood poisoning that's just about killing you? See, I tried to warn you."

"He gave me three prescriptions and told me to make sure I take them as prescribed," Scotty squeals.

"He is a vet—not to be confused with a real doctor. Someone needs to let him in on that fact," Jarod states bitterly.

"I'm so confused. He seems so honest and all," Scotty says.

The Outrageously Ridiculous Adventures of Scotty J. Fahrenheit

"The devil looks honest too," Jarod offers.

"You're really scaring me, Jarod. Let's change the subject."

"Okay, I promise I won't say anything more about your life-threatening illness. You do what you think is best for you. In the meantime, keep in mind my warnings." Looking up at the clock on the wall, Jarod brightens, "Hey, it's time to call it quits." He looks back at Scotty and adds, "By the looks of things, you best go home and take care of your eyes. I can't imagine doing this job blind."

"Thanks for the warning," Scotty says. "I'm going to finish cleaning the cages and then I will head out," he motioned to the cages to the side wall which they hadn't finished yet.

"Work is over at five o'clock. Why would you stay any longer?"

"I want to make a good impression," he says as Jarod walks out of the room.

Scotty keeps on cleaning the cages, squinting to see through his bad eye.

The doctor hears noises so he heads in the grooming room. "I didn't expect you to still be here. You were done at five. Did my son forget to tell you that?"

"Oh no, he told me. It's just that I owe you time because of my eye. So here I am finishing up on the dirty cages."

"Thank you, Scotty. That is very thoughtful of you. Did my son put you up to the shenanigans today?"

"Sir, I don't know what you're talking about. I did the best I could today, and I hope I did it well."

If he wasn't convinced before, he was definitely convinced now—Scotty is a real idiot.

FIRED!

***

On the way home, Scotty stops to get his prescription filled. With a throbbing eye, he makes his way home. When he walks into the kitchen his mother takes one look at him. "Oh, my God! Son, what happened to you?"

"Nothing much," He responds.

"That doesn't look like nothing much. Your face looks horrible. Now do you want to explain what exactly happened?" She pries.

"I was grooming this cat and she got a little feisty. No big deal," he shrugs.

"Follow me to the bathroom," She orders.

"For what now, Ma?" He asks, following behind.

She lifts the lid up on the toilet seat. "Sit down."

"Why did you put the seat up if you want me to sit down?"

"Because your rear end will snap the seat. That's why."

"Makes sense."

She walks over to the medicine cabinet and takes out something that is just marked "Dad's Magic Solution." Scotty takes a look at it and asks, "Is that the magic potion?"

"Why do you ask?"

"Mom, anything but that stuff. It burns on contact. With all the pain I am going through now, I think that stuff may burn my eye out."

"Hush your mouth and lean over to me," she says before dabbing the homemade remedy in his eye.

The Outrageously Ridiculous Adventures of Scotty J. Fahrenheit

Scotty does so reluctantly and starts screaming from the excruciating pain. "Please, Ma, enough. Can you rinse this poison out of my eye?" He wriggles around in pain. "Ma, you're going to blind me." Against all sane logic he says, "While you are at it, why don't you do the other eye. Better to be blind in two eyes than one."

Mable shrugs and applies the medicine in the other eye too.

"Someone help me! I can't see a thing!" he screams, immediately wishing he hadn't said anything.

Mable rolls her eyes and says, "Please stop with the drama. I know it burns. That means it's doing its job. Here, take my hand and let me lead you to the living room. You can lay down on the couch until your vision comes back."

Scotty huffs, "You mean if it ever comes back. I may be on the couch for the rest of my life." He says, holding his mother's hand while walking into the living room.

It's just Mable's luck that Scotty falls asleep, allowing her to prepare dinner in peace.

As she is finishing up in the kitchen, Scotty walks in.

"You sure look a heck of a lot better," she remarks. "I can see the eye isn't as swollen."

"Yeah, my eyelid is beginning to crack open. I can see through a small slit."

"I made you mac-and-cheese. Do you feel alright to eat?"

"I ain't that ill," Scotty says, suddenly famished. "I would have to be dead before I said no to dinner."

Mable gets a chuckle out of him. She walks over and gives him a hug. "Okay, have a seat and eat before your dinner gets cold."

Chapter 31

Back at Stanley's house, he is explaining to his wife that things seem to be looking up. "Honey, Scotty made it through his first day without getting terminated. Do you think I should call Dr. Spinelli in the morning with a progress report?" he asks happily.

"Oh, Stanley, don't you dare. It's like stirring up a swarm of killer bees."

"I don't get what you mean?" he says, confused.

She puts a hand on her hip and says, "How can I put this? You don't want to disturb the hive. If you call, you might be letting Dr. Spinelli know there's something wrong with Scotty. I mean, he's going to start to critique his every move. It's better out of sight, out of mind."

Stanley considers his wife's words, "You got a point. Trust me when I say that it's hard for Scotty to ever be out of sight. Thank you for your great input." He says with a smile before gathering the family around the old wooden dinner table.

***

Meanwhile, over at the Ryan's house, Stanton is getting grilled. "Well, how's my boy doing?"

"I'm sure you're referring to the competition."

"Son, why would you think I'm just asking about that? Can't a father simply wonder how his son is doing?"

"I'm feeling great—" He gets out before the father interrupts.

"Enough about your health. Are you beating Stanley?"

Stanton shakes his head, "Like I said, you only care about the competition. I'm following your playbook and things are going as planned."

"That's exactly what I want to hear," his father says, clapping his hands together. "Great news! Let's go into the kitchen and hopefully find your mother. She will be ecstatic with the update."

Stanton is pretty sure that his mother probably isn't in the kitchen. When the senator is home she likes to find solace away from him.

Sure enough, the senator comes back and tells Stanton she's not in the kitchen. "Gee, there is one thing about living in a mansion."

"What's that?" Stanton asks, confused.

"It's too hard for me to locate your mother. The house is too big; she always MIA."

Stanton wants to tell his dad that it has nothing to do with the size of the house. She would find a way to get lost in a camper. His overbearing ways have taken a toll on his mother and she has become like a wallflower, robot wife.

Finally, Stanton and his parents take their seats at their oversized, custom-made dining room table. Butlers and maids are on hand to wait on their every need.

***

Unlike her husband, Judy Ryan didn't come from wealth. Just the opposite. She grew up in poverty. To help support the

FIRED!

family, she worked as a waitress at the local diner. Her sweet nature and good looks caused the patrons to love her.

Everything changed the day Bryant Ryan was on business in the area. It was a cold and dreary day. The dark sky gave way to torrential downpours. Many drivers pulled to the side of the road, waiting for the rain to subside. Bryant was having a hard time managing to drive in the heavy rain so when he spotted the little diner, he decided to stop and pulled in.

He took a seat and an older woman walked over with a menu, rattling off the daily specials before asking, "What brings you here?"

"I have a business meeting, but the rain has plans of its own."

"Yeah, it really looks bad out there. Can I start you out with a drink?"

He ordered a coffee and watched the torrents of rain out the window while waiting.

The woman came back with a cup of piping hot coffee, but as she's about to put the cup down, another patron ran into her, causing the coffee to spill on her hand. Bryant quickly ran to the counter to get a cup of ice. He put it on her hand, and the old waitress thanks him before excusing herself. Seeing the commotion, the owner ordered Judy to take over the table. The second she walked over, Bryant was completely taken with her.

"Hi, my name is Judy," she said, introducing herself. I'm sorry for any inconvenience, but I will be taking over Lucy's place as your waitress.

"Inconvenience?" Bryant said to himself dreamily, "On the contrary. I'm not glad Lucy burnt herself, but I sure am glad you're my waitress." He thought as he gave his order to Judy.

Infatuation is certainly alive and well. Her beauty and shyness captivated him. There was no way he was going to leave without getting her phone number.

When he finished eating, she dropped off his bill and smiled before walking away. He got her attention and called her back to his table. "Would I be out of line if I asked for your phone number?"

Judy hesitated and told him she didn't have much free time. She went on to explain that when she wasn't at the diner, she was taking college classes. Just then the owner summoned her over to bring an order to another table. She smiled at Bryant before walking away.

Bryant took out his wallet and left his money on the table. As soon as he walked out, another waitress noticed the money, picked it up, and hurried over to Judy. It was a $100.00 tip! Judy immediately rushed out to thank him. Thankfully, the rain subsided and she caught up to him just as he's getting into his dark blue Cadillac.

"I want to thank you for the generous tip. It will sure come in handy," she says thankfully.

"Oh, you don't have to thank me. You gave me great service. I wish you well in college. Take care," he says, not wanting to ask her for her phone number again.

"I don't want you to think I was being rude for not giving you my phone number, but there is a reason for that, and I'm embarrassed to tell you why. If you want to get ahold of me, I can be found here every weekend and most nights."

"That's great to know. Trust me, I will see you soon," He says.

FIRED!

"Maybe you should tell me your name," she joked, calling out before walking back in the diner.

"My name is Bryant. Have a nice day," he called back before she walked away.

For days on end, he couldn't get his mind off her.

During the week, Bryant's father Ted called him in his office.

"Father, is there something you need?"

"We're in the business of selling brakes. Speaking of breaks, I've noticed you have put the brakes on your work. What's that all about?" he asked.

"Dad, it's about a girl—"

"Isn't that always the case?" Ted interrupted.

"Let me tell you, it was as if I was looking at a real, live angel."

"You should invite her up to the house for dinner."

"I would love to, but she lives in another state."

"Son, are you unaware that there is something called telephones?" he laughed at his own joke.

"Dad, please; this is no joking matter."

"Wait, don't tell me that she wouldn't give you her number?" he asked incredulously.

"She told me I could see her at the diner."

"And where would that be?"

"Virginia," he stated flatly.

His father paused and then said, "Oh, now I get it. You fell in love with some waitress while you were on your business trip."

"Dad, I can't stop thinking about her. It's been one week and I'm going crazy. What should I do?"

"You better win that girl over, unless you want to be looking for another job," his dad said seriously.

"Wow, that's harsh," Bryant acted hurt, but realized quickly that his dad meant business.

"Harsh is your productivity level tanking since you met that girl."

"And just how am I supposed to win her over?"

"Son, I can't believe that just came out of your mouth," his dad said, shaking his head.

"I'm here and she's there," Bryant replies, motioning with his hands to show the distance.

"Easy. Get in your Caddy, and pay her a visit," his dad offered.

Bryant is taken back for a moment and said slowly, "And you would really be alright with that?"

"I don't say things I don't mean. Now get the heck out of here. And don't come back until you settle things. Do you understand me?" His face broke into a smile.

Returning the smile, Bryant got up and hugged his father. "Dad, how can I thank you?" He scrambled to get his things together and started making plans for the trip. As he is about to leave the room, he turned and said, "Oh, and by the way, her name is Judy."

"Great. I hope to meet this Judy girl very soon."

On his way to Virginia, Bryant decided that buying her something is always a plus. He is torn between flowers or chocolates. Taking no chances, he stops at a candy store and buys

FIRED!

the biggest box of chocolates that the store has. Upon arriving in Virginia, he stopped at a flower shop and bought a dozen red roses. Leaving the flower shop, he made it to the diner in record timing. He looked around the small place, hoping to spot Judy.

Lucy walked over to his table. "Nice to see you again, Sir. I heard about the great tip you left Judy. She is a sweetheart. I can tell you that tip certainly went to good use. What can I get you today?"

"Honestly, I am really here to see Judy."

"Oh, that's too bad. Usually she's here on Tuesdays, but there was a situation that came up."

"I asked her for her phone number, but she didn't give it out. I wish she had."

"I don't know if I should be telling you this, but there's no phone at her house."

"I thought everyone has a phone," he said, surprised.

"I can tell by looking at you and the car you drive that you have no idea how the other half lives."

"Please forgive me if I come off like that," he offered.

"I hate to say this, but most rich people seem to be out of touch with the poor. As for Judy, her family is just that. They live on a farm, and because of a bad accident, her dad is bound to a wheelchair. What's worse, just before the accident, her dad took out a government loan to purchase new equipment. Because he couldn't work, all the farm equipment was auctioned off for pennies on the dollar. Now her family owes a massive amount of money."

"That's terrible. I wish there was something I could do to help."

The Outrageously Ridiculous Adventures of Scotty J. Fahrenheit

"Whatever you do, please don't tell Judy I told you any of this. She would be so embarrassed," Lucy pleaded.

"How can I get ahold of her?"

Against her better judgement, Lucy gave him Judy's address.

Bryant got in his car and headed to the nearest gas station for directions to the farmhouse.

The directions led him down a dirt road. He is flabbergasted when he arrives at the old, rundown farmhouse. Immediately realizing that he can't just show up with flowers and candy, he turned his car around and headed back to the diner. Where he gave Lucy both the candy and the flowers and thanked her for the information.

When Bryant got back home, he explained the situation to his dad. Of course, his father wasn't buying any of his excuses. "Us Ryans do whatever we have to, to get what we want. Now get right back in your car and make your way back to Virginia. Don't come back unless you have Judy in tow. Do you understand me?"

"Dad you're always right. I don't know what I can do or say, but I promise I will not give up."

"Now you're talking like a Ryan. Stop wasting any more time."

Arriving back in Virginia, his first stop was the diner. Again, Judy wasn't working, but Lucy was there. She informed him that Judy Walton's farm is being auctioned off. He headed to the local property tax department, where he was given the name of the bank that held the mortgage and liens.

With little time to spare he went to the bank, demanding to speak with the bank manager.

FIRED!

A tall, middle-aged man walked over. "May I help you, young man?"

"Yes, I am here to inquire about the Walton's property."

"If you're looking for money owed, I can tell you that the bank will retrieve its money before any other lender."

"That's not the case," Bryant admitted.

"If you are here looking for the list of assets that will be auctioned off, I can help you with that."

"When is the auction taking place?"

"The end of the week, but the family has been advised to leave the premises immediately. We usually board the place up so the family has no choice but to vacate. Being that John Walton is in a wheelchair, we have decided to be more lenient. However, they are aware that the property will be auctioned off this Saturday. We just hope the family is vacated by Friday evening."

"Is there anything that can be done to stop this auction?" Bryant asked.

"Technically, yes," The bank manager said reluctantly.

"Can you explain?"

"If the Waltons come up with twenty-five thousand dollars, they can stop the auction. Otherwise, the house and all its contents are sold to the highest bidder."

"What if the house auctions for less than twenty-five thousand? What happens then?"

"That's usually the case. The bank writes off the difference. Who knows? The house may go anywhere from one dollar on up."

"So why don't you just let the Waltons live in the house and write off the debt they owe?"

"Because that is not how the bank works."

"I can clearly see how the bank works."

"Sir, if we are done here, there are things I have to catch up on," the banker said, obviously getting agitated.

"How many other people are you throwing out of their homes?" Bryant insisted.

"That will be enough. I will ask you to leave," the banker said, tight-lipped.

"Oh, you don't have to worry about that," Bryant replied and walked away.

He went back home and headed to the local bank. There he took out a large sum of money, put it in his briefcase, and headed back to Virginia.

Exhausted from all the driving, he found a small roadside motel. He settled in a room and tried to sleep, but tossed and turned. Unable to sleep, he found his way to the Walton's place. When he gets there, it looks as if everyone is gone. He walked up to the front door and noticed a letter affixed to the door. Curious now, he began reading it.

> *To the new owner of this house. We are sorry the house is in this kind of shape. We had a few setbacks that prevented us from fixing it. We wish you the best. This has been a great house for us, but we know it's time for someone else to take it over and (hopefully) restore it.*

FIRED!

Bryant took the letter and put it in his pocket. Soon people started arriving for the auction. Then the auctioneer and the bank manager showed up. They both stood in front of the crowd and explained the process. The auctioneer started the bidding at a ridiculous bid. Nobody bids. He continued to try to start the bidding, and gets all the way down to one hundred dollars, which finally gets the bidding started. Of course, the bidders continued to drive the amount up. Eventually the bid is up to four thousand dollars and it looks like Bryant is the last bidder, but just then another man bids again. The bidding went on until it was up to seven thousand dollars. Finally Bryant won the auction for the house. The crowd finally begins to walk away.

The bank manager walked up to Bryant. "So you wanted to get all the information so you could see what was owed on this house. Well you must feel good about stealing this house from the Waltons. To think you had the gall to call out the bank. How are you planning to pay for this?"

Bryant opened his briefcase, exposing the money. "I'm sure cash will do."

The banker smiled. "There are a few forms you need to sign. What do you say we go in your new home and find a place to sign them?"

"I don't feel that it's right to walk into another man's home without permission," Bryant explained.

"As soon as you give me the money, it becomes your home."

Bryant handed the bank manager the seven thousand dollars.

"I need for you to give me your exact spelling so I can have it recorded on the new deed," the banker explained.

The Outrageously Ridiculous Adventures of Scotty J. Fahrenheit

Bryant took out the sheet of paper and wrote down "John Walton."

"No, no. John Walton no longer needs to be on anything. I don't think you understand the process," the bank manager concluded.

"Look here. I understand the process perfectly. You will not have to change any of the paperwork. You need to leave everything as is. Do you understand me?"

"I guess I do, but I really don't know why you're doing this. There has to be an underlying motive here. Everyone has their price, and I am sure you're no different."

Just then Bryant understood exactly what the banker was referring to. He did this for one reason and one reason only—seven thousand dollars was the price he was willing to pay to win Judy over.

Bryant told the bank manager to get a hold of John Walton and give him back what was almost taken from him.

"And another thing," he added. "Here is an extra three hundred dollars." Bryant said, telling him to have the Walton's phone service turned back on.

"I don't think it would cost $300.00. What do you want me to do with the rest of the money?" He asked.

"Buy them a new phone, and give John the rest."

***

Within one year, Bryant and Judy were married. Though Bryant was always kind and giving to Judy's family throughout the years, she secretly questioned his generosity. Just once she hoped to see him give to others without ulterior motives.

Chapter 32

The next morning, Scotty awakens to his mother knocking on his door. "Scotty, get up. I want to check your eyes."

He walks over to the door and opens it to see his mother's concerned face immediately look relieved.

"Son, your eye looks so much better. Thank the Lord, it's no longer swollen shut."

"Ma, I need to get ready for work. I don't want to be late."

"It's music to my ears to hearing you say that," she remarks with a smile.

Jarod is the first person Scotty sees when he gets to work.

"Hey man, you have no idea how happy I am to see your face. I really thought the grim reaper was coming for you," Jarod says, relieved.

"Trust me, buddy, nothing could take me away from this job." Scotty says as he gives Jarod a bear hug.

"Have you checked our schedule for today?" Scotty asks.

Jarod walks over to the desk and retrieves it. "Looks good we have some really good patients."

The Outrageously Ridiculous Adventures of Scotty J. Fahrenheit

The tech brings in the first grooming job of the day. "Hi Scotty, meet Firefly. Try your best to chipper the poor pooch up." She secures the dog on the grooming table and leaves the room.

Scotty takes a good look at the dog and says to her, "Okay, so I am going to give you the works. First, I am going to trim that hair of yours. A girl must always look her very best. Why are you not very chipper? What can I do to change that?"

He picks up the electric razor and begins cutting the dog's fur. He leaves the dogs hair near the face long and cuts the rest of the fur very short. He cuts the hair on the tail really short except for the very bottom of the tail, which he leaves really long.

Scotty sets Firefly down on the floor and walks her over to a full-length mirrored wall. Suddenly, the dog seems to get a pep in its step. "So, you like the look?" he asks her. "What can I do next?" He says looking around. Soon his eyes are fixed on a shelf holding bottles of nail polish.

"You are going to have to help me. I am going to show you a bunch of colors. When you see one you like, bark or maybe wag your tail," he says, holding up different bottles.

Finally, when Scotty shows Firefly the florescent pink bottle, the dog starts to howl. "I am taking that as a definite yes," he says with a smile

Scotty suddenly starts singing the lyrics from a popular song on the radio about being a natural woman, and Firefly howls with every word. In turn, Scotty keeps singing the same lyrics over and over as he applies the nail polish to her nails.

"Ah, now for the finishing touch." He ties a pink bow on top of the dog's head.

FIRED!

After a few minutes the tech knocks on the door. When she walks in she is blown away by the dog's lively behavior. "Listen to this." Scotty says just before he starts singing. Once again, Firefly howls along with Scotty's singing.

The vet tech is in awe. "Scotty, this dog was in severe depression! How can grooming the dog like a bitch cause such happiness? It's truly unbelievable!" she says as she gathers Firefly and takes him back out to his owner.

"I just know what to do with these dogs. But you really should apologize for calling the dog a bitch," Scotty says seriously.

"Scotty, you are so funny. I just hope Mrs. Jones is okay with her dog wearing pink nail polish and a pink bow. By the way," she adds with a smile as the door is about to close, "I'm glad to see you're feeling better."

This makes Scotty grin as he starts putting away the grooming tools.

Soon the vet tech rushes back into the room. "Charlene Jones wants to talk to you about her dog."

Scotty walks out to the waiting room where Charlene is holding her dog. "I don't know how you knew. You would think I would have picked up on it—" she says before Scotty interrupts.

"Know what? I bet you didn't know your dog is a singer. Listen up," he says before breaking into the song again.

The dog starts howling along with him and Charlene bursts into tears. Dr. Spinelli rushes over, wondering what all the commotion is about. He can't believe what is going on in his waiting room.

Charlene speaks up through her tears, "My dog, Firefly, has been living a lie. No different from me. I, too, was like Firefly.

The Outrageously Ridiculous Adventures of Scotty J. Fahrenheit

I have something to confess, my name hasn't always been Charlene. I used to be Charlie. I, too, use to mope around until I channeled my real inner self. I may have been born a man, but since dressing like a woman, I freed myself. It's obvious my poor Firefly has been suffering with the same problem." She said, embracing her ecstatic dog.

Jarod comes in at the tail end of Charlene's speech.

Just before she walks out with her dog, once again she thanks Scotty for curing her depressed dog.

Clapping breaks out in the waiting room as all the clients and employees give Scotty a standing ovation. Dr. Spinelli is not as enthused. He looks around and yells, "What is wrong with you people? I'm beginning to think my entire staff, as well as my customers, are all a bunch of lunatics."

The clapping comes to a halt and Dr. Spinelli orders everyone back to work.

Just as Scotty and Jarod are walking away, the vet tech walks over. "Soon June Bug and Killer will be arriving. Which one of you wants Killer?"

"Honestly, I really don't feel like taking Killer," Scotty says. "I had so much luck with Firefly, it only seems logical for me to take on a dog named June Bug. Fly or bug, they're both closely related," Scotty rationalizes.

Jarod pipes up, "Hey man, I was going to ask you if you wanted to do the coin toss on this one. But if you insist on taking June Bug, there's no need for it. We have a deal." They both shake hands and walk to their prospective rooms.

Suddenly, a loud bark comes from the hall. Scotty opens the door and sees one of the vet techs with a ferocious Doberman

FIRED!

Pinscher sporting a spiked collar around its neck. The other tech is walking a white small poodle wearing a pink diamond-studded collar.

Jarod walks over to Scotty and says, "Looks like Killer and June Bug are here. Scotty takes one look at the Doberman's clipped tail and pinned ears before assuming, "Oh, that must be Killer."

"What do you say we take the dogs for a walk?" Jarod asks.

"I think it is going to be hard for us to keep up with you," Scotty remarks with a snort.

"You got that wrong," the vet tech says, handing Jarod the poodle named Killer.

"You mean that's June Bug?" He shouts in shock as the male tech hands him the leash to the Doberman.

"You better have a good grip on him. That's Tony Buffo's dog," Jarod gets out before the dog starts growling and snarling at Scotty.

The vicious dog doesn't take his eyes off Scotty.

The vet tech chimes in, "He is really skittish when he first meets someone. He reacts to 'let's go.'"

All of a sudden, June Bug takes off with the leash wrapped around Scotty's hand. He races down the hall through the office and squeezes through the front door that was opened just a crack. Holding firmly to the leash, Scotty gets pinned in the doorway. He tries to scream for someone to help, but nothing comes out of his mouth. Instead, the strong Doberman pulls so hard that he frees Scotty from the doorway.

The Outrageously Ridiculous Adventures of Scotty J. Fahrenheit

Running as fast as his massive weight allows him to run behind the dog, Scotty screams out, "Help!"

By now the dog is running down Erie Boulevard, one of the busiest streets in Syracuse. Two women driving by in a luxury car get a glimpse at Scotty and June Bug. "Look at that half-crazed idiot. Is he kidding?" one woman says.

"That's just another jerk. Don't even look at him," the other woman replies.

"Why would you say that?"

"He's probably just trying to show off how fast he can run. I feel so sorry for that dog. That's what animal cruelty looks like."

"You know that is probably the only way he can attract a woman. I mean, look at him! He's the poster boy for the word *desperate*."

"The only person he's going to attract is one who's in love with Doberman pinschers. I thought they were vicious dogs, but seeing this has changed my mind," the woman continues.

"Please, boy, slow down! You're killing me!" Scotty yells as his shirt comes untucked.

A man and his girlfriend pass by in a red convertible. The man shakes his head and yells out, "Fool, fix your shirt!"

His girlfriend chastises him, "Hey, you can't fault the guy for trying to exercise. It's obvious he is using the dog to help him get the weight off. I'll give him credit, unlike you," the thoughtful girlfriend angrily remarks.

"That's a strange thing to say, coming from you. You obviously don't have any idea what it's like to be heavy," the boyfriend assumes.

FIRED!

"Oh yeah, what if I tell you I weighed over 250 pounds? A German Shepard named Rosco helped me lose my weight," She confesses. Scotty is still in earshot, so as a normal runner cheering on each other, she encourages him with a thumbs up and yells, "Great job, dude! You've got this!"

Suddenly, June Bug takes a sharp turn onto Seeley Drive. Some people may refer to it as a hill, but it would be more appropriate to call it a mountain. By this time, Scotty is sweating profusely. Without slowing down, June Bug starts running up the hill.

"Please stop, June Bug," Scotty manages between labored heaving breaths. "There ain't no way I can make it," he says, gasping for breath.

With his heart beating like a drum and his legs unable to keep up, Scotty has no choice but to let the leash go. But as he tries to let go he realizes that the leash is stuck on his hand.

To make matters worse, the dog starts to pick up speed. Two men who look like marathon runners are working their way up the hill as well. When June Bug and Scotty approach, Scotty yells out, "Move out of the way, mad dog coming through!"

After they pass one of the athletic runners comments, "Did you see that?"

"How is it possible that he is passing us?" The other wonders.

"We should catch up and ask him if he wants to join our running team."

"Honestly, I don't think we can catch up to him. Check it out, they are just about over the hill," the runner admits.

At the top of the hill, Scotty continues begging June Bug, "Please…have pity on me…you bastard. If you…keep this up…

you will be…dragging a dead man," he gets out between huge, wheezing gasps of air.

June Bug stops just long enough to sneeze. Scotty looks ahead, noticing the rest of the road—only this time it goes downhill. Scotty is ecstatic thinking how much easier this is going to be.

Starting back up, the dog picks up serious speed. He has Scotty racing down behind him. While Scotty is running at a high rate of speed, June Bug comes to an abrupt stop, sending Scotty airborne—literally flying over the dog before landing on the ground.

He looks back at June Bug, wondering what made him stop. "You are out to kill me. You go full speed up the damn hill, but stop on the way down. You are one screwed up dog," he remarks angrily, wiping bits of pavement out of the scrapes he just procured from the fall.

June Bug just stands there, chomping on a piece of pizza crust left on road.

As soon as the dog is done eating, he puts his head up and starts running again. "Not again," Scotty screams as he is pulled up from the ground.

All of a sudden, a squirrel crosses the road. That's all it takes for the fearless dog to dart into the middle of the street.

An old man racing down the road in his old Ford has to slam on his brakes to avoid hitting Scotty and June Bug. "What is wrong with the both of you? I could have had a heart attack," the old man yells.

FIRED!

A young driver who witnesses the entire incident pulls over to check on the old man. "Are you alright?" he asks, "I saw what just took place."

"I feel a bit ill but I'll be fine. Thanks for stopping," the old man say kindly to the younger person.

Scotty is still running behind June Bug, who is still chasing the squirrel. This leads the both of them in the woods. June Bug jumps gracefully over a tree branch. Scotty, not being so lucky, trips over the branch and gets his foot wrapped around a vine. He crashes to the ground, smashing his mouth on the branch and chipping his front teeth. June Bug continues running as Scotty drags along the ground behind him. Finally, the leash breaks free from Scotty's hand.

At first, Scotty feels exhilaration. But after a moment he realizes he is responsible for the dog. "Here, June Bug, here boy," he yells while lying on the ground. "You big nasty dog, get over here now!" he orders the mutt over and over as he stands up slowly.

After ten minutes the dog comes back. He jumps on Scotty, causing him to fall to the ground. June Bug puts one leg on Scotty's chest and begins snarling and growling. A man walking in the woods spots the situation. He rushes over to Scotty and begins shewing the dog away. "Hurry up come with me," the stranger offers.

"No, no, don't do that. You don't understand who that dog belongs to," Scotty says in a panic.

The man leads him to his old truck and asks Scotty where he is headed. "Please, sir, I have to go back in the woods and find that dog," he tries to explain.

The Outrageously Ridiculous Adventures of Scotty J. Fahrenheit

"You are in shock. That dog was trying to rip you to shreds. If I didn't come along you might have been killed! That type of dog can be vicious," the man replies. "Where are you supposed to be right now," he coaxes from Scotty.

"I work at Dr. Spinelli's veterinary office, but—" he gets out before the man interrupts.

"Okay, then that's where I'm taking you," he insisted, putting the truck into Drive and taking off.

Chapter 33

When Scotty walks into Dr. Spinelli's office, everyone gasps. "What happened to you?" one of the vet techs asks.

"The heck with what he looks like. Where is June Bug?" Doctor Spinelli worries.

Jarod walks over. "Where in the world did you go? A walk means about twenty minutes, not all day."

"Scotty, where is June Bug? I am not going to ask you again," the irate doctor demands an answer.

"I, I don't know," he whistles out of his chipped front teeth.

"You better know. Do you understand me, Chipper?" Dr. Spinelli says, mocking his teeth.

"After everything he's been through, you have the audacity to treat him like this?" Jarod scolds his father.

"Actually, Son, if he doesn't tell me the whereabouts of June Bug, I may do things to this man that I have never done to any animal."

"He's gone," Scotty shouts out.

"Gone where?" the doctor says, now with his hands around Scotty's neck.

The Outrageously Ridiculous Adventures of Scotty J. Fahrenheit

Jarod runs over to his father. "What's gotten into you? Take your hands off him."

Dr. Spinelli releases his hands, screaming, "You both have no idea what is going on. Buffo is going to retaliate for this. That rotten dog is his pride and joy. I don't know what I'm going to tell him. I may have to go into the witness protection program!" he exclaims, a bit crazed.

"Don't you think you're exaggerating just a bit?" Jarod asks.

"Your brain is just as fried as that idiot's." The doctor says to his son. Then turning his attention back to Scotty, he demands again, "Now tell me what happened to June Bug!"

"Father, take a look at him. He looks like he was hit by a freight train," Jarod remarks.

Scotty starts to explain the story of what happened, "I tried the best I could. I kept up with him as long as possible. The leash finally came off my hand while I was being dragged through the woods. I swear to you all, I never meant for June Bug to get loose."

"You will find that dog before Tony Buffo gets back. I mean that. Do you understand me?" Dr. Spinelli warns, pointing a finger in Scotty's face.

"I will search for that dog as long as it takes. I don't know what else I can do," Scotty cries.

"Why did you tell Jarod you wanted to take June Bug in the first place? What were you trying to prove? Tony Buffo is not the type of man you want to mess with. You have less than a week to find that dog before Buffo gets back into town. If you don't find him, we may find you floating in the Erie Canal." The doctor lectures.

"I have only one question to ask," Scotty says, looking at the doctor.

FIRED!

"What may that be?" the doctor rudely inquires.

"Would you like me to stay and finish up my shift?"

"The only thing I want you to do is open the door and get out. The only time I want to see your face with your stupid chipped teeth is when you deliver June Bug back to this office. Do you understand me?"

"All I can say is I'm sorry—" Scotty says before Dr. Spinelli interrupts.

"Don't say another word. At this point, I feel like I could kill you," the doctor says, picking up a silver letter opener with a crazed look in his eyes.

When Scotty gets ready to leave, he tells all the staff goodbye. The female employees begin to cry. "We will miss you," one of the techs admits.

"You can say that again," the receptionist chimes in.

"I will definitely miss you the most dude. You were the bomb," Jarod admits.

Dr. Spinelli walks in and rolls his eyes. "Please stop with all the drama. Are you all going to feel bad when I lose my license? Instead of crying for this man, you all may be crying on the streets when we get closed down."

Scotty, humiliated and sad, crams his massive body in the driver's seat of the van and worries what he will tell his mother.

He decides to take another trek through the woods to look for the lost dog. He begins calling out for June Bug. After wandering in the woods for over an hour without any luck, he gets in his van and heads home.

The Outrageously Ridiculous Adventures of Scotty J. Fahrenheit

As he nears his home, Scotty spots a bunch of cars parked in his driveway. He has no clue as to why they are there.

Opening the door, he is startled by a group of people yelling, "Surprise!"

"Ma, I don't understand. Why are all these people here?"

"Son, all my friends came over to celebrate your new job. Now be happy and thank them for coming."

One of her friends brings in a large cake with a Doberman Pinscher on it. "Congratulations!" she yells out. Everyone else joins in.

"Of all dogs, why did you put that one on the cake?" Scotty cries out, throwing his hands up in the air, his words whistling a bit through the chipped teeth.

"I thought it was appropriate for a man who landed a dog-grooming job," she explains.

"Son, you need to thank Mary. Take a look at what she wrote on the cake. 'To the world's best groomer.'"

"Ma, ever since I was a child, I begged you to throw me a party. Why, out of all the times, did you pick today? You invited your friends to throw me a party on the worst day of my life!" he moans.

"Whatever are you talking about?" one of Mable's friends asks.

"Within a few days, I may be dead," Scotty cries.

"Why are you talking so crazy?" his very embarrassed mother asks.

FIRED!

Scotty just shakes his head and says, "I hope you all kept your receipts, 'cause you will need to take all your gifts back," he states before heading up to his room.

Mable is feeling grief stricken and hands back all the gifts, apologizing as her friends begin to file out of the home with kind pats on her arm.

"Mable, you know Donny is diabetic. If I take the cake home, he will eat it all and probably go into a diabetic coma. So I think Scotty will enjoy it later." Mary offers, finding a place to set the cake down in Mable's refrigerator.

After all the guests leave, there is a knock at the door. "May I help you?" she asks the man who is standing there when she opens the door.

"Hello, my name is Stanley Rogers."

"Oh, you must be Scotty's job coach. Come on in."

"Is Scotty home right now?"

"Yes. He is upstairs and won't come down. Maybe it has something to do with his chipped teeth," she begins. Stanley listens to Mable spew out the details. "I thought throwing him a surprise party would be such a pleasant gesture. But we were all shocked by Scotty's behavior. I still have no idea of what happened. I mean he has been distraught over finding a job. Now that he has one, something triggered his negative attitude. I wish I knew what it was."

"That's why I am here. Would you be so kind as to to get Scotty?"

"Sure, just take a seat and I will tell Scotty you are here," she gestures to a sofa in the living room before heading upstairs to get Scotty.

Mable knocks on his door.

"Ma, please go away. I just want to be left alone," Scotty whistles from behind his door.

"Son, there is someone in the living room who needs to speak with you."

"I understand Mary decorated a doberman on the cake. There's nothing more I can say. Would you please go back downstairs and tell her to go home?"

"Scotty, it isn't Mary. It's a man named Stanley."

He swings the door open, "Did you say Stanley, as in my job coach Stanley?"

"That would be him in the flesh, sitting in our living room."

"I wonder what he wants. Tell him I will be right down."

"No, you follow me down and talk to him yourself."

Scotty obediently follows his mom down the stairs. He takes one look at Stanley and asks, "Does this have anything to do with my job?"

"I certainly believe it does," Stanley replies.

"Do I really have to go over it now?" Scotty asks.

Mable sees her cue to leave the room. "I'm going to go into the kitchen to put away all the party stuff. You both need some privacy," she says before exiting.

"What are you doing here?" Scotty asks.

"I think you already know. I got a call from Dr. Spinelli."

"Was it that bad?"

"Are you actually asking me that question?" Stanley says, baffled.

FIRED!

Scotty just stood there like a wounded animal.

"I knew you were going to be tough, but never did I imagine this tough. Tell me if any of this sounds familiar. First, you were supposed to groom Peaches the cat. Instead you end up shaving the cat's backside bare. Did you do that?"

"Did the doctor tell you about the huge dingles dangling from her butt?" Scotty asks.

"What are you talking about?"

"Didn't think so," Scotty replies. "All I did was relieve the poor cat's anguish. Did the doctor tell you how happy the owner was? She even gave me a twenty-dollar bill as a tip!"

"No, but let me tell you what the doctor did say."

"Have at it, cause it can't make me feel any worse."

"Actually, he said you got into a scuffle with Peaches, which caused your eye to get infected."

"Did he also tell you how I stayed after hours to clean the cages?"

"He told me you were the one who advised his son to put cat fur on a dog that had bald spots."

"There we go again. I see he forgot to say how happy the owner was," Scotty remarked.

"Then he said there was the issue with you grooming a male dog like a bitch."

"I didn't do such a thing. I just did my job. Don't put the blame on me. No way. He was the one that chose the pink nail polish. And how dare you use a swear word with my mother in the kitchen?"

"The final insult to injury was what happened with Tony Buffo's dog. Do you have any idea what you did?"

"Funny how you won't bring up all the terrible things that happened to me."

"None of that matters. It's all about Tony Buffo and his dog"

"Please, Stanley, I'm sick of hearing about Tony Buffo. It's like he is God or something."

"He is like God, in that he can take your life at any given time."

"Stanley, what can I do?"

"You can start by finding June Bug. Dr. Spinelli is threatening to sue us. Honestly, I don't blame him. Dr. Spinelli says if you don't find the dog before Buffo gets back, I will be responsible for your actions. Do you understand me?"

"I should make Spinelli responsible for what Buffo's dog did to me," Scotty replies, pointing to his chipped teeth. Then he said, "Oh, one other thing, does that mean I ruined the chance for you getting the bonus?"

"Not only did you ruin my chance of winning, you singlehandedly will be responsible for me getting fired."

"Please, Stanley, I wouldn't want to be the cause of that. Can I please talk to your boss?"

"No. I beg you to keep your mouth shut with those chipped teeth."

Scotty replies with his lips closed, making his voice sound muffled and funny, "I will. I promise."

Stanley just shakes his head as he turns to leave without another word.

FIRED!

After Stanley leaves, Mable hurries into the living room. "Now you and I are going to have a talk."

"Come on, Ma, not you too."

"Do you want to explain the stunt you pulled in front of your guests?"

"Stunt? You call that a stunt? You should have seen me running down a hill and flying over a dog. Now that was a stunt."

"Son, have you been using illegal drugs? Your actions tonight make me wonder. I heard drugs rot your teeth. I look at you and I can only assume the worst."

"Ma, let me give it to you easy. I lost this dog, which, may I add for the hundredth time, belongs to Tony Buffo. Because of that, I lost half of my front teeth as well as my job. And if I don't find June Bug, I may lose my life. Dr. Spinelli warned that I may be found floating in the Erie Canal."

"Of all places, that cesspool? Your body will never be found. That canal is full of every chemical known to man."

"Thanks a lot, Ma," Scotty mumbles. "I feel so much better knowing my body will rot in record timing."

Mable shakes her head and says, "Son, you must stay positive. Think of your next strategy."

"My next strategy should be buying a one-way ticket out of here," Scotty remarks, crossing his arms over his large chest.

"Stop with such ridiculousness," she says, waving him away.

"Buffo will be out to kill me, and you call it ridiculousness. Ma, you've got to get a grip."

"Your negativity is too much for me to handle. I think it would be best for you to go up to your room."

"That is exactly what I tried to do earlier."

"I can see you need time alone. Time to sort the entire day out. Go over what you could have done differently. That way you will be able to avoid any of this in the future," she adds.

"I'm just about ready to end it, I mean, you know, call it quits—offing myself and the whole nine yards," he mumbles, scaring his mother.

"Are you actually contemplating suicide?" she probes.

"That would be correct. Send me to my room while I am in a state of an emotional breakdown. You're telling me to go over what happened today, forcing me to relive the whole rotten thing. I don't want to go over it now, tomorrow, or ever! Ma, I know you're always right and I'm always wrong, but this time I refuse to follow your advice."

Mable hugs her son, saying, "God has another purpose for you. You have to believe it."

"And what purpose might that be?"

"Son, I said God has a purpose for you. But I'm not God, so I have no idea what it is."

"You're not God, so how would you know he has a plan for me?"

"Okay, Son, you're being very hostile and disrespectful. I'm just trying to defuse this terrible situation."

"The only thing that can help is finding that vicious dog. Everything else is useless," he says before heading to his room.

Chapter 34

The next day Mr. James has a meeting with Senator Ryan.

"I bet you have good news for me," the senator hopes.

"I called you in like I promised to give you updates," Mr. James says.

"I appreciate you doing that."

"I knew that Stanley's guy would screw up. I just never knew how bad," he says, smiling.

"How bad is bad?" the senator persists.

"On a scale from one to ten, this one is at the tippy top of ten."

"That bad?"

"Yeah, that bad and even worse. If it weren't for Stanton, I would have no other choice but to kick this Scotty out of the program. We may be sued if that nitwit doesn't find Tony Buffo's dog."

"Do you mean Tony Buffo, as in the mob boss, Buffo?" the senator asks.

"That would be the guy. Seems Scotty got a job at Spinelli's. I guess he took the dog for a walk and the dog never came back."

"I hope you stick to what you just said about not taking Scotty out of the program. That would mean Stanley would be given another candidate. You need to make sure Scotty doesn't leave. You remember what I told you about my son winning this competition?"

***

In the meantime, Stanley is on his way to his office. He fears what the boss is going to say.

When he gets to his cubicle, the boss rushes over. "Good morning, Stanley. How is your day going so far?"

"Let's cut to the chase. I know where this is going," Stanley assumes.

"Sit down for a bit. I want to go over a few important things with you. First of all, you do know that I received a call from Dr. Spinelli?"

"I received one as well. You really don't have to waste your time reiterating the same broken record." Stanley blurts out.

"Excuse me, Stanley, I don't like the tone you are using," Mr. James remarks.

"It just seems you are here to fire me for Scotty's actions."

"Of course, you probably know that Dr. Spinelli will sue us should anything happen to Buffo's dog?"

"Yes, I am aware of that. I want you to know that I did the best I could with Scotty. Now I understand it wasn't enough."

"You've got it all wrong. I value your work effort. Continue to try a little harder with Scotty."

"Can you please repeat what you just said?" Stanley asks, dumbfounded.

FIRED!

"You must understand that all people are created differently. Scotty may have some problems, but I'm sure they can be resolved," Mr. James continues.

"Let me get this straight. You're not going to fire me, and you're going to leave Scotty in the program?"

"Yes, to both of your questions," Mr. James answers with a straight face.

"You've got to be kidding. May I ask you for a favor?" Stanley asks, astonished.

"What may that be?"

"Could you please take Scotty off my case?" Stanley begs.

"Absolutely not. You're doing a fine job with him. After all, wasn't it you who got him the interview, which inevitably got him the job?"

"Frankly, I am stunned with your reply. I don't think Scotty is right for this program. Actually, I think you should refund him his money and send him on his way," Stanley explains.

"Our motto is that we can find anyone a job. Scotty is that anyone. You are one of my best job coaches. After all, I gave you Scotty because I have the utmost faith in you," he says, patting Stanley on the shoulder.

"What if I tell you I can't take much more of him? I feel I was given an unbeatable task," Stanley admits.

"I want you to feel like all winning boxers do when they walk into the ring. They have faith that they can come out the victor. That is how I want you to feel," Mr. James says before walking out, throwing punches.

The Outrageously Ridiculous Adventures of Scotty J. Fahrenheit

Stanley grabs the phone and calls his wife. "Cindy, you will never believe what just happened," he says.

"Clue me in."

"My boss is losing his mind. The entire conversation with him was ludicrous. He thinks finding Scotty a job is somehow related to a boxer in the ring," Stanley whispers.

"Can you specify what you are talking about?" Cindy asks, confused.

"I am referring to either me getting fired or Scotty being tossed out of the program."

"Please tell me it's Scotty getting taken out of the program."

"Now here's where it gets wild. He's not firing me and he's not taking Scotty out of the program. He thinks I can come out as a winner. Cindy, if I didn't have a family I would tell him what he can do with this job," he says, lowering his voice as Mr. James walks by his cubical.

"Cindy I have to let you go," he says, making eye contact with his boss.

"I want you to know I called Scotty's house," Mr. James says as he nears Stanley's cubicle. "I spoke with his mother. She explained that Scotty was in a dire state. She feared he was going to be taken out of the program. When he got on the phone he apologized for what happened. He said he did all he could," Mr. James adds, hoping to make Stanley feel guilty.

***

The next day Scotty is called to come into the office. When he arrives he greets Stanley by saying, "Hi Stanley, I don't know what I'm doing here, do you?"

FIRED!

Stanley just sits speechless.

Mr. James walks in. "Hi, Scotty. I'm so glad to see you today."

"I just want to tell you both that I'm sorry for the mistake I made at Spinelli's. I know that was a big one, and it cost me my job," Scotty admits.

"You don't have to explain. That job just wasn't right for you. I'm sure Stanley will find one that better suits your needs. Keep your chin up, pal," Mr. James says before leaving the cubicle.

"I haven't a clue as to what job fits your needs," Stanley explains.

"Does that mean I'm not fired?"

"Yes, unlike me, Mr. James believes there's a job out there that will suit your needs. The problem is that I can't come up with any."

"Hopefully I can come up with a couple," Scotty says cheerfully.

"I can't figure you out. How do you live your life? You haven't shared one good thing that has ever happened to you. Maybe we should get you a job at the suicide hotline. Seeing all the things you went through, I am sure you would definitely be an inspiration. I mean, could you imagine what a suicidal person would think once they heard *your* life story?"

"No, what would they think?" Scotty asks, unaware.

"They would think their problems were nothing compared to yours. They would most definitely decide that if you can live without killing yourself, so can they," Stanley preaches.

"Hey, that's a great idea. Do you think they're hiring at the suicide hotline?"

"I wouldn't want to take that chance," Stanley explains.

"What chance?"

"If anyone at the suicide hotline suffers from depression, your presence may throw them off the edge."

Stanley starts searching for jobs on his list. "I don't see anything that you are qualified for. Most of these jobs require a little bit of skill and knowledge. Two things you don't have."

"Are you saying there isn't one thing on that list that has my name on it?" Scotty so positively wonders.

"No," is all he says.

"I think I should leave. You don't seem to be in a good mood. If you happen to find something, just give me a call," he says before walking out.

Scotty heads for the woods, hoping to find June Bug. "Here doggy, doggy," he calls out.

He walks for about an hour and has no luck. He gets back into his van and notices cars are being detoured due to an accident. Being unfamiliar with the road causes him to get lost and Scotty winds up downtown. There, he spots a bunch of people picketing in front of the local pesticide company. He slows down to see what all the commotion is about. "What's wrong?" he yells to one of the men holding up a sign.

"Read it," the striker yells to him. Scotty looks at the sign and pulls his van to the side of the road.

He gets out and starts a conversation with an elderly woman. "What's going on here," he asks.

"Unsafe practices and too little pay," the woman explains just as Scotty spots a car the exact color of his Valiant driving by,

FIRED!

reminding him of his car in the shop. He runs back to the van and decides to call the garage. He goes into the corner store and asks to use the phone. The girl at the counter hands him the phone and he calls Vinny's garage.

"Vinny's garage, may I help you?" the man on the other end of the phone asks.

"Yeah, I am calling about my car."

"We have a bunch of cars here you want to tell me which one you are calling about?"

"It would be the green Valiant."

"Hold on a minute. I'll get the mechanic who's working on it," the man says before throwing the phone down.

Within a few minutes the mechanic comes on the line, clearly agitated. "What did I tell you? Didn't I explain that I would call *you* when the car was ready?"

"Yeah, I can most definitely remember you telling me that."

"If you remember me saying it, then why are we having this conversation," he asks before Scotty panics and hangs up the phone.

Scotty decides to take a drive and winds up at a park. There, he takes a seat on a bench close to a brick building. After a few minutes he notices two guys coming from behind the building. "Hey, you got the stuff?" one of the men asks, showing Scotty a wad of money.

"Excuse me?" Scotty says.

"Come on, don't do me like that," the guy continues, shoving the money in Scotty's face.

"Buddy, we were told to hand you the cash, and you would give us the stuff. Where is it?" the stranger says, now flashing a gun.

"Oh, you mean the *stuff*," Scotty bluffs.

Not understanding what the men want, Scotty pretends he has the stuff in his van. "Come on, fellas, follow me. I got the stuff," he nervously says as he gets up.

The shady-looking men follow him to his vehicle. "It better be good stuff. We were promised the best."

"That it is," Scotty remarks, still not sure what he's going to do when he gets to the van.

When Scotty makes it to the van one of the men waves his gun around and yells, "Get the powder, we're in a hurry."

Scotty, thinking fast, wonders what he can do to get out of this mess. Suddenly a park ranger pulls in the lot. "Let's get out of here," one of the guys says to the other before they flee.

The park ranger pulls next to Scotty. "Everything alright here?"

"Actually, no," Scotty answers nervously.

"What seems to be the problem?" the ranger wonders.

"I don't know if you realize it, but you probably just saved my life. Those guys that were just near me had guns and a whole lot of money. They thought I had some kind of powder. I really got the feeling they were up to no good," Scotty explains.

All of a sudden, the Ranger rushes to his car and races away.

Feeling like this was a good time to leave, Scotty gets back in the van and heads out of the park. While driving away, Scotty

FIRED!

spots the Ranger's car. Then he sees the two men outside the car being handcuffed. They spot Scotty passing, and one yells out, "You're dead, fat boy."

Scotty notices a big hawk in the sky. "Wow, why couldn't I be a bird? A bird as big and strong as you. Every time things would get bad, I could just fly away. I mean far, far away. That sounds so good."

When he gets home, Mable is waiting in the kitchen for him. "How was your day today?" she asks.

"Stanley was in a very bad mood. He was a bit, what do you call, standawayish."

"You mean standoffish?" she says, correcting him.

"I am running a bit behind with cooking tonight. Go watch a little television before dinner is ready," she offers.

Scotty turns on the local news and they are showing the workers at the plant picketing. "Ma, come quick!" he yells as she hurries in the room. "I was driving by that place today. I saw a lot of those people carrying the same signs."

"Looks like the people are on strike," she explains.

Just before Mable was about to leave the room, a headline proclaiming "Breaking News" flashes on the screen. "What is that about?" she wonders.

All of a sudden, the news reporter announces, "Two major drug dealers have been apprehended. We are trying to get more information on this situation."

Then the park ranger who spoke to Scotty comes on the television. "I am trying to locate the man that I spoke to earlier. If anyone has any information on this man could you, please call the local police department," he says, holding an artist's sketch of Scotty and describing the vehicle the sketched man was driving.

"Son, if I'm not mistaken, that drawing looks a lot like you. The ranger even described that yellow van. What kind of trouble are you in now?" she scolds.

"Do you really think that guy in the picture looks like me?" he asks.

"Can there ever be a day without chaos?" Mable cries out.

"I'm just going to let this all go away."

"You're considered a fugitive, and you think it's all just going to go away?"

"What does that mean, and what do you expect me to do?"

"Turning yourself in would be a good start. Come on, I'll go with you. I'm sure this is all just a misunderstanding," she believes.

When they get to the police station, the police officer in the lobby recognizes him. "Come on with me," he says, leading Scotty to the interrogation room while Mable is told to stay in the waiting room.

Soon the main detective comes into the room. "Can you please tell me your relationship to the two men who were apprehended today?"

"Relationship? No, I'm not that way. I'm in love with a girl named Charlotte who dumped me."

"Okay," the detective says, scratching his head, "let me go about this another way. What were you doing in the parking lot with the two men?" he continues his interrogation.

FIRED!

"They wanted powder from me. I didn't have any. Then the ranger showed up."

"So, if I am understanding you correctly, you didn't have the powder at that time?" the detective continued.

"Correct," Scotty answers.

"Where was it?" the detective asks.

"I don't know," Scotty replies.

"Why don't you know?"

"Why all the questions?" Scotty asks, all confused.

"Should I start reading you your rights?"

"Can you please call my mother in?" Scotty asks.

"Is she a lawyer?"

"She is everything."

They bring his mother in. "Mable Fahrenheit, your son was involved in a large drug deal that was thwarted by Ranger Bob Jossel. The two men we have in custody said Scotty was responsible for delivering the drugs."

"You must be mistaken. Scotty has never touched drugs—" Mable gets out before Scotty interrupts.

"Then why did you accuse me yesterday for being on drugs. You said my teeth looked like a drug addict's. Remember, Ma?" Scotty says, making things worse.

"Did you actually say that to your son? Are you going to admit he is taking drugs?" one of the officers continues with the interrogation.

"Yes, I did say that," she admits.

"I take that as an admission. Right now, I need to tell you that it's time you retain a lawyer."

Mable asks to speak to the detective in private. He accepts, and she explains how Scotty is in no way responsible for committing any crime.

"Ma'am, we have drug dogs on the premise. Did you come in the yellow van?" the detective asks.

Mable tells him yes, and he says that he will have the police dogs check the van. If they smell the least scent of drugs, Scotty will be arrested.

The dogs go out to the van and they don't pick up any drug residue.

"Looks like you are clear for now. But we're asking that you stay local until this case is closed," the detective says before releasing Scotty.

When Scotty and his mother leave the station, Mable is filled with questions.

"Ma, I really think there is an evil spirit following me around," Scotty says honestly.

"Hush, right this minute," Mable reprimands." I will not have you speak like that in my presence. Actually, the Lord God forbids you from such thoughts."

"Then what would you call everything that's happening to me? I need answers right now."

"Listen, the best thing you can do is forget about today and look forward to tomorrow," she says, trying to cheer him up. Her efforts work, and for the rest of the evening Scotty puts the incident behind him.

Chapter 35

The next morning Scotty rushes to the office and spots Stanley in his cubicle with another client.

Scotty waits outside but continues to peek his head around the cubicle wall.

"Yes, Scotty, I see you," Stanley replies after about the fourth time with a roll of his eyes. "Would you please go back to the waiting room? I'll call you when I'm done here."

After twenty minutes, the man who was working with Stanley comes walking out.

"Hey, how's it going? Got a job yet?" Scotty asks.

"I remember you; you're Scotty," the friendly man replies.

"That would be me," Scotty replies with a grin.

"How's the job search going for you? I was the one who talked about liking antiques and everything old."

"I bet you're like me and you've got an oldie but goodie at home waiting for you. I live with an old broad myself. She's in her seventies," Scotty says to John, referring to his mother.

"Just how old are you?" John asks.

The Outrageously Ridiculous Adventures of Scotty J. Fahrenheit

"I really don't like to give my age away. But if you insist, I am thirty-six years old. I know, I know; I act a whole lot younger," Scotty brags.

"How's that working out?' John wants to know, assuming that Scotty is talking about his wife or girlfriend.

"Works out with what?" Scotty asks, confused.

"Living with someone who's twice your age."

"Oh man, I love it. She does everything for me. Like all the cooking, cleaning, paying all the bills, and everything else you could ever imagine." Then he leans a bit closer and lowers his voice to say, "The best part is that she treats me like a king," Scotty nods his head as he tries explaining.

John just shakes his head and says, "I never understood the sugar-momma thing. But now that you explained it, I completely understand. Having a sugar momma seems to be a really sweet deal for you—and everyone else in that type of relationship." Looking at his watch, John says with a smile, "Well, it's been nice talking with you, but I have to let you go. I have a second interview in an hour."

Scotty sobers and says, "Looks like they aren't really sure about you. That bit about the second interview should scare you. I went on the first interview, and, dang it, I was hired on the spot!" he brags.

John pauses and thinks a moment before he says, "If you already got a job, why are you back here?"

"Long story, but, as I can see, you don't have enough time for me to get into all the rotten details."

"Can I ask what type of job you had?"

FIRED!

"I was an animal groomer—and I did one heck of a job!" he keeps bragging.

"Why don't you still have the job?" John wonders.

Scotty starts feeling suspicious and asks, "Mr. Taylor, is there a reason you are sounding like the detectives who questioned me last night?"

John's eyes grew wide for a moment before it hit him. "You're right," he says, shaking his pointed index finger in the air. "I've got nothing more to ask you. Have a great day. Good luck on…er…whatever it is that you end up doing next," he adds feeling very uneasy and wanting to get away.

Scotty just huffs and says, "You're the one who needs the luck."

Soon Stanley comes out into the waiting room. "Scotty, can I help you with anything today?"

"Yeah, I am here wondering if you came up with anything?"

Stanley blows out a slow breath and scratches his head. "Let me tell you something. I spent the entire night trying. I looked at a thousand jobs. I read into each job title and the requirements needed to get the job. Out of one thousand jobs, can you guess how many you actually qualify for?"

"I would guess a lot of them," Scotty guesses.

Stanly leans forward and puts both of his hands in the form of an "O" as he says, "Zero. Do you understand what *zero* means?" he adds angrily.

"It's really that bad?"

The Outrageously Ridiculous Adventures of Scotty J. Fahrenheit

"Let me break it to you in layman's terms. I'm a man in a sinking ship with only one other person in the boat—" Stanley says before Scotty interrupts.

"Gee, that stinks for both of you," Scotty ignorantly responds.

Stanley closes his eyes and puts a shaking hand to his forehead as he replies, "Are you completely brain dead? The other person in that sinking ship is you," Stanley explains, pointing directly at Scotty.

Scotty crosses his arms over his massive chest and chuckles, "You're wrong. That would never be me. Cause I would never be alone with you on a ship—let alone a sinking one," Scotty informs him.

"What is *wrong* with you?" Stanley wonders.

"Hey, look on the bright side," Scotty replies. "If we were on a sinking ship, at least we would have each other," he offers, trying to make Stanley feel better.

"If that were the case, I think drowning would be a better plight than being stranded on a sinking ship with you," Stanley mumbles, realizing that he's getting nowhere with Scotty.

"Just think, we could drift to a far-out island and spend the rest of our lives together," Scotty says, gazing off in the distance and smiling and nodding as he pictures the two of them laying on the sand and drinking refreshing milk out of coconuts under the shade of leafy palm trees.

Stanley breaks through his relaxing thoughts. "That gives credence to the statement *hell on earth*," he says bitterly.

Scotty shakes himself back to reality and looks hurt. "I'm sensing a bit of hostility coming out of your mouth."

FIRED!

"Hostility is not the only emotion I am feeling. How the heck else should I be feeling," he says, throwing his hands in the air. "You and your bright side are unbelievable. Put this in your little brain, there is no bright side in trying to find you a job. It's all dark and grey."

"I do have some news. After I tried to find June Bug yesterday, I took a wrong turn and wound up in the city. A bunch of people were standing outside holding up signs. They were saying that the conditions weren't good and the pay stunk."

"Yeah, so? I saw that on the news. The manager of the company was on the news talking about all the money they are losing each day the strike goes on." Just then Stanley's face brightens. "Ah, yes, they're losing money because their people aren't working!"

"Yeah, so?" Scotty asks, not getting what Stanley is seeing.

"That just gave me a great idea. Why don't you go over there and ask for a job? I understand it is a union plant, which means anyone who works when the union is on strike is referred to as a scab," Stanley says with a grin on his face.

Scotty shakes his head. "Well, I've been called much worse things in my life. What's so bad about being called a scab? I've got a few on my arms from Peaches."

"You know, if you break the line, you can sustain bodily injuries from angry strikers. That might not be so bad. If you wind up in the hospital, maybe they will take you out of my group."

"I promise you, Stanley, even if I am dying, I will not let them keep me in the hospital. Finding and keeping a job is what I am all about."

The Outrageously Ridiculous Adventures of Scotty J. Fahrenheit

Stanley and Scotty go back to his cubicle, where he takes out the phone book and looks up the phone number for the pesticide company. Stanley instructs Scotty to not say a word while he makes the call. It's not long before he is transferred to the HR department. "Hello, my name is Stanley Rogers."

"Mr. Rogers, if you're a news reporter, we are not giving out any more info about the situation here," the woman remarks kindly.

"No, that's not the reason for my call. You see, I work for an employment services agency. I have a client who is in desperate need of a job."

"Sir, I don't know if you are aware of this, but the union is on strike."

"Yes, I understand that. Please, can you just give this man a chance."

"Does this man have any reservations about breaking a strike line?"

"Hold on, Miss," he says. He turns to Scotty and asks, "Do you care what happens to you if you break the strike line?"

"No, I don't care," Scotty replies.

"Could you say that a bit louder so the woman on the phone can hear you?"

"I don't care what happens to me," Scotty yells loudly so she can hear.

"Miss, you heard him. What do you say?" Stanley begs.

"Well, I guess I'll put you through to the head of the department. Normally I would make the decision myself, but during the strike I have no control over the hiring process," she says before connecting him to the manager.

"Good afternoon, Michael Deni here. How may I assist you?"

Stanley went over his entire spiel again. Mr. Deni tells him that he will give Scotty a shot and to make sure Scotty arrives before the strikers come in the morning.

When Stanley hangs up the phone he relays the news to Scotty. "I promise, Boss, I will do all I can to follow the directions. I ain't going to lose this job."

"Stop calling me 'Boss.' And whatever you do, don't call Mr. Deni that either. Your job is in jeopardy before you even walk through the door."

***

When Scotty gets home, his mother is sitting on the front steps. "What are you doing out here?" he asks.

"I'm so sick and tired of hearing the phone ring. Dr. Spinelli's office keeps calling. I think they have our number on some sort of redial."

"Did they tell you what they wanted?"

"No, they just said it was imperative that you call the office as soon as you are available."

"Well, I just won't be available," Scotty says smugly.

She stands up and points her finger at her son, "You will walk into the house and go directly to the phone. You will call Spinelli's office ASAP. Do you understand me?"

"Yes, Mother," He says meekly, following her into the house.

Scotty dials the number and within a few rings a woman answers.

"Dr. Spinelli's office. Can I help you?"

"Is this Joanie?"

"Yes, who is this?"

"Hi Joanie. It's me, Scotty."

"Scotty how are you doing? It's not the same without you here. We all miss you. Well, almost everyone. I know why you're calling. The doctor wants to speak with you. Hey, take care, and I hope things turn out for you," she says before connecting him with the doctor.

"Is this you, Scotty?"

"Yes, it's me. But is that you, Dr. Spinelli?"

The doctor sounds immediately angry, putting Scotty on edge. "Listen up, Punk. Tony Buffo called earlier, advising me he was cutting his business trip short. He said he would be picking up June Bug earlier than expected," Dr. Spinelli's voice gets louder the more he talks.

"What do you want out of me?" Scotty asks defensively.

"What do I want out of you? I want you to get out there and locate that dog," the doctor yells into Scotty's ear. "Scotty, this is no joke. Do you want to know why his business trip was cut short?"

"Yeah why?"

"Because he probably whacked the guy off sooner than he thought."

FIRED!

"I was only whacked one time in my life. It was when my dad found me picking up his shot gun. Boy, did that hurt."

"Listen, Bozo, I'm not joking around. Just find the flipping dog, or else!" he yells before slamming down the phone.

Scotty hangs the phone up and thinks out loud, "Funny he should mention Bozo. I loved that clown. I wonder what ever happened to him?" he asks his mother standing right beside him.

"I always thought when you got fired or quit a job, that was the end. I mean you were through. Not for that Spinelli guy. He is going to haunt me until the day I die. Speaking of which, I might endure a little bodily harm with the new job I landed," he says, startling his mother.

"I was going to ask you if you had one shred of good news today. It seems like every day is a repeat performance of the previous. And now you're talking about bodily harm," she cries out.

"Remember the pesticide company they showed on the news?"

"You mean the one on strike?"

"Yup."

"Don't even tell me you got a job there," his mother said, crossing herself.

"I won't, but I did," Scotty states, grinning.

"Do you think that is a wise move, Son?"

"Are you kidding? I need a job! without one, I will never get Charlotte back. Why can't you ever have faith in me?"

"Last time I had faith in a man was your daddy, and we all know how that turned out," she mumbles.

"I don't," Scotty says.

Changing the subject, Mable offers, "Why don't you head back out and try to find June Bug?"

"I was thinking about that. Maybe I should just tell Buffo what happened. Ya know, be honest about the whole thing. Ma, do ya think it would be alright if I offered to buy him another dog?"

"Do you want to be buried in the plot next to your father?" she asks flatly.

"I thought that was your spot."

"It won't be if you don't find Buffo's dog. Now get out there and search," she says, walking him to the rusty yellow van. Looking at that rust heap again, she asks, "By the way, when are you supposed to get your car back? Haven't they had it long enough?"

Scotty just shakes his head and says, "Let's not talk about that. I nearly got my head chewed off asking the mechanic that same question."

"Maybe we ought to take a drive there and see just what is taking so long," she offers as he stuffs his large body behind the wheel of the van.

"I have to tell you the truth, Ma. I fear that mechanic more than Buffo," Scotty says, closing the driver's side door.

Taking a deep breath, she shakes her head and says, "Son, just do your best to find the dog."

"I'll try, Ma. I'll try." He says before driving away.

Chapter 36

When Scotty arrives at the spot where he lost June Bug, he sits on the ground and starts calling for the dog. Hearing something rustling through the woods, he stays completely still. The sound is getting closer and closer.

Just then he spots what he thinks is a dog. "Ah, there you are! Come here, little doggy," he says, opening up a pack of crackers.

The supposed dog walks up to him with matted fur and saliva dripping from his mouth. Only the dog was not a dog at all—but a rabid raccoon! Upon realizing it, Scotty gets up and starts running. The rabid raccoon chases him until he falls, grabs the crackers from his hand, and comes eye-to-eye with Scotty. Scared out of his wits Scotty screams out, "Help!"

Out of nowhere, June Bug comes to his rescue. He takes his powerful paw and smacks the raccoon, sending the creature airborne. Thankful, Scotty tries to pet the dog but is met with snarls and growls. The dog grabs the crackers that the raccoon dropped and runs away.

Shaken and baffled, Scotty gets off the ground and hurries back to the van.

The Outrageously Ridiculous Adventures of Scotty J. Fahrenheit

After this awful episode, he decides he needs a pick-me-up. He heads over to the local ice cream shop. After waiting for just a moment he is given a seat near a window.

"Hi, Sir, may I help you?" the friendly waitress asks.

"Yes, I will take one of these with everything on it," he says, licking his lips and pointing to the picture on the menu of a very large sundae with tons of candy and toppings piled up on top.

Looking him over, she said, "That's just the one I thought you would order. Our Super-Mega Candy Sundae is one of our best sellers," the waitress says while writing his order on her pad.

Scotty knows the rules. His mother is always telling him to wash up before eating. He heads to the men's room to wash his hands. On the way back to his table he spots a young couple sitting in a booth laughing. He looks over at the two and doesn't even realize the woman is Charlotte. He just smiles and keeps walking. When he sits down, it hits him. He springs from his seat and hurries over to her. "My God, is that actually you, Charlotte? Have you any clue how damned depressed I have been?"

She just looks over at him and puts her head down.

"What's that all about?" he begs.

"Buddy, we would appreciate you leaving us alone," the man with Charlotte speaks out.

"Do you even realize who I am?" Scotty replies.

"I don't care, and neither does Charlotte. So if you would be on your merry way, I will forget this altercation ever took place."

"Hey man, If you are looking for a fight, bring it on," Scotty provokes.

FIRED!

The man gets up from the booth and says, "Take a look at these arms. I work out five hours a day. Do you think I am afraid of you?" He flaunts huge arm muscles.

"Oh yeah, I've got a big stomach," Scotty says, lifting up his shirt and allowing the bulging mass of his belly to flop out.

The man laughs, "I don't know what kind of and idiot you are. But you are monkeying with the wrong guy."

"I would never monkey with anybody. Who's the idiot now?" Scotty asks.

The man just looks at Scotty in awe, shaking his head.

Scotty speaks again, "You know what? I take that back. There sitting across from you is a girl I thought loved me. That makes *me* the real idiot," he finishes glumly as he hangs his head and begins walking away.

The guy starts feeling bad about the situation and reaches for Scotty's arm, stopping him. "Look man, you don't have anything to worry about. Trust me on that," the guy tries to explain.

"You're the one sitting by the love of my life all giddy and stuff," Scotty says, motioning toward Charlotte.

"Buddy, like I said, you have nothing to worry about."

"Why is that?" Scotty wonders.

"Because Charlotte would never be my type."

"Oh, I get it. You are just out to use her."

"It's got nothing to do with Charlotte," he says in a low voice, trying to explain.

"Oh, then it must be her money you're after. If her father finds that out, you're finished," Scotty says.

The Outrageously Ridiculous Adventures of Scotty J. Fahrenheit

"Okay, okay. I can't take your hassling anymore. Look, I'm gay."

"That makes matters even worse. Isn't that what all women want, some gay guy?" Scotty remarks.

"I can see this is getting us nowhere. Please go back to your seat and leave us alone."

"You know, Buddy, I will go back to my seat. I just have one last thing to say."

"What stupid thing might that be?"

"You think you can brag about being gay because you got Charlotte. If I was sitting with her I would be gay too." Scotty turns to Charlotte and says, "Charlotte, I promise I will get a good job. I'm going to win you back, and then you will see just how gay I can be. But for now, I will go back to my seat, but instead of feeling gay, I will feel miserable."

Charlotte is so saddened by the whole thing that as soon as Scotty walks away, she begins crying.

"If I did anything to hurt you I am sorry," her friend apologizes.

"Matt, I have never stopped having feelings for Scotty. He has said and done things for me that no one else has."

"You mean you actually like that guy?" he asks, stunned.

"I do. I really do," she admits.

"Hmm, I think I just found out the real reason I am gay."

"What's the reason?"

"To be completely honest. I can't understand women. I mean look at you. You're actually crying over a guy like *him*. What's up with that?"

"You wouldn't understand because you don't have that kind of connection to a woman."

"Maybe it's good you women think the way you do."

"Why do you say that?"

"Because no gay man would ever want *him*."

"Then it's a good thing women and gay men are looking for different things in a man," she replies.

***

By the time Scotty sits down, his sundae is melted. Instead of using a spoon, he brings the bowl up to his mouth like a cup and begins drinking it down. After he's finished, he leaves the last of his money on the table.

When he gets home, his mother demands he tell her some positive news. She explains how sick and tired she is from all the negativity.

He tells her the situation with the raccoon and June Bug.

"What great news to know the dog is still alive," she remarks. "Now all you have to do is catch him."

"Ma, you make it sound so easy. Like all I have to do is clap my hands and the dog is going to magically appear. It took a foaming raccoon with a cracker in his mouth to get the dang dog to come over."

"Son, what have I told you about swearing?"

"Come on, Ma. *Dang* isn't a curse word, and you know it!"

"Oh, please, I beg you, no more bad news."

"Then I won't tell you that I went into the ice cream shop and spotted Charlotte with another guy."

"Well, you know exactly what you have to do to get her back. It's pertinent to concentrate on your job and not get caught up with other distractions."

"Do you call Charlotte laughing and having a sundae with a gay guy a distraction?"

"Look, it's not polite to call somebody that. I thought you were better than that. Lately, I just don't understand what has gotten into you," she says, disgusted.

Exhausted from trying to explain himself, Scotty calls it quits. He goes upstairs to his father's closet in search of another dreadful outfit for his meeting at the pesticide company. He finds an old pair of Levi jeans. Although it's summer, he chooses a tight, blue wool turtleneck sweater.

He puts the outfit on and then realizes that he needs to find a pair of shoes. His eyes light up as soon as he spots his father's old white patent-leather shoes. He squeezes into them before gazing in the mirror, deciding that he looks awesome. But his happiness soon fades when thoughts of Charlotte race through his head.

He decides to go to bed early in hopes of taking his mind off of her. Kneeling at the side of his bed, Scotty begins to pray. "Dear God, my life is going down the tubes. I know you know. But do you know how bad I feel? Let me tell you, I feel awful. How can I ever make things go right for me? God, I am really getting tired. My mom is getting so sick of me. I don't know what she has planned if I don't stop being so negative. But gee,

FIRED!

God, how can I be positive when everything around me is so negative?"

After a moment of being quiet he adds, "One last thing, God, will I ever get my car back? I wish just once I could hear you answer me. I kind of understand what it's like to be deaf. All I get from you is silence when I ask a question. Maybe I should stop asking. Well, goodnight and sleep tight. Don't let the bedbugs bite," he says before jumping into his twin-sized bed and falling fast asleep.

Chapter 37

At four o'clock in the morning, Scotty wakes up and rushes to get dressed. "You look marvelous, you sexy beast," he says, eyeing himself in the mirror.

He quietly leaves the house, making sure not to wake his mother. He makes it to his van and soon realizes it's not starting. "Not now," He screams, pounding the steering wheel.

He continues turning the key with no luck. Feeling helpless, he runs in the house, screaming for his mother.

She hurries downstairs, startled by his screaming, still disoriented from being jolted awake so early. "What is all the commotion about?" she mumbles.

"Ma, that piece of crap won't start. I tried about fifty times, and nothing," he screams out.

"Calm down," she says, taking out her black book of numbers.

"Are you serious right now? I'm in trouble, and all you can do is call one of your friends?"

"Son, please. I am calling the tow service to come and jump the van."

FIRED!

"Whatever you do don't—and I repeat, don't—call the jerks from the Five Brothers towing service." He remarks as his mother motions for him to quiet down.

"How many times have I told you not to interrupt me when I am on the phone? You do understand how very rude your behavior is?"

"Ma, I don't want that slime ball coming to do anything for me. He wouldn't give me a ride to the shop. Dad told me never to tolerate nasty people."

"Well, I have no idea who Triple A is going to dispatch. If it's Five Brothers, then it's Five Brothers."

"I guess you're right. I'm so sorry, Ma."

Mable walks over to a small drawer and takes out a bottle of aspirin. "I hope you don't mind if I go back upstairs. My head is pounding right now."

"I'm going to wait in the van for the tow guy to show up."

After what seems like an eternity, the tow truck pulls in. The driver notices the van door is open, so he walks over. He takes one look at Scotty and remarks, "You again?"

"I tried to warn my mother," Scotty tells the driver.

"What's that supposed to mean?" the driver asks, upset.

"It means you are a very rude guy, and I didn't want to deal with you again. That's what I mean."

"Here goes, Jerk. I own the company, because of that remark, you can go back inside, call Triple A, and tell them that you want someone else dispatched," he says, slamming the van door and walking away.

"Wait, I beg you not to leave," Scotty says, chasing the man to his tow truck.

"You have no clue how sick and tired I am of rude rejects like yourself. I don't have to do anything for you," the driver explains.

"I'll do anything to get you to jump this van. Please, I'm desperate. Whatever you want from me, just ask," Scotty pleads.

The guy stops a minute and thinks before saying, "You got a deal. There's just one thing you can do for me," the guy negotiates.

"Sure, anything; what do you want?" Scotty agrees.

"I want you to promise me that you will keep your pathetic, big mouth shut."

Scotty puts his fingers to his mouth and makes a sign as if he is sealing his lips.

"Good. You're understanding very well," he says as Scotty shakes his head yes.

They both walk over to the van. The tow truck driver asks, "What's the van doing?"

Scotty refuses to speak. Instead he mouths "My lips are sealed."

"Get out of the way," the tow truck driver replies before he pushes Scotty aside and gets into the driver's seat. He takes one look at the shifter and realizes that the van isn't all the way in Park. He pushes the shifter back into Park and then turns the key. The van starts immediately.

"There, all fixed. Now I need you to walk over to the tow truck and sign a paper," he says.

FIRED!

He hands Scotty the paper and responds, "You can thank me now."

Scotty keeps to his promise not to speak and just nods his head while signing it.

The tow truck driver grabs the paper, gets back in his truck without another word and peels out, giving Scotty the finger as he does so.

Now that that crisis is over, Scotty hops into the van and heads over to the pesticide company.

His dreams of avoiding the strikers is crushed. Not only does he have to walk past them, but he is confronted by one of the strikers.

"Hey, Buddy, grab a sign and join in," the guy orders.

Not knowing what to do, Scotty grabs a sign.

One of the strikers walks over to Scotty. "I don't think I've ever seen you in the plant. It's really awful how we are all struggling while these rich cats have no concern for us."

Another striker walks over. "Hey man, I'm almost ready to crack. Striking is great, but living without a paycheck sucks."

"What are you going to do?" Scotty asks.

"As long as the plant has no workers, they are hemorrhaging money too," the desperate union worker replies.

"I really have to use the bathroom. What am I supposed to do?" Scotty says, coming up with a scheme.

"Walk over to that guy in the front and tell him you need to use the restroom. He'll let you in. That's the only reason we're going into the building," the picketer explains.

The Outrageously Ridiculous Adventures of Scotty J. Fahrenheit

"Thanks, man, I'll do just that," Scotty says, hurrying to the huge man in the front of the line.

"I was told you are the man I need to talk to. Let's say you walk me to the bathroom," Scotty says.

"I was wondering when you were going to show up. I called days ago, what the heck took you so long?" The guy asks, mistaking Scotty for someone else.

"These things take time," Scotty bluffs.

"Follow me. I'll lead you inside. There you can complete your clandestine mission. You'll see what I'm talking about. We're all aware of the many safety hazards that this company refuses to address. I've got to admit, you would be the man I would least expect to be going undercover. I mean, with that outfit and all, you come off as an idiot. Makes sense though. They would never assume you were from OSHA trying to site them for safety violations. It's funny how people can get sidetracked just by someone's appearance. You really nailed it," the man says with a chuckle while walking Scotty into the building.

"I got this covered," Scotty pretends as Mr. Deni walks over.

"You must be Scotty," Mr. Deni assumes, extending his hand.

The man that led Scotty in looks over, winks, and mouths, "Thank you."

Scotty winks back as the man assumes Scotty has already infiltrated the plant.

"I'm sorry if you were hassled by the strikers. They can be very forceful. Speaking of agitators, the guy who walked you in is ruthless. He stops at nothing. Looks to me you know how to hold your own," he says, walking Scotty to his office. "Have a seat," Mr. Deni offers before he continues, "I want to thank

FIRED!

you for taking on this challenge. As you can see, all work is on hold for the time being. This strike is really affecting our business. That's the reason you are here. Since the strike started, the factory has been shut down," Mr. Deni explains.

"If the factory is closed, what do you want out of me?"

"You'll be responsible for spraying chemicals on lawns. We have accounts that have to be serviced. Usually there is only one man per truck. But considering the circumstances, you'll be paired with another man. It will be very beneficial for both of you," Mr. Deni advises.

Scotty is taken to the personnel department where a woman gives him an application and other papers needed for employment.

Scotty looks at the papers blankly and says, "Gee, I just filled all these papers out at my last job. Why can't you just get them from Spinelli's?" he ignorantly asks.

"That's not how it is done. Please fill out the papers and bring them back up to me when you're done," the woman replies.

After he gets the papers filled out, Scotty is led to a large conference room. There's a group of men sitting around a table. Scotty interrupts their conversation to introduce himself.

"Hi guys, I want to say how happy I am to be here today. Just when I was ready to call it quits. You know, I was ready for the rope, the old bottle-of-pills trick, large body of water, or the knife-to-heart gig. I mean, what an opportunity. This job just came so easy! What brings you all here?" Scotty says, shocking the men.

A tall, muscle-bound man speaks up first. "Me, I'm doing this as part of my parole sentence. I already did my time in the

The Outrageously Ridiculous Adventures of Scotty J. Fahrenheit

pen. Actually, those brutes on the strike line are worse than the dudes I dealt with in prison. I should have brought my knife. I almost got the crap kicked out of me when they found out I was going to take a job," he explains.

"Wow. What saved you?" Scotty asks.

"I told the strikers the truth."

"What was that?" another man asks.

"I was forced by the judicial system to be here. I told them about being on parole after accidentally killing a man. I promised when my hours were met, I was gonzo," the parolee explains.

"How about you, Sir?" Scotty asks, pointing to a feeble elderly man.

"I'm on Social Security and it's not enough to live on. Years ago, I worked at the old steel mill. That was before the economy hit the skids and the old mill closed the doors. So I took a job at the nearest burger joint. It was impossible for me to feed my big family. I worked two other minimum-wage jobs just to keep the family from freezing."

Everyone kept listening to his story as the old man continues, "But when I got on in age, I wasn't as fast. That was the nail in my coffin. All three jobs let me go. My wife and I live off basically nothing. Every day we volunteer at the local soup kitchen just so we can eat. Or we go to the library, that became our second home," he chuckles. "We go there for free heat and air-conditioning. It's great, except I read so many books that now I have serious eye problems. I can't read anymore and my eyes are always in pain."

Scotty has been taken back by his story and is starting to feel emotional.

FIRED!

The elderly man keeps talking. "To think I have to go back to work at this old age," he says, shaking his gray head slowly. "I put my application in at so many places. Nobody wants a crippled old man like me. Of course, that was before I applied to this place," he explains.

Scotty breaks out in tears.

"What's up with the waterworks, Amigo?" a young man who is probably in his twenties asks Scotty.

"That has got to be the saddest story I have ever heard. I can't imagine eating soup every day, living in a library, and going blind over it. Now that the man is crippled nobody wants him. He is treated like a reject. How horrible!" Scotty continues wailing.

"Amigo, didn't you say you were suicidal? I don't think it gets much worse than that," the young guy remarks.

A man in a silk suit comes in the room and begins giving the men some instructions. "I will make this very brief. You are all going to be doing basically the same thing. The only difference is where you will be doing it. You will each be given a truck filled with chemicals. Those chemicals will be applied at each individual lawn. Each stop uses a different application. You will be given the list with what yards need which chemicals. Some stops are non-toxic, which means they only get organic fertilizer. Other stops need toxic chemicals sprayed on their lawns. It is imperative that you don't make a mistake," he says while looking directly at them all.

He continues with the instructions, "Each hose is labeled to what it is. It isn't hard to remember. The hose marked "Toxic" with cross-bones means just that. The fertilizer is marked

The Outrageously Ridiculous Adventures of Scotty J. Fahrenheit

"Green" with a four-leaf clover emblem. It's very simple. Your job is to keep the customers happy."

"That seems simple enough," Scotty says to the other guys. They agree.

"Now I am going to pair you men up," the man in the silk suit says. "Todd and Scotty, I will put you two together. You are going to be given the east side route. You have to be extra careful because they are the upper-class crowd. They pay a lot of money and demand extra-special service. We can't afford to lose any customers—especially that crowd."

After everyone is paired up, he explains a few more things. "When you get to each stop, make sure you knock at the door first. You don't want a customer to have any animals outside while you're spraying. If the customer isn't home, then spray the application and leave the bill taped to the back door. And whatever you do, don't forget to put the yard signs up. Any questions so far?"

"Yeah. What signs are you talking about and where are we supposed to get them?" Scotty asks.

"The signs are in the back of the truck. There's more than enough to go around. Now if you are all set, go down the hall to the locker room where you will find uniforms. You are welcomed to take six uniforms home with you. Then head to the personnel office down the hall." Looking at his watch, the man jumps and says, "I really have to end this, so if there are no more questions, good-bye and good luck," he adds. Nobody asks anything more so he hurries off.

Chapter 38

While Todd starts walking down the hall, Scotty chases after him. "Hold up and wait for your partner, dude. We will sure make one heck of a team," Scotty says, patting him aggressively on the back.

Todd just about falls on the floor. "Easy, boy, you just about took me out with that forceful slap on my back. And for crying out loud, why are you sweating so much?"

"Sweat is the right word for it. Check this out," Scotty says, revealing his sweaty belly and back.

"No not another dude with swamp crack," Todd says, shaking his head.

"What is swamp crack?" Scotty asks, confused.

"You ain't the first fat guy I've worked with. That swamp crack stinks to high heavens. It's a real killer! When your smell starts getting really strong, I will demand you powder your smelly swamp crack. Do you understand?"

"Okay. I'll stop at the store when I'm done today to get some swamp crack powder," Scotty agrees.

They both head over to the locker room, where there are just a couple of suits left. Todd holds up a suit and remarks how he would be swimming in it. Scotty takes the other one and wonders how on earth he will be able to fit into it. Todd quickly suits up.

"What's the hold up?" Todd asks Scotty.

Scotty is having a hard time getting the suit over his massive, bulging stomach. Todd rushes over and tells Scotty to hold his breath. Scotty tries his best, but there is no way that suit is going to go over his enormous belly. "Now what do we do?" Scotty worries.

"Just lay on the floor," Todd advises.

"What does lying on the floor have to do with anything?" Scotty questions.

"Can you please just shut the heck up?" Todd says, trying to push Scotty down.

Scotty gets on his knees and eases down. "Okay, I am on the floor. Now what?"

"Shut your mouth and hold your breath," Todd says, trying to zip the way-too-small uniform. After much effort it zips tightly.

"There we go. Now stand up," Todd says, helping Scotty up.

"Man, this suit is so tight it's almost impossible to breathe."

"Just be glad it's on. My suit doesn't look much better," he says, motioning to the baggy suit hanging on his body. "Now let's get going."

Suddenly they hear a loud ripping sound.

"What was that?" Scotty asks, slowly walking past Todd.

Todd immediately notices the huge rip down the back of his suit.

The more Scotty walks, the bigger the tear gets.

FIRED!

"Alright, Dough Boy, let's get this show on the road," he says, not telling Scotty about the condition of his suit.

While walking down the hall, one of the workers takes one look at them and laughs. "Guys what's up with your uniforms?"

"Don't even go there buddy?" Todd says.

"You better mind your manners or else," Scotty threatens.

"Or else what? heart attack ready to happen, boy?"

"Hope you're having fun. We're going to be the best dang team known to this company. Do you understand?" Todd replies.

"We are the superheroes of this place. No if, ands, or buts!" Scotty yells out.

The guy just laughs. "Butt is what's hanging out of your way-too-small uniform. You look like a stuffed sausage! Now go start your route. "

"Gee, Todd, what did that jerk mean about my butt?"

"Don't listen to that jealous fool. Let's go find our truck."

"Thanks for sticking up for me. I've been made fun of my whole entire life. Look how great you look in your uniform. I mean, you're so lucky to be that skinny. You must really keep to a diet. Man, that's too hard for me. I mean, my ma cooks all this great food. I just can't control myself."

"You think this uniform looks good on me? Look again; the thing is falling off me! No matter what I do, I just can't gain weight. For years my mom said it must be some kind of metabolic problem."

"Is there any way that can be contagious? I mean, I would love to have that problem," Scotty asks.

"Trust me, it's no fun for me. It's like I am constantly forcing food down my throat so I don't lose too much weight."

"I want that disease! Just how did you get it?" Scotty asks.

"Hey, dude, this isn't something I asked for. I just wound up with it. Enough about this. We need to find the truck so we can start our route," he says, shutting Scotty up.

It doesn't take long for Todd to locate the truck. "Looks like this is the one."

"You wanna flip a coin?" Scotty offers.

"Flip a coin for what?" Todd asks.

"To see which one of us gets to drive."

"Dude, I would love that, but I ain't got a coin in my pocket," he says before Scotty takes out a quarter.

"Heads or tails? You go first," Scotty offers.

"Let's do this. Heads, you win; tails, I lose. Does that sound fair to you?" Todd asks.

"It sure does. So if I win this time, you can drive next time," Scotty says, not comprehending that he would win no matter how the coin landed.

"Seeing that the coin toss went right over your head, I have a confession to make," Todd says.

"Oh, no. Please don't tell me you're going to quit already?" Scotty panics.

"Nothing of the sorts. I either keep this job or…let's just say that I had a bit of a run-in with the law. So I lost my license, and now I can't drive."

FIRED!

"Gee, I hope I never lose my license. I never want to forget how to drive. How odd is that?"

Todd just looks over at Scotty and rolls his eyes.

"How the heck do they know if you can drive or not?" Scotty asks, confused.

"That ain't the problem. Actually, I am a really good driver."

"Then why are you listening to the law? They don't seem to know jack."

"I would love to agree with you, but really, I ain't gonna take any chances. See, I am on parole right now. Once false move and I'm back in the slammer," Todd admits.

"So do you or don't you have a legit license?"

"Let's just leave it with you being the driver."

"Sounds great to me," Scotty smirks.

When they get into the truck, Todd grabs the folder with all the stops for the day. "Holy cow, are these people crazy? How are we supposed to get all these lawns done in one day?"

Scotty takes a look at the list and shrugs it off. "That ain't bad."

"As opposed to what? You really think this ain't no big deal? What, may I ask, do you consider a big deal?" Todd asks.

"Getting a job and keeping it seems to be a big deal."

"Sounds like a personal problem," Todd jokes.

"Let's concentrate on where we're going," Scotty explains.

"I guess we're supposed to go from the top to the bottom," Todd assumes.

"You know how to get to all these places?" Scotty asks.

"Do I look like a map to you?"

"No, I just assumed that, being a man of the town, you would know."

Todd picks a ledger with the directions to each stop.

"No problem, copilot. Just lead the way," Scotty says, acting witty.

"Dude, I would love to, but being in so many fights kind-of ruined my eyesight. I mean, things look extremely blurry. There must be another way to figure how to get to where we are going."

Scotty looks around in the van and gets an idea. He grabs the two-way radio and screams. "Hello? Hello? This is Scotty. Over and out," he says, banging the receiver on the steering wheel.

"Yes, Scotty, what's the problem?" a young woman answers.

"I need the directions to where I'm going. You have any idea?"

Todd grabs the radio and says, "Look, I am half-blind and can't read the directions. We need to know how to get to our first stop."

"No problem. Give me a minute to locate your route," she comes back on with directions for them to follow.

When they get to the first stop, the owner tells them to go ahead with spraying the application. She can't stop laughing after noticing the split down Scotties uniform. "Oh, by the way, boys, make sure to use the fertilizer," she says, trying to contain herself from laughing in Scotty's face.

So far, so good. The first job seems to be going without a hitch.

FIRED!

When they pull up to their next job, they are amazed at the enormous house. Scotty rings the doorbell, but nobody answers. Todd decides they need to walk around the house to make sure nobody is outside. They immediately spot a middle-aged woman sunbathing in a tiny bikini. Scotty walks over to her and puts his hands over his eyes. "Miss, we are here to spray your lawn. You better go in so you don't get sprayed."

"Where is my usual weed-killer guy? He always meets me at the pool," she says with a lazy smile.

Todd comes rushing over. "Miss, you don't have anything to worry about. Me and Scotty will do an outstanding job on your lawn."

He looks at Scotty and asks, "Why the heck do you have your hands over your eyes?"

"I don't like to look at a woman who is half dressed," Scotty admits.

"Who the heck cares what she's got on. We're here for a job—that's all," Todd whispers to Scotty.

"Miss, we are here to do a job. The sooner you can go inside the quicker we can get it done," Scotty says, his hands still over his eyes.

"I'll go inside if you can join me. I mean, that was the routine with my other pesticide guy."

"Thanks for the invite, but I have to get my work done," Scotty remarks.

"If you would remove your hands from over your eyes, you would see she was talking to me. And Scotty, I will take this beautiful woman up on her offer. Remember what we were told?"

"No I don't recall."

"It went something like 'we have to do anything to keep the customer happy.' That is exactly what I intend to do," Todd explains.

"So what am I supposed to do?" Scotty asks.

"You are supposed to spray the lawn. By the time you're done, I'm sure I will be done. Just make sure to do a thorough job, because I will be inside doing the same."

"You've got me all confused," Scotty says, walking away.

While Todd is inside, Scotty is trying to figure out the hose situation. For some unknown reason, the hose is clogged and he is unable to get it to operate. He spends the entire time pressing buttons in vain that have nothing to do with the hose.

***

Inside, Todd asks the woman to please put something on over her bathing suit.

She goes upstairs and comes down with a fancy robe on. "Is this better?"

"Yes. Thank you."

"Now it's your turn. I really don't want the chemicals coming off that suit," she admits.

"No problem," he says before taking the suit off, leaving him wearing his street clothes.

Soon the woman leads Todd to her husband's library. "Can I fix you something to drink? I will be having a screwdriver. How about yourself?" She asks taking out a bottle of vodka before reaching into a small refrigerator to get a carton of orange juice.

"I'll take my screwdriver without the vodka. I gave up the booze and the one-night stands," he confesses. Then he continues, "It sounds like the verse from one of my favorite songs. You know that song Baker Street by Gerry Rafferty."

"I don't think I remember the song," she agrees.

Todd, trying to refresh her memory, starts singing the lyrics, "He's got this dream about buying some land. He's gonna give up the booze and the one-night stands and then he'll settle down in some quiet little town and forget about everything."

Suddenly she burst into tears.

"I didn't mean to upset you," Todd says.

All teary-eyed, she admits. "It's not you. That song is exactly what my husband promised me. The only true part of it was he did buy some land. As for the rest, nothing has changed."

"Don't count on others to change. The only person you can change is you," he says.

"You're so right. I never drank until things got so bad between Jerry and me. I am no different than him. I have one-night stands just to get back at him for all his infidelities. Actually, I am embarrassed to say that's the reason I invited you in."

"If I was my old self, I would definitely have taken you up on your offer. It's got nothing to do with you," he tries to explain.

"What do you mean when you said your 'old self'? How did you change?"

"It's a long story, and I don't want to bore you with the details." He looks around at all the books in the library. "Hey, is one of these books a Bible?"

The Outrageously Ridiculous Adventures of Scotty J. Fahrenheit

"You certainly change subjects quickly," she says, finding the Bible and taking it down.

"You asked me how I changed. This book is the way I did that. Before my mom died she made me promise I would read it and abide by the words written on each page. She told me that the Bible had the answers to any question I had."

"Are you serious about the Bible really helping you?"

"I would never lie about something like that. Why don't you read it? I promise it will change your life like it has mine."

Just then, Scotty starts ringing the doorbell. "That must be Scotty," he says, putting his uniform back on.

Scotty opens the door and yells, "Is anybody home?"

Todd comes rushing into the foyer with his uniform undone.

"Hey, Todd, I know you have a hard time seeing and all, but for some reason, your uniform isn't buttoned. If you come over here, I'll give you a hand," Scotty offers.

"Thank you, but I can handle dressing myself. Have you put the lawn signs up?" Todd asks.

Suddenly, a women's voice can be heard. "Todd, I'm going to call the company and request you every time. I am going to tell them how much I appreciate what you've done for me."

"Thank you. I sure take that as a compliment," He remarks, smiling back at her.

"Ma'am, thank you for putting that robe on," Scotty says. "Now I don't have to cover my eyes."

Todd grabs Scotty by the arm. "Look, we got so much more to do. Get those signs up now."

FIRED!

"I got bad news for you. While you were in there, I was having trouble getting the hose to spray."

"What did you do?" Todd asks.

"Come on, let's figure this out and get this lawn finished," Scotty says.

"I'll make a deal with you," Todd offers.

"What's that?" Scotty asks.

"I'll spray the lawn if you put the signs up. Do we have a deal?"

Scotty shakes his head yes.

Chapter 39

Todd starts with the front lawn and then heads to the back while Scotty starts putting signs up. As soon as Todd is done, he heads to the truck. He looks at the front yard and can't believe what Scotty did. "Are you really serious right now?" he yells out, motioning toward the front yard.

"What's wrong?" Scotty asks clueless.

"Why are there over a hundred signs in the front lawn?" he asks, shaking his head.

"I wanted to make sure the owners are aware the lawn has been sprayed," he so innocently responds.

"Just get in the truck and let's go," Todd says, shaking his head and opening his door.

"Now you got me nervous that I put too many signs in the lawn. Maybe we'll get fired."

"Are you really that naïve? Don't you understand we are scabs? That place is just lucky to have us. We're doing them the big favor. Trust me, they need us more than we need them," Todd explains.

"So we can't get fired?" Scotty asks again.

FIRED!

"No, we'll get beat up by the strikers before we get fired," he says, trying to reassure Scotty.

"Alrighty then. Heck with the signs. Let's just go."

"That's the most intelligent thing you've said all day," Todd says, giving him a high five.

On the way to the next stop Todd confides in Scotty, "I know you're probably judging me for what you assume I did with that woman."

"I would never judge you or anyone. It ain't my job

"I shouldn't have said that. You're probably the only person who hasn't asked me the details about my incarceration."

"Whatever that's supposed to mean."

"You know when I was in prison?"

"Oh, yeah. You did mention that."

"Here's the scoop. One day me and my brother, Odel, were on the street corner waiting for the light to change. All of a sudden, a big thug walks up to Odel and demands he hand over his wallet." Poor Odel, stricken in a wheelchair, begins to panic."

"Why was he in a wheelchair?"

"He's got cerebral palsy."

"Did the guy end up robbing Odel?"

"I walked over to the criminal and told him to leave him alone. The guy just wouldn't heed to my warning. Instead, he put his hands up and tried to punch me."

"What did you do?"

The Outrageously Ridiculous Adventures of Scotty J. Fahrenheit

"I pushed him away and he lost his footing. I never meant for him to hit his head on the curb and drop dead."

"What happened next?"

"I was charged with manslaughter and spent over seven years in prison."

"Didn't your mother stick up for you and tell them how her son, I mean, your brother was being robbed?"

"No, because she doesn't know him."

"How can she not know her own son?"

"Because he's not her son."

"Then why did you call him your brother?"

"See, Odel is a black man, and it's kind of a custom for black guys to refer to one another as 'brother.' Even though I'm not black, I felt really close to Odel, so when he started calling me 'brother,' I did the same," he explained.

"I see," said Scotty.

"Anyway, when I was in prison, my mother visited me two times a week. I'll never forget the time she came with a troubled look on her face. I knew something really bad was up. She told me she was diagnosed with some kind of cancer and didn't have long to live. I was so upset. I didn't know what to say or do."

"So what did you do?"

"I just listened while she confessed the sins from her past. I had a hard time hearing her tell me that when she was young she got addicted to drugs and prostituted for her habit. If that wasn't bad enough, she admitted that me and my three brothers were all half-brothers."

FIRED!

"Did she tell you who your real mother is?"

"Are you serious right now? There is no question that she was our mother. How come you don't understand that we all had different fathers?"

"Did it ever occur to you that Odel really is your brother, and your real father is black?"

"You are totally unbelievable," Todd says in disbelief.

"Just certain things about you."

"Like what?"

"Well, look how tough you are. You are a real ladies man. You are so athletic. I mean, you sprayed that lawn in no time. I bet you're a really good singer and dancer too—" Scotty says before Todd interrupts.

"Gee, I take all that as a compliment. If I wasn't so white, that could be a real possibility. But me having freckles, very blonde hair with blue eyes kind of proves I am not a black man," he says, smiling and exposing a gold tooth.

"I really have to disagree with you on that," Scotty says. "That gold tooth is a dead giveaway. You're more black than any black man I know! You wouldn't want to make a bet with me, now would you? Oh, how's you mom doing?"

"The last time I saw her, she brought me a present."

"I like presents. What was it?"

"It was an old Bible. The thing she credited for turning her life around."

"That's awesome."

The Outrageously Ridiculous Adventures of Scotty J. Fahrenheit

"What's even more awesome was that I was allowed to keep it in my prison cell. Mom told me the answers to all my questions could be found within its pages. She made me promise I would read it and follow the Word of God."

"Well, did you stick to your promise?" Scotty presses.

"Yes, I did. And I still do. That's why what you may think happened with that rich woman in her house didn't."

"It didn't think anything about seeing your uniform undone and all."

"Let's just leave it at: nothing happened," Todd says before they get to the next stop.

Scotty gets out of the truck and looks around at the lawn. "How are we supposed to spray all these gardens? I mean, what gardens get what spray?"

"Please, for just once, can you try to make sense? We don't have to spray the gardens. We just have to concentrate on the small lawn. We should be done in a snap," Todd happily announces.

"Great. It's my turn to spray the lawn now," Scotty offers.

Todd gets to the side of the truck and watches Scotty dragging the huge hose around. "Let me know when you're ready for me to turn it on," Todd yells.

"Ready anytime you are," Scotty says, holding the hose.

"Okay. All set?" Todd yells.

Scotty realizes nothing is happening screams out, "Nothing is coming out yet."

"Okay, how about now?"

FIRED!

Scotty waits a few seconds and yells, "Still nothing."

Todd turns off the sprayer and walks over to Scotty. "What's your problem now?" he asks.

"You treat me like I'm some kind of an idiot."

Todd grabs the hose and shows Scotty how to operate the nozzle. "All you have to do is turn the lever to this position. Now it should be ready to go."

"Seems simple enough," Scotty remarks.

"Wait. I'll leave the lever in the ON position. Then you should be all set. I'm going to go back to the truck and turn the system back on. Make sure to keep the hose facing down."

As Todd is walking back to the truck, Scotty drops the hose. He doesn't notice that when the hose hits the ground, the lever gets jarred, causing it to turn to the OFF position.

Scotty picks the hose back up and Todd yells, "Are you ready?"

Scotty tells him to turn it on. Unfortunately, nothing happens. Scotty waits a few seconds and assumes something is wrong with the hose. While thinking the hose is in the ON position, he takes no chances and turns the lever to what he believes is off and points it directly at his face. Within seconds, chemicals begin spraying all over his face. He drops the hose and begins trying to wipe the toxic liquid from his drenched face.

Just as Todd is ready to get in the truck, he spots Scotty. "What the heck happened to you?"

"Didn't I tell you there was a problem with the hose? I turned it off and the stuff went all over me."

"Calm down. Just get in the truck and relax," Todd offers before finishing the job.

In no time, he is done. When he gets back to the truck he tells Scotty, "We can't take any more chances. From now on, I will spray the lawns."

Finally they are done for the day.

As they drive back to the pesticide plant, Scotty starts feeling a bit queasy but ignores it.

When he gets home his mother notices that he just doesn't look right. "Son, is everything alright with you?" she asks.

"Really, Ma, this day just wiped me out. I think I'm going to call it quits for the night."

"Are you really going to miss dinner? That's a first."

"Let me lay down for a bit. If I feel better, I will come down and eat."

She brushes it off as Scotty not being used to working so hard, as he heads upstairs to rest. When he doesn't come down the rest of the night she assumes that he was very tired from hard work.

Chapter 40

In the middle of the night, Mable hears a loud bang against her door. She swings it open, and there stands her son clutching his throat. "Let me guess, eating in your sleep again?"

With no response, Scotty falls into her door before falling to the floor. "Come on, you practical joker, this is no time to be funny. Now get up and move away from this door. You know I have claustrophobia."

Thankfully, he is able to muster himself just a few inches, just enough for Mable to squeeze her way out. "Son, are you having an anxiety attack?"

He shakes his head no.

"Please tell me what is wrong with you."

"I can't," he says in a whisper.

"What do you want me to do?" she asks.

"Get help," he manages.

Mable calls the ambulance, and soon they arrive.

"What seems to be the problem?" one of the medics asks Scotty.

After no response, they ask him another question. Again, no response.

"We have to get him to the hospital. He is laboring to breathe."

"Oh, my God, will he be alright?" she cries out.

"Sorry, Mrs. Fahrenheit, we won't know until the doctors can look at him."

Mable cries as the two thin medics try—unsuccessfully—to pick him up. "Maybe we can roll him on the stretcher," one of the men wonders. When that doesn't work, Mable steps in to help but they try to shoo her away. "Your son is very heavy. If we let you help, we risk you going into cardiac arrest. Then what?" the other medic advises while moving her out of the way.

"Desperate times call for desperate measures. Boys, let me help," she says, stepping in.

Finally, they are able to pick him up with Mable's help. Unfortunately, when they get him to the stairs, one of the medic's hands begins to weaken. He drops the stretcher, causing it to fall down the flight of stairs.

"Oh, my Lord," Mable screams, covering her eyes.

When they finally get him settled in the ambulance, she climbs in to ride to the hospital with her son, thanking the medics. "You will be alright, Son," she says with tears running down her face as the ambulance races to the hospital, lights on and sirens blaring.

When she gets to the hospital and in an emergency room cubicle separated by curtains, she becomes distraught over seeing her son laying there. "It's all my fault. How could I have missed the clues? Maybe I could have overlooked the fact of you going to bed so early, but there is no way I should have ignored the most obvious clue. I mean, you've never skipped a meal in your entire life! That was the clue of all clues!" she says, crying at his bedside while clenching his hand.

"I presume you are Mrs. Fahrenheit?" Dr. Brown says as he pushes the curtain aside, extending his hand.

"Yes, doctor. I'm Scotty's mother. I want you to know that he is all I have left in this world. If something happens to him, I don't know what I'll do."

"Unfortunately, something has happened, and it is up to me to find out what it is. We are running tests, and it will take some time for the results. Do you have any idea what could have taken place?"

"I know he has been upset about holding down a job. He was fired just recently."

"Is there a possibility he tried to commit suicide? I don't mean to be so crude. I'm just trying to figure out what he put in his system," the doctor pries.

"He just started work at another place."

"And where would that be?"

"It's at that pesticide company."

"I thought that plant was on strike."

"Yes, Doctor, you would be correct. As Scotty puts it, they needed 'scabs' to fill in for the striking union workers. I can't tell you how happy he was to be given a job."

"You have helped me immensely. If I am correct, your son is suffering from chemical poisoning. I am going to call the pesticide company and find out what chemicals they use. Then I will contact a doctor proficient in chemical poisoning. Be positive. We are going to do the best we can to get Scotty fixed up," he says before rushing out of the room.

Luckily, the doctor was able to identify the chemicals. A poison-control expert was called in, and he gave the protocol for the proper treatment. He commends her for giving Dr. Brown the key information about Scotty's new job. "Your son is not the first person working for the pesticide company to be admitted to this hospital. Actually, it has happened quite often. I would think that place would be fined for such a dangerous work environment. Anyway, your son will soon be on the mend. We are flushing out the chemicals while keeping him hydrated. Hopefully, he will regain consciousness very soon. I would advise you to go home and get some sleep."

"Thank you for all that good news. I don't want to go home until he wakes up and sees me here. Is that ok with you and the doctor?"

"That's fine. You take care, and make sure that son of yours is more careful while working around such dangerous chemicals."

"I will definitely relay the information," she assures the doctor.

Within an hour, Scotty wakes up. He looks over and sees his mother in an unfamiliar room with him.

"Ma, where am I? And what are all these things attached to my body?" he says groggily.

"I'm so glad to see you up and speaking," she says, grabbing his hand.

"That doesn't answer my question. Wait a minute I must be in the middle of a nightmare?" he assumes.

FIRED!

"No, you are laying in a bed in the hospital. According to the doctor and poison control expert, you got poisoned by the chemicals at your job."

"Oh, yeah. That must have been from when the hose went crazy. I mean, I really got soaked."

"Why didn't you tell me this in the first place?" she asks, annoyed.

"Cause I didn't think anything of it."

"Look, I am not going to lecture you," she says, calming herself down.

"Why not?" he wonders.

"Because you have been through enough. By the way, the poison control guy said a lot of workers from that place seem to come to this hospital with the very same problem. I just thank the dear Lord for watching out for you," she says before kissing his cheek.

Scotty begins to worry about missing work after just one day.

Thankfully, Dr. Brown comes into the room and discusses the situation. He explains how it was a close call, but nothing to worry about now. Scotty asks him when he would be able to go home.

The doctor says to his mother, "Mrs. Fahrenheit, now that your son is on the mend, I find no reason for you to stay. Sleeping on the chair makes for a very uncomfortable night. As for you, Scotty, I want you to spend one more day here just so we can make sure everything is alright."

Mable decides she is going to stay by her son's side.

The Outrageously Ridiculous Adventures of Scotty J. Fahrenheit

"Ma, please go home. There is nothing you can do for me here. I am in great hands. I want you to go home and get some sleep. I will be fine here. As a matter of fact, I think I will just chill for a spell."

"You are the most unselfish man I know," Mable admits to Scotty." Honestly, this whole ordeal has drained me. My back is hurting from helping the medics pick you up. You were dead weight."

"Gee Ma, talk about dead. I am so lucky to still be here. What if—" he says before being interrupted.

"Let's not get into the 'what-ifs.' Just be thankful everything turned out okay," she smiles.

"If you don't mind, I really am going to try and get some shut-eye. Go home and I'll give you a buzz later," he says, trying to get her out so he can conjure up another scheme.

Seeing that Scotty is okay, Mable calls a friend to come take her home. She only has to wait about thirty minutes before her ride arrives. She says goodbye and gives Scotty a kiss on the forehead before she makes her way out of the hospital and home.

Chapter 41

As soon as Mable leaves, Scotty starts figuring out a way he can escape from the hospital. But what about all the monitors he is hooked up to? He pressed the button to call a nurse. Soon an old nurse comes in and asks, "What can I help you with?"

"Looks like I got to use the bathroom. I was wondering if you could unhook me from all these machines."

"I'm sorry, but no. However, I will get you a bed pan so you can relieve yourself," she says before leaving the room.

That didn't work. So now what? When the nurse walks back into the room, he tells her the feeling just went away. She tells him to ring the bell if he needs her. By this time, she has already figured out that he was going to be a problem.

It was time for an alternative plan. He had to find a way to unhook the monitors. He rings for the nurse again.

"Do you feel you have to relieve yourself now?" she asks, holding the bedpan.

"Look, I'm really shy, and besides, my irritable bowel is acting up. I can tell you right now, that bedpan will not be enough to hold all the crap I got inside of me. Isn't there a way

I can walk to the bathroom? I mean, a way you can unhook me from the monitors."

"I can unhook you from the monitors, but I can't unhook you from your IV fluid drip."

"How is that possible if you said you won't remove my drip?"

"Your liquid bag is hooked to something we call a stick. That stick is mobile. You can walk to the bathroom with it."

"Great," he says as she starts unhooking him from the monitors.

"Let me know when you're finished in the bathroom, and I will hook you back up," she says, helping him up.

She advises him not to close the door so she can make sure he is alright, "I won't be able to go with you staring at me," he says, not wanting her to realize he never had to go to the bathroom in the first place.

Suddenly, she hears screaming in the hall. One of the nurses comes in the room and tells her she is needed in the room next door.

"Scotty how are you doing in there?" she calls, "Are you almost done?"

Desperate for her to leave, he tells her it is going to be a while before he can get off the toilet. She says that she will be right back and for him not to leave the bathroom.

The minute he hears her leave, he springs into action. Hooked up to his fluid bags and dragging the stick along, he hurries out of his room and to the stairway. He puts the stick in his hand and carefully makes his way down the stairs. When he gets to the bottom, he opens the door and follows the signs to

FIRED!

the parking garage. With his entire backside exposed, he walks through the desolate parking garage, trying to figure out what his next move will be. Suddenly, a black sedan pulls alongside him. "Hey, buddy, do you need a ride to your car?" a deranged-looking weirdo in the car offers.

"Oh, no. My car is at home," Scotty says to the stranger.

"Then what are you doing walking through the parking garage in a hospital gown?"

"I just broke out of that holding tank. I've got no time to waste. I just got a new job, and I can't get fired. By the way, what are you looking for?"

"You—hop in," the man says, unlocking the doors.

Scotty believes this is his way out—an answer to his prayers. He tries to get in the car but has trouble getting the stick inside.

"What's up with you walking around with that stick?"

"Just a little problem. You think you could help me unhook the bag from this stick?"

"Just put the stick and bag in the back seat. Looks like there is enough cord for you to still get the liquid from the drip bag."

After Scotty gets situated, the driver slowly leaves the parking garage. "I hope I'm not too much trouble."

"No, actually you just made my night," the driver says with a smile.

"What brings you to the hospital?" Scotty asks.

"I come here every night, hoping to find someone like yourself."

"Now isn't that a kind thing to do. I was hoping to find someone like you too."

"Most people don't have that same feeling," he says under his breath.

"Why would that be?" Scotty asks, confused.

"Most people take one look at the car and freak out."

"Are you kidding? When you offered me a ride, I looked up and realized you are an angel sent from heaven."

"Trust me, I'm anything but an angel," the weird man scoffs.

Within a few minutes, Scotty tells the man he has to make it home.

The man continues driving, smoking one cigarette after another.

"Um…you're heading in the opposite direction," Scotty worries.

"Look, can you just calm down?" the man barks.

"No, I am super nervous that I will be late for work."

"What's great is because you escaped from the hospital and everyone is going to think you don't want to be found. Call that the perfect situation for me," he says, blowing smoke in Scotty's face.

"I know it's your car, but could you please lay off the cigarettes. I just about dropped dead from not being able to breathe," Scotty says, coughing.

"I guess you're lucky, cause I just smoked the last one."

"That's good news," Scotty assumes.

FIRED!

"Not so fast. I will be stopping at the first gas station. When I pick up someone, my anxiety level goes through the roof, and I can't stop smoking," he admits, pulling to the side of the road.

"Look, I won't say another word. Please don't throw me out," Scotty begs.

"Why would you ever think that?"

"Then why did you just stop at the side of the road?"

"Cause I got to take a piss." He says before getting out to relieve himself.

Scotty's nose begins to run. He opens the glove box in hopes of finding a tissue. He takes out a picture and what looks to be an insurance card. He continues looking until he spots the driver approaching the car. He slams the glovebox shut and quickly puts the picture and the card in his hospital socks. There's no way he wants the man to know he was looking through his stuff. He worries the stranger will throw him out.

They start driving again and soon Scotty sees a gas station. "Are you going to stop?" he asks as the driver is just about to pull in.

After the driver buys the cigarettes and starts driving again, Scotty tells him he has to go to use the bathroom.

"Why didn't you go when you had the chance?" the man asks, agitated.

"I didn't have the cramps yet!"

"Well, you're just going to have to deal with the cramps," he rudely advises.

Scotty does his best to clench his buttcheeks.

The Outrageously Ridiculous Adventures of Scotty J. Fahrenheit

Just as he is about to pull away, Scotty lets out a huge fart. The driver stops the car and rolls down all the windows, "I haven't smelled anything that bad in all my life!" he exclaims, gagging.

"If you don't let me sit on a toilet, you're going to smell a lot worse," Scotty says as his face begins to sweat.

The man pulls the car right up to a bathroom at the back of a gas station building and becomes irate. "You better hurry up. After all, you're the one in a hurry to get home. Remember you can't be late for work," he says. Just as Scotty is getting out of the car, he inadvertently unhooks himself from the drip. He hurries out of the car, hoping to make it to the toilet on time.

Scotty seems to be taking an awful long time. Getting nervous, the driver decides to see what is going on. He quickly goes into the bathroom where he hears Scotty making all kinds of noises. "Hurry up," he orders.

"I'm sorry! I have irritable bowel problems. There's no way of rushing these kinds of things," he says.

A young, buff weightlifter comes in the bathroom. He notices the weird man just standing there. "Excuse me, but is there a problem in here?" he asks, flexing his muscles.

With no weapon in his hand, the stranger becomes very nervous. He worries that Scotty will come out and run his big mouth. He wasn't going to take any chances, so he darts out and speeds away.

Scotty walks out of the stall. "Hey, where did my ride go?"

"Honestly, dude, I don't know what's your gig, but that guy is a real creeper. I took one look at his car parked directly in front of the bathroom. I thought he was in here doing terrible things to someone."

FIRED!

"Yeah, he did look a little strange. I just escaped from the hospital and I needed to find a ride home."

"Would that be a mental hospital?" the man genuinely asks.

"It's a long story. If it's no problem, can you please give me a ride home?"

The stranger kindly obliges and takes him home.

"I don't have any money to give you, but if you give me your name, I will make sure to look you up," Scotty tells him.

"You don't have to do that. Besides, if I tell you my name, how are you going to remember it?"

"You got a pen or something?" Scotty asks, taking the stranger's insurance card from his sock.

The young man gives him the phone number. Scotty writes down the info on the back of the insurance card before putting it back in his sock.

Chapter 42

After the kind bodybuilder drives away, Scotty walks to the doorstep and takes the key from under the mat. He tries his best to be quiet as he opens the door and goes inside. When he gets upstairs he walks over to his mother's room. He stands there, just looking at her. Suddenly, he coughs. She is startled as she sees him standing in her doorway. "Am I dreaming? Oh, my God! You died and now you are an angel," his half-asleep mother surmises.

"No, Ma, it's me. I'm not dead."

"Come over here so I can touch you," she says, needing to verify his earthly existence.

She starts asking him one question after another, but Scotty interrupts her. "I would love to sit around and chat, but I've got to get ready for work."

"Son, you still have that pick line in. Do you want me to call Lois?"

"Ma, it's no big deal. Just pull it out. I'm sure I will be alright."

Mable decides she is not able to get the line out. She tells him that by the time he gets dressed, Lois will be over to help him.

Sure enough, her friend comes to the rescue.

FIRED!

"I am shocked the hospital released you with this still in."

"Lois it's complicated. Can you just get this out?" Scotty begs.

"Is it okay if I ask how the job search is going?"

"You want to know the truth? I don't know."

"Keep positive. You know the old saying about how good things come to those who wait," she says just as she is removing the pick line.

Scotty thanks her before rummaging through his father's closet. Again, he picks out another ill-fitting outfit. This time it's a polyester shirt with many different dogs on it. The pants are knee-length forest green.

Looking at his watch, Scotty realizes that he's going to be late if he doesn't leave immediately. While still wearing the hospital socks he puts on a pair of sandals. He dashes to the beat-up old van and hurries to his job.

When he pulls up to the building, he is surprised by all the cars in the parking lot. He rushes to the gate, where the guard tells him the news. "Good news! The strike is over and all the workers are back on the job."

"That's terrific. So will you please let me through the gate?"

"I am sorry to tell you, but you no longer have a job here."

"What did I do?"

"You didn't do a thing. The company just hired you temporarily until the strike was over. I thought you realized that."

"Now I see why we were called scabs. Did all of us scabs get fired?"

"All but one."

"Who would that one be?"

Just then Todd comes waltzing over. "Hey, dude, why the long face?"

"You just wait. You are going to get the terrible news."

Then Todd gives his name to the guard and is let through the gate.

"How is it you are not fired?" Scotty asks with his face against the gate.

"Remember the woman near her pool?"

"How could I forget her? She was wearing a way-too-small bathing suit. I mean her thing-a-ma-bobs were hanging out."

"That's the one. Seems she called the company and told them what a hard worker I was. She went on and on about the terrific job I did," Todd brags.

"Terrific job? You did nothing there!" Scotty says angrily.

"Are you for real? That woman and her problems wore me out," he said before walking away.

***

With nothing left to lose, Scotty decides he has one last thing to do. He must go to Buffo's and face the consequences. It was more than evident he would never get Charlotte back, nor would Stanley win the Best Coach award. Feeling like a complete failure, he takes out the directions Spinelli wrote down and heads over to Buffo's.

Nearing his destination, he begins praying out loud. "Dear God, I know you're there. I got to tell you though, sometimes I have a hard time believing you can actually see me. That in

FIRED!

itself is a mystery. Let's face it, God, I'm one fat guy—makes it difficult for you or anyone not to see me. Let me get back on track. Maybe I am going to face my ending very soon. I've heard all about this Buffo guy. Can I ask one last favor from you? I know you don't have to answer, but I still have to ask. Will you please spare my life? You see, I just want to amount to something. So far, I've been a total failure. It's like everything I touch either breaks or breaks away from me. I can't tell you what an idiot I feel like."

Scotty pauses a moment and then continues, "I know I don't have to tell you this cause you are all-powerful and knowing. Well, God, I am just about here. If it's your wish for me to die today, can you tell my mom I really love her and I will miss her?"

Almost finished with his prayer, Scotty adds, "One last thing, God, I want to tell you I'm sorry for all the things I did that hurt you. I don't want to go down in flames and spend eternity with the…wait a minute, I won't say his name. Just the thought of him makes me terrified. It's your call—either my life ends today or it doesn't. I am hoping you chose the second choice."

Finishing up his prayer, he adds a quick, "Wish me luck," heavenward as he pulls up to a huge, black steel gate. He opens the driver's side door and leaves it open while he walks up to the gate. He jumps when he hears a man with a raspy voice ask, "May I help you?"

"God is that you? Cause if it is, I just went over what I want—or I should say need, from you," Scotty says, assuming it is God because he can't see anyone else around.

"Are you some practical joker, or are you high on that wacky stuff?" the man continues.

"I'm neither, but I sure as heck am confused. How can you be talking to me? I mean there is no such thing as invisible people. Or maybe that thing about aliens is true."

"Look to your right. Do you know what a speaker looks like?"

"Oh yeah, now I see it."

"That's what you are hearing me through."

"I'm still confused as to how you knew I was here."

"Every time a car pulls up a bell rings to notify us someone is in the driveway. The speaker is always on so we can hear what's going on," the annoyance can be heard in the man's voice as he explains.

"Oh, I get it now."

"Great, so what are you here for?"

"I am Scotty J. Fahrenheit here from Dr. Spinelli's office," he says, trembling.

"Pull right up, I will unlock the gate."

"How can you do that from in the house?"

"There is a button that I press. It's really simple."

Scotty is unaware that something has jumped into his van and he quickly gets in and closes the door. All of a sudden, he feels something breathing down the back of his neck. He turns around and goes into panic mode when he realizes that it's June Bug. That causes the dog anxiety and the hair begins to stand up on the back of the dog as he begins to growl, showing his massive, sharp teeth.

Scared to death, Scotty revs the van through the gate and skids, almost hitting two men standing in the driveway. He

FIRED!

quickly opens the door and June Bug immediately jumps out and rushes over to one of the men, who is ecstatic to see the dog. "You're the first person to ever bring my precious dog to me. Nobody—and I mean nobody—would ever be so brave to drive with my dog in the car. Everyone knows he can be just as vicious and ruthless as his owner. It's obvious my precious dog respects you," Buffo says in disbelief while petting his beloved dog.

Scotty takes one look up at the sky and realizes that God answered his prayers. Under his breath he whispers, "Thank you."

"Johnny, take June Bug in the house and give him some water," Buffo orders.

Buffo points at Scotty's top and says "Your shirt; I really like it. That dog looks just like June Bug when he was a little pup."

Taking a closer look at Scotty, he says, "You know, I think I like you. Your shirt proves you're a true dog lover. Something tells me you're just the man I'm looking for. What do you say I offer you a job? You would be a great addition to the family." Then Buffo acts like he forgot something and says, "Oh, how rude of me. I should introduce myself first."

"You don't need to introduce yourself. I've heard all sorts of things about you," Scotty remarks.

"All good, I hope."

"Actually—" Scotty gets out before Buffo interrupts.

"I can see you are a truthful man, just by the way you started that sentence. You were going to admit you heard a lot of bad things about me. All the more reason to have you on my team. I need someone like you who's going to tell it like it is. My guys, I love them, but they have a habit of keeping those things from me."

The Outrageously Ridiculous Adventures of Scotty J. Fahrenheit

"I tell it like it is, alright. But do I got this right? You're really offering me a job?"

"Look, I know your worrying about leaving Spinelli, but I have a much more lucrative position. I understand working with animals is very rewarding, but sometimes it can be a dirty job."

"You got that right."

"Trust me, it's no different than working in my line of business. The animals we deal with make this job super action packed. So, what do you say?"

"Gee, Mr. Buffo, I don't know what to say."

"Then say yes."

"I guess yes," Scotty says, accepting his offer without hearing any of the details.

Buffo takes him into the house and introduces him to the guys. "This is our newest addition to the family. I picked him because he's a fearless man. Look at the size of him. I get the feeling nobody is going to want to tango with him."

The five guys shake his hand and congratulate him.

"Now that you're an official member of the family, it's only right that you be given a nickname," Buffo insists.

Everyone agrees, and, of course, Buffo does the honor of picking out a name that he deems fit. "What does everyone think of 'Scotty Boy'?"

Nobody is about to disagree—doing something so trivial could be detrimental to one's health. They all congratulate Buffo on his great choice.

"When do you want me to start?" Scotty asks.

FIRED!

"There's no better time than the present. I'm going to make you a courier. Your first job will be going to Reno Calaperi's, better known as Fish-Hook Pockets. That swindler has been stealing from my organization. He needs to be put in his place, and I think you're just the one to do it. He stopped paying his dues, and I am getting pretty sick of it. Here is his address. Now head over and see what you can do."

"If you give everyone nicknames, what name did you give yourself?" Scotty asks, looking directly at Buffo.

"I prefer to be called 'Boss.'"

Scotty is so glad to actually be able to call someone by that name. "Okay then, Boss. I will see you in a few," he says happily before leaving the room.

Chapter 43

Two of the guys whisper as soon as Buffo leaves the room. "What do you think of this 'Scotty Boy' character?"

"I think he's an absolute train wreck."

"Me too, but isn't that what we thought of Baccala?"

"Yeah, but we were right about him. Buffo thought he was the best thing since, well, I don't know what."

"Maybe Buffo sees a resemblance between Scotty and Baccala."

"Come on, Baccala had thick, curly black hair. Scotty Boy is a thinning blonde."

"I guess the only comparison is that they're both way overweight with some kind of idiot problem."

"I have to agree with you there."

"Buffo tried to take Baccala out of the slums. Instead, he ends up putting him in the ground."

"Terrible thing how Baccala got in-between that line of crossfire."

"Yeah, he never truly got over Baccala."

FIRED!

Buffo goes into his desk and takes out a gun. He yells for Scotty.

"Yes, Boss, what it is?"

"I forgot to give you this. No man of mine will ever go unarmed," he says, handing him a 44-magnum pistol.

"Thanks, Boss."

Not understanding the magnitude of a powerful loaded weapon, Scotty just tosses it in the front seat. He follows the directions, and when he arrives, he parks his car on the street for some reason. The red Caddy parked in the driveway gives him the impression that someone must be home. After ringing the doorbell ten times, he realizes he may be wrong. Walking around the house makes perfect sense. In the backyard is a huge olympic-sized pool. Scotty spots someone swimming.

"What do *you* want?" Reno stops swimming and asks.

"You," Scotty replies.

Reno gets out of the pool and reaches for a towel.

"You look like you're in great shape."

"I swim every day for an hour. I am not too happy with you showing up in the middle of my workout. Like I asked you before, what is it you want from me?"

"It's not what I want, it's what the Boss wants."

"Wait a minute, are you the latest stooge working for Buffo?"

"No I am called 'Scotty Boy.'"

"What does Buffo think *you're* going to do?" Reno says, laughing at him.

"Really I haven't the slightest," Scotty says, going on about his entire life story.

"You know, you remind me of my son David. He would have been okay if the damn nurse didn't drop him on his head when he was a baby. Made him out to be a simpleton. Kind of like you. Anyway, the poor kid had a heart of gold. Me and his mother doted on him. There wasn't a thing we wouldn't do for that kid. I even let him work in the family business. But things changed when he met his so-called 'Charlotte.'"

"You mean my Charlotte?" Scotty bristled.

"No, I am just making a comparison between your story and his. The girl he fell in love with was named Sarah."

"Thank God for that," Scotty said, relieved. "I was worried he was the gay guy in the ice cream parlor."

"Believe me, my David was the furthest thing from being gay."

"Those kinds of guys always end up getting the girl," Scotty ignorantly believes.

Reno chuckles, "You're one hell of a joker. Anyway, my David tried his best to court her, but when her father found out who he was, he forbid her from seeing him. He said that no daughter of his would ever date someone working in the family business."

"What did he do?"

"He did what most people have to do. He quit working for me and got a job as a school crossing guard."

"How did he like it?"

FIRED!

"I guess a lot. His main concern was to prove to Sarah's dad he was worthy—"

"Well did he?"

"Stop being so impatient. If you would give me a minute to finish the story."

"Sorry bout that."

"Anyway, it was the last day of school. All the kids were excited about summer break, but David was excited about something else—"

"What was that?" Scotty asks excitedly, interrupting again.

"One more of those and I am going to stop with the story. Can you shut up for one minute?" Reno asks as Scotty nods his head.

"So before I was rudely interrupted, I was trying to say that David shared with me and his mother that after work he was going to go to Sarah's house and win her back. My wife was so excited that she went into the safe and took out one of her rings. She told David to give it to her after he asked her back."

"I know I said I would shut my big mouth, but can I just ask you one more question?"

"I guess you're gonna ask it anyway, so have at it."

"Where's your wife?"

"Now that's a whole other story."

"So what happens?"

"Well, he was walking to his car when he spots a dog on the other side of the street ready to cross the busy road."

"Don't tell me the dog got hit."

"Fortunately, the dog didn't. Too bad I can't say the same for my son."

"But you just said the dog was okay."

"The dog was okay because my son risked his life by darting out in front of a truck."

"That was a good thing your son did that."

"Not at all," he said bitterly. "It was a stupid mistake that cost him his life."

"You mean the truck hit your son instead?" Scotty probed.

"Not just hit him; it ran him over," Reno explained, sadness etched in his features.

"Oh, that's so awful," Scotty remarked.

"You wouldn't believe all the people who showed up for his funeral. Cindy-Lou had the most emotional eulogy."

"She probably was as kind as Cindy-Lou Who," Scotty says.

"I don't think I know her," Reno replies, bewildered.

"Come on, everyone knows Cindy-Lou Who."

"Trust me, I don't," Reno goes on.

"You mean to tell me you never read *How the Grinch Stole Christmas?*"

"You're just a laugh a minute. Yes, I did read it."

"Admit I am right, because she is the most adorable kid ever."

"Yes, that's one time I can agree with your stupidity. Now let me go on with the story."

"No, you don't have to."

FIRED!

"You don't want to hear the rest of the story?" he asks, ticked off.

"I read it every year before Christmas."

"How the hell does Buffo put up with you? I think his mind is going, just like his mother's. I'm trying to finish my story, not the damn story about some fictitious green miserable monster!" Reno says angrily.

"Gee, you really have to calm that temper of yours. Go on with your story."

"Cindy-Lou, the petite ten-year-old explained how her family was struggling after her dad became hurt really bad in an automobile accident. She told everyone how every day David would give her and her twin brother lunch money. Then she said on Fridays, he would give each of them twenty dollars. Little Sarah said that they used the money to help pay their family's bills."

As Reno finishes his story, tears start falling down Scotty's face. "That is so touching," he cries. "Your son was a saint. I betcha he was smiling from heaven that day. That's too bad for Sarah and her family. How did they eat lunch after he died?"

"A teacher called me and explained how David was giving them money. When I heard about that, I found out just how poor they were."

"So did you do anything?" Scotty probes.

"You could say that. Nothing a large brown envelope full of money couldn't help," Reno says with a secretive grin.

Scotty, relieved, asks, "I take it that helped out?"

"That and then some," he shrugs.

The Outrageously Ridiculous Adventures of Scotty J. Fahrenheit

As he finishes the story, Reno leads Scotty into the mansion. "Wait right here," he says before leaving the room.

He comes back with two things in his hands. "I want you to give this to Charlotte once you win her over," he holds a gorgeous diamond ring between his thumb and index finger. It glitters in the sunlight streaming through the windows, casting rainbows around the room. "That's the ring my wife gave David...we found it in his pocket the day he died," he adds as he hands it to Scotty carefully.

Scotty's eyes light up as he accepts the ring gingerly. "It's beautiful! he says, admiring it. "I promise I will give it to Charlotte. How could she ever say no to this? Can you please thank your wife?" he asks, gazing at it for a moment longer before putting it carefully in his pocket.

"I would...but we're not on speaking terms."

"If she's so kind, why won't she talk to you?"

"After David died, we did nothing but play the blame game. All we would do was think of David. Living together became too painful. It took a toll on our marriage and we found ourselves in the divorce courts."

Now Reno hands Scotty the other item he had in his hands, an envelope. "This envelope is your out. Give this to Buffo. And don't wait around to get your woman like my son did. Charlotte's father is no different than Sarah's. They think they're so much better than everyone else. You go and get her."

"If I could only be half the man your son was," Scotty says truthfully.

"Thank you for that. David was one heck of a man," he states proudly. Then he says, "I know you probably have other stops.

FIRED!

There is just one more thing I want to show you before you leave," he says, walking up a large flight of stairs.

Scotty follows him into a large room enclosed in glass. "This is beautiful," he says, admiring the room.

"I had this built for my son. He loved looking through this telescope. Pointing out the constellations made him so happy," he recalls with a far-off look in his eyes.

Reno opens the door and they both walk onto a stone deck built above the edge of the pool. "I just had this built. What do you think?"

"It's totally cool," Scotty says, walking toward the stone wall.

"No, don't get too close," he warns quickly. "The walls are still not set yet and the tiles are a bit slippery," he says, pointing to where some rain water had collected. I wouldn't want you to fall."

Scotty steps back from the wall, looking around at the excellent stone craftsmanship.

"Well, let's go back down," Reno says. "You've been here long enough."

Scotty walks off the deck and back through the glass room and down the stairway, assuming that Reno is right behind him.

Reno takes one more look around the deck for a few moments, then he slips on some water and forgets the wall is still unstable, putting his hands on it to hoist himself up. Suddenly the wall gives way, causing Reno, Fish-Hook Pockets, to fall to his death, unbeknownst to Scotty and everyone else in the house.

Chapter 44

Back at Buffo's house, one of Buffo's associates gives him a call, saying, "Boss, I've got some news for you."

"Yeah, go ahead, but this better be important."

"You know my housekeeper is the sister of Fish-Hook Pocket's maid."

"Look, I'm pretty busy, so bothering me with this lunacy is outrageous," Buffo rudely remarks.

"Please, give me a minute."

"Your minute is almost up. Hurry it up."

"My maid's sister—" He tries to get out before Buffo interrupts again.

"What don't you understand about 'I don't care about the maid'?"

"What if I told you Fish-Hook Pockets was found dead by my maid's sister?"

"For Pete's sake, why didn't you say that in the first place? Please, tell the details."

"Apparently, Maria the maid found Fish-Hook Pockets face down in the swimming pool."

FIRED!

"Holy crow, I sent Scotty Boy over to his place to pick up some money!" Buffo remembers.

"Do you think he had something to do with Fish-Hook Pockets demise?" Antelmi asks.

"I don't know, but at this point, I sure hope so," Buffo admits.

Buffo hangs up the phone and turns the television on.

Within a minute a news flash comes across the television. Mary Pickens the newscaster is seen standing in front of Reno's mansion. She starts reporting, "We have breaking news that the notorious mobster Irving Horowitz, who went by the name of Reno Calapari, was found dead in his swimming pool. We have no further information at this time and will keep you informed with any updates," she says before going to a commercial break. By now people are calling left and right to make sure Buffo knows the news or to come clean on the debts they owe to Buffo.

Soon Scotty pulls up to the mansion. Buffo is standing in front of the window and runs out to greet him. "I knew you were the man for me. "My phone hasn't stopped ringing. I got people who are offering to pay more money. You got everyone nervous. They don't want to meet the same fate as old Fish-Hook Pockets."

"I got something for you," Scotty says, giving Buffo the envelope from Reno.

Buffo opens it up and can't believe his eyes. "What did you threaten him with?"

"I just gave him the truth."

"You're the man," Buffo says, smiling from ear to ear.

Johnny Spano comes rushing into Buffo's mansion. "What do ya think of Fish-Hook Pockets not being Italian?"

"I should have known the day he had us all over for dinner. His sauce made me sick for days," Buffo explains, rubbing a hand on his belly.

"As for the meatballs, rocks were softer than those things. That was the first time I didn't eat anything on my plate," Spano goes on.

"There isn't an Italian dead or alive who would have ever tried to pass that crap sauce off," Roberto Antelmi chimes in.

Donny Brasso walks into the room. "Hey, Donny, it's so nice to see you. Any info on your son?" Roberto wonders.

Brasso starts getting very emotional. "I had to leave the house. The walls are closing in."

"What's wrong with him?" Scotty whispers to Johnny.

"Donny's son, Donny Junior, never came home. He's been missing for over a week—disappeared without a trace."

Just then Scotty's foot starts to bother him. He takes the insurance card and the picture out of his sock.

Johnny spots the picture. "Where did you get this?" Johnny says, grabbing the picture and giving it to Buffo.

"Donny, look at this," Buffo says, handing it to him.

"That's my Donny Junior!" Donny yells, getting irate at Scotty, "How and where did you get this?" he asks, now with his hands around Scotty's neck.

"Easy, Donny. Take your hands off him and let him explain," Buffo orders.

FIRED!

Scotty starts telling his story. "I got poisoned and was rushed to the hospital. I didn't want to miss a day of work so I escaped and got picked up from some weirdo in a big black car."

"What does that guy have to do with the picture?" Donny asks.

"I don't know. He pulled over to take a pee. I needed a tissue so I went into his glove box. I picked up the picture and this card thing, trying to find a tissue. When I saw the weird guy walking back to the car, I did some quick thinking. I slammed the glove box shut and took these," Scotty explains.

"Let me see that card your talking about," Buffo orders, taking it out of Scotty's hand.

Buffo looks at it and announces, "Looks like Randal Woodson is our man."

Buffo calls one of his friends at the police department. Mary Joan is happy to give Buffo the information on Woodson.

"Scotty, since you aced it with old Fish-Hook Pockets, you are going to go on another mission. If I am correct, this pervert from the insurance card has Donny Junior. Let's just hope and pray we find him in time," Buffo worries.

"The plan is put in place. Donny, we need you to stay behind. This is too close to home for you," Buffo once again orders.

"Tony please bring my son back to me," he begs with tears in his eyes. "You got it," Buffo promises.

Scotty is ordered to follow Buffo to Woodson's house. As soon as he pulls up to the old dilapidated farm house, he hands Scotty a baseball bat and gives him strict instructions not to kill Woodson. They need to find out where Donny Junior is and if Woodson dies, Donny Junior may never be found.

The Outrageously Ridiculous Adventures of Scotty J. Fahrenheit

Buffo is a bit concerned that maybe they are at the wrong house. He tells Scotty, "When you make it in, give us a sign so we know if we're at the right place." Then he adds, "Look, we can't take any chances. If we blow this, we may never have another opportunity to find him alive," Buffo instructs Scotty.

Scotty walks to the door and knocks. Nobody answers, so he breaks into the house. Woodson hears the loud noise and finds Scotty standing in his living room. Scotty takes one look at the freak and opens the curtains.

Buffo takes that as a sign they are at the right place. He picks up his car phone and calls the police.

Inside the house, Woodson says to Scotty, "I should have known all along that you were a ploy. I must have been crazy to think that someone would be foolish enough to be walking around in a parking garage in the middle of the night wearing nothing more than a tiny hospital gown," Woodson assumes.

Scotty gets upset at this and starts chasing him with the baseball bat.

Woodson yells out as he runs away from the mad, crazy fat man with the baseball bat. "Look, I really screwed up abducting Donny Junior. I knew something was really odd about you. I should've know you're part of the mob coming to kill me."

"Stop talking," Scotty orders, "you're taking me off my game." Finally catching up to him, Scotty takes the baseball bat and brings Woodson to his knees.

The police arrive within a few minutes. Buffo, Spano, and Antelmi wait in the car to see what unfolds. Soon they see the police walking out with Woodson in handcuffs. Buffo and the boys try to go into the house, but the police tell them it is off limits because it's a potential crime scene. Buffo tries to tell them Scotty is somewhere in the house. Unfortunately, the police don't seem to be listening. Ten minutes later, Scotty walks out with someone at his side. At closer inspection, the men realize the man with Scotty is none other than Donny Junior. Buffo and the guys rush over to him. "Thank God, you're alive!" Buffo tells Donny Junior, who immediately breaks down and begins to shake. "Uncle Tony, I knew you would never let me down."

Soon the ambulance shows up, and Buffo orders Scotty to ride in the ambulance with Donny Junior.

Meanwhile, Buffo and the boys head back to the mansion where Donny is anxiously waiting. "Did you find my boy?" he asks eagerly.

"Get yourself together and get ready to go to the hospital," Buffo advises.

"Why to the hospital? You're scaring me. Tony, tell me my son is alright."

"Don't worry, he was only taken to the hospital for precautions. Nothing is going to happen to him with Scotty by his side."

"I have to apologize to Scotty. I really thought he was involved with my son's disappearance."

"Scotty Boy is the best thing that could have happened to us. Look at all he's done in just one day; this man is a miracle worker! Without him, Donny Junior wouldn't have been so lucky," Buffo explains.

When Donny and the guys get to the hospital, Scotty is standing guard by Donny Junior like a trained police dog. Donny rushes over to his son's bed. "Words can't say how I'm feeling right now. My world is complete now that you are safe."

The Outrageously Ridiculous Adventures of Scotty J. Fahrenheit

"Dad, you're the reason I'm alive," Donny Junior says, confusing his father.

"Actually, it was Scotty Boy who saved your life," Donny tells his son.

"See, Dad, as soon as that weirdo got me to his house, he brought me down into this cave-like room in his basement. He took the tape off my mouth, saying if I screamed, nobody could hear me. I told him who you were and who you worked for. That got him nervous. I told him that if he did anything to me, you and the whole gang would come looking for him, and that you wouldn't stop until you found him."

"That was brilliant," Donny tells his son.

"Dad he told me he wouldn't do the dirty work. He was out searching for someone he would pin my murder on. He was going to have that guy kill me, then he would kill that guy."

"Scotty, that is why he picked you up! I assume you were chosen to kill Donny Junior, and then Woodson would kill you before pinning the murder on you," Buffo figures.

"Scotty, how did you get away from Woodson?" Donny Junior asks.

"It all took place in a gas-station bathroom. I'm just sorry I didn't know that the guy had you sooner."

"You're the real hero here," Buffo admits before leaving the room to make a phone call.

In the meantime, Woodson has been booked and incarcerated.

In the hallway, Buffo calls Mary Joan at the police department. She gives him the update as to where Woodson is being held.

FIRED!

She also gives him the number of the man he needs to talk to at the prison. After she gets off the line, he calls Ted Reese.

Then Buffo calls Scotty out in the hall with him and tells him he has one last job for the day.

"I got to admit, you sure didn't lie to me," Scotty remarks.

"What do you mean?" Buffo asks.

"I've never had a job with more action than this," Scotty admits excitedly.

"Great! So here's your next assignment. You need to go Jamesville Correctional Facility."

"Isn't that a jail?"

"Yes, it's the one Woodson is being held in."

"What do they want with me there?"

"There's a man named Brian Kempt who will be waiting for you. When he comes to the gate, you need to give him this," Buffo says, taking out three one-hundred dollar bills.

Buffo tells Scotty that after he gives Kempt the money he can go home and get some rest. "Make sure you are back at the mansion by ten in the morning. No worker of mine will ever miss Sunday mass. The only reason I will accept anyone missing mass is if they're six feet under. Me, mom, and the boys go to the cathedral, which I think is the nicest catholic church around. Remember, ten a.m.—and don't be late."

"No problem, Boss," Scotty says before he heads out to finish up his last job and head home.

Chapter 45

Upon arriving home, Scotty finds that his mother is very worried that things didn't go well. She's surprised when he tells her that the job is everything he was looking for.

"I am so proud of you, Son. Seems you finally found something you're really good at," she says, unaware of what took place.

"I really think I found the perfect job," he says excitedly. "I like the guys I work with. The boss is Tony Buffo, and Ma, he is such a smart and kind man. I'll tell you more about it later on. Right now, I got to try to get some shut eye. The boss said we all must meet at his house in the morning so we can go to the Catholic church together."

"Did you tell him you're not Catholic?" she asks. Then she thinks again and adds, "Oh, maybe that's not the right thing to say. I'm happy the man you work for is such a religious man."

"Really, Ma, why would I say such a thing? God is in that church too."

"I guess you're right. It's just that I will miss you not being at service with me. I feel like I am losing you already…" she trails off as she gives him a hug goodnight.

FIRED!

Both Scotty and Mable get up early. They sit and have breakfast together.

"You know, Son, I said something last night that might have seemed I was against you going to the Catholic church. I don't have a problem with that. As a matter of fact, shortly after me and your father got married, we had the most wonderful neighbor. Her name was Carmella Masaro. She was one of the most religious people I ever met. Her husband died years earlier and she wore a black dress until the day she died. Believe it or not, she left me a small box with a few things in it. Follow me upstairs and I'll show you."

Scotty follows her and Mable takes out an old shoebox and reveals its contents. First, she opens up a little black prayer book. Scotty notices a handwritten sentence on the page.

"Ma, I can't understand what that says."

"I can't either because it's written in Italian. However, I can read where she signed her name."

"What else is in that box?"

She takes out a pair of rosary beads.

"What are those?" he asks.

"Catholics say something called the Rosary."

"What does that mean?" he inquires.

"They put their fingers on each bead as they pray certain prayers," she explains.

"Do you know how to do it?"

"I wasn't brought up Catholic, so no."

"Boss told us his mother was going to church with us. Maybe I will ask her how it's done."

"That's a great idea. I'm sure she can help you."

Next Mable takes out a plastic box. "What's that supposed to be?"

"Carmella told me it was a healing box. The box was blessed by a priest, and the cross inside is a religious relic of sorts," Mable tries to explain.

"If it's a healing box, I bet it can heal just about anything," Scotty believes.

"And here is the last thing she left for me. It is something she used to wear on her head when she went to church."

"This is absolutely beautiful," Scotty says, watching his mother hold it up.

"Notice how she sewed in a small comb so it wouldn't fall off during mass."

"Why don't you wear it to service?"

"Like the rosary beads, we are protestants, so we don't wear mantillas."

"I think I'm going to like being a Catholic. They seem to do cooler things than us."

Mable smiles at her son. Looking at her watch, she says, "Why don't we finish our breakfast so you aren't late."

"Good idea, Ma. I can't be late or Buffo will get mad!"

As they are walking down the stairs, Mable remembers something, "Oh, I forgot to tell you that Stanley called yesterday."

"What did he want?"

FIRED!

"He was so kind to ask what happened to you. I explained you got poisoned and were rushed to the hospital," she tells Scotty as they get back to the kitchen.

They sit back down as she continues, "He said today at three o'clock the best coach is going to be awarded the bonus and a trophy. He was so humble when he said he doesn't blame you for him not winning. I guess some guy named Stanton is the winner. Anyway, he said the award ceremony is taking place on the green. The place is beautiful. Looks like no rain, so it being outside will not pose a threat. He invited us, but I didn't know if you would want to go."

"Ma, I want you to go. I bet they are going to have great food. I don't know if the Boss is going to want me to work today. I'll try to do my best to show up. Give Lois a call and have her take you."

"I just might do that," she says, giving him a hug. Then she adds, "Oh, don't forget this," handing him the shoebox from Carmella.

When he arrives at the mansion, Buffo tells him he is very early. "You are the second one here."

"Oh man, I wanted to be here first. Who beat me?" Scotty jokes.

"That would be my mother. Come on in. I'll take you to meet her. I just have to warn you that she is in a catatonic state."

When they get in the oversized dining room, Scotty walks over to Buffo's mother, having no idea what a catatonic state means. "Well, hello there. My name is Scotty Boy, and who, may I ask, are you?"

The Outrageously Ridiculous Adventures of Scotty J. Fahrenheit

She just sits in her chair, not saying a word. Scotty asks her again. Same thing—no response.

"After seeing my dad get whacked, she had a stroke and has been in an unconscious state ever since."

"Gee, seems like a lot of bad things happen to good people. Can you tell me her name?"

"Sure, it's Carmella Antonina Florencia Maria Antonetta Buffo."

"Holy crow, she must have had a hard time writing that name in grade school. Wait a minute. Did you really say 'Carmella'?"

"Yes, why?"

"Because I have something that might chipper her up." Scotty says innocently before going to his van and retrieving the shoebox.

When he gets back, Buffo excuses himself to make a phone call. Scotty is left alone in the room with Tony's mother. He walks over to her with the box in his hand. First, he takes out the rosary beads and puts them around her neck. Next, he takes out the mantilla and tries to put it on her head. At first it slips off. Then he remembers the comb is supposed to be used to hold it in place. But as soon as he finishes, he trips on one of the table's legs and loses his balance, causing him to stumble into Carmella's wheelchair. Her frail body gets jolted out of the chair and her head smacks the floor.

Panicked, Scotty gets on the floor and asks her is she is alright. Being that her eyes are closed, he fears that she is dead. He rushes to the shoebox and takes out the healing box. He places it in Carmella's hand. He begins shaking her, telling her she has got to wake up because she is holding the holy healing box.

FIRED!

Suddenly she opens her eyes and looks around, panicked. She yells in a heavy accent, "What on God's green earth am I doing on the floor? Who the heck are you?" she yells, looking at Scotty.

"I'm so sorry. My name is Scotty, but you can call me Scotty Boy."

"Only if you get me off of this floor."

Scotty picks her up and goes to put her back in the wheelchair. "Do I look like some sort of invalid?" she asks him.

"You're darn right," he replies, "you don't need no dumb wheelchair."

He puts her into one of the dining room chairs instead.

"Thank you for that," she says, calming.

He pulls his chair right beside her and starts to ask her about the Catholic Church. "I have some things I want to show you."

"Are you referring to the healing box in my hand?"

"Oh yeah, that too. But wait, that's not all," he says, taking out the old prayer book.

"That looks just like the prayer book my mother used to have," she says, putting a hand to her chest and getting emotional.

Scotty opens it and asks her, "Can you tell me what this says?"

She leans over and starts reading, "To my dearest friend. Let God be the answers to all your problems," she says, translating it.

"Look at the name of the woman who owned the book?"

"Yes, her name is Carmella, just like mine."

"Isn't that something?" Scotty says, smiling.

"It sure is," Carmella replies.

"Look, I have something else for you," Scotty says, putting the black rosary beads around her neck.

"No, these are not to be worn like jewelry," she says, quickly taking them off.

"Gee, I'm sorry. I didn't mean to offend you," Scotty says, remorseful.

"Why are you apologizing? You didn't do anything wrong. Now hold these in your hand, and I will teach you how to pray the Rosary."

"Can I show you the last thing before you teach me?"

"Sure, what is it?"

Scotty picks the mantilla that dropped on the floor when Carmella fell. "I want you to have this."

"You are so kind," she says, putting it in her hair.

"You look beautiful. Now if you don't mind, can you teach me about the beads now?" he asks, picking them back up.

Just then Buffo walks into the room and he is taken back by what he is witnessing. His mother hasn't been able to communicate for over fifteen years. "Mother, I can't believe this. You are alright!"

"Yes, I am fine now," she says with a smile. Now be quiet and mind your manners while I teach Sonny Boy how to say the Rosary."

"It really is you. How could I ever forget your sharp tongue? This is an absolute miracle!" he exclaims, hugging his mother.

FIRED!

"Look, if you have to interrupt me, I want to start by telling you to get that darn wheelchair out of my sight. And, Son, I don't mean tomorrow—I mean now."

"Yes, Ma'am," he replies, still in awe that his mother is okay. He immediately wheels the chair out of the room and takes it down to the basement.

By the time he gets back, the guys begin to arrive. He doesn't let them in on the secret of his mother's miraculous recovery. Instead, he waits until they are all seated at the oversized dining room table.

Not one of them has realized yet that Carmella isn't sitting in her wheelchair. "Well, Boys, aren't any of you going to say hello to my mother?" he asks with a grin.

They all look at him like he's lost his mind. "Sure, Boss. Good morning, Mrs. Buffo. I like the mantilla your wearing. It looks really good on you."

"Thank you. Sonny Boy here gave it to me," she says, motioning to Scotty as everyone looks mortified.

"Yes, guys that's my mom," Tony says proudly. "She has come out of whatever state she was in. The doctors said this could never happen, but look how wrong they were!"

The men are all in awe, just staring at the miracle in front of them. Finally one of them asks, "How did it happen?"

"I can tell you how. This here Scotty Boy has miraculous powers. He was the instrument God used to heal her," Buffo says.

"Heal me? What the heck do you mean about healing me?" Carmella asks, all distressed.

The Outrageously Ridiculous Adventures of Scotty J. Fahrenheit

"Mom, you have been in an unconscious state since your stroke. Don't you remember?"

"I had a stroke? Is that what the wheelchair was all about?" she asks.

"Ma, I am so sorry to say yes to both your questions."

Scotty leans over and hugs her. "You are so sweet and kind. Besides my mother, nobody has ever taken the time to teach me anything, until today."

Carmella looks at Scotty and says, "When I look at you, I see something so different. There is a mystical aura around you. I can just feel it. You're special, and I'm glad you're with us," she cries out emotionally.

"If it weren't for your son giving me a chance, I wouldn't be," Scotty replies truthfully.

"Scotty, you've been so kind to all of us. I have something special for you. Wait here, I'll be right back," Buffo says before leaving the room.

He comes back with a very expensive suit and gives it to Scotty proudly.

"Wow!" Scotty says, taken back by the quality of the clothing he's holding. "This is out-of-this-world nice! How much do I owe you?" he asks.

"Nothing. It's a gift from me. You see, I always have my clothes custom made. Rocco the tailor only designs clothes for me. I don't want anybody running around with the same suit as me. I pay the guy plenty so he stays with me."

"How did you know my size?"

FIRED!

"Well, I had this kid named Baccala who used to work for me. He told me he could never amount to much. He said that only men like me could wear suits made by the best tailor in the world. When he took all his pay and helped those in need, I had my tailor make him a suit—one that looked just like the most expensive one I owned. This is that suit. Unfortunately, Baccala didn't get to wear it," Buffo says sadly.

"Why?" Scotty asks.

"Just a very unfortunate death. I loved that boy like a son," Buffo says, getting emotional.

Carmella interrupts the sad moment, "Speaking of a son, where in heaven's name is my precious little grandson, Anthony Junior?"

"Ma, little Antony Junior isn't so little anymore."

"Did he run away or something?"

"No such thing, Ma."

"Then where is he?"

"I made a promise to Rosa on her death bed that Anthony Junior would never be involved in the business, and I kept to my promise."

"I'm glad to hear that. So answer me, where is he then?"

"He's at a private boarding school, safe and sound."

"That's wonderful, Son," she replies. Looking at the clock on the wall, she adds, "We all better shut up and eat. I will never be disrespectful and show up one minute late for church."

With that, the whole group of them quiet down and finish their breakfast.

Chapter 46

After they finish eating, Buffo tells Scotty to change into the suit.

Scotty goes upstairs into one of the bedrooms to change. When he comes down the stairs Carmella remarks. "Sonny Boy, you look like a million bucks. I'm going to sit by you in church. I can help you find your way," she says, complimenting him.

Tony looks around at the other guys and says, "Can we all agree that my mom has a better name for Scotty?"

It's unanimous that Scotty will now be called 'Sonny Boy.'

Scotty follows along during mass the best he can. When the priest is saying the homily, Scotty begins to cry. The priest is describing the story of the widow's mite. He explains how she had very little, but gave it all away.

When the basket comes around, Scotty is ashamed that he doesn't even have one penny to put in. Carmella goes for her purse and realizes she doesn't have it. "Tony, where is my purse?" she panics.

"Ma, please, not now," Tony says, taking out of wad of money from his pocket before discreetly putting it in the basket.

Soon everyone is lining up for communion. When the priest takes one look at Carmella standing up and alert, he is in awe.

FIRED!

After he places the host on her tongue, she not only tells him, "amen." She goes on about her son forgetting to bring her purse to church. "Father, I would never forget to put my envelope in the basket. Please forgive me."

At that, the priest just smiles.

After mass, the priest stops Tony Buffo outside and asks him how his mother was cured.

Buffo points to Scotty and tells him it was a miracle. The priest stands in awe before explaining to Scotty that God uses people to carry out his work. He called Scotty a disciple of the Lord, telling him to rejoice by kneeling and giving thanks to God Almighty. Immediately, Scotty falls to his knees. He looks to the sky and yells out, "Dear God Almighty, thank you."

Many of the parishioners can't believe what Scotty just did and just look on.

Carmella, taken by his actions, falls on her knees, saying, "God, thank you for bringing this miracle-worker in my life. Through your power, I have been healed!" At this, Buffo's men drop to their knees.

Now some of the parishioners are so astounded that they all quickly follow suit. By now, the priest doesn't know what to think. He begins by blessing all those on their knees. Things start to escalate as one man beings speaking in tongues.

Scotty gets up and walks over to the man. "I can't understand a word coming out of your mouth," he says to the man, who is in a trance-like state. Another woman raises her arms and starts speaking in tongues. Unbelievably, many of the other parishioners join in.

Seeing all this, Scotty decides that it's his turn to join in. He drops to his knees and starts speaking jibberish.

"This man is speaking the word of God. We must take heed and circle around him," Carmella says as she stands up and places her hand on Scotty's shoulder.

The new deacon of the church looks at the priest, asking, "What's so special about that man?"

The priest replies, "That man is a true miracle-worker. Carmella Buffo has come here for years stricken to a wheelchair and suffering from an issue that has made her unconscious. But now look at her; she's on her feet conversing with the congregation!" he exclaims, pointing her out.

The deacon says, "Father, I'm sorry for my harsh words. I've just never heard the words coming out of his mouth."

"Deacon Bob, anything and everything is possible with our Lord. We just need to have faith. Obviously, Carmella is proof of that. If only all of us could have her faith," the priest says meekly.

Tony interrupts the moment, saying, "Scotty, let's wrap this up with God. I'm a very busy man and I need to get back."

Carmella holds out her hand to help Scotty up, but Tony quickly steps in. "Ma, come on. You just got cured! Do you want to end up right back in that wheelchair?"

"Son, you should be worrying about where my purse is. You know your father always told me to carry a wad of cash in case something should come up. But now here I am, left completely vulnerable because of you. To top it off, I feel naked without my red lipstick. What have you turned me into?"

FIRED!

"Sonny Boy, would you please take me home so I can get my purse? Great going, Anthony Christopher. Without my purse, I have no keys to get in my house."

"Mom, I have something to tell you," Tony says.

"What now? More bad news?" she wonders.

"It's about your house…" he trails off.

"What about it?"

"You…uh…don't live there anymore."

"Son, I think you're as crazy as your aunt in the insane asylum. So tell me then, where do I live?"

"Ma, years passed, and you weren't getting any better. I had no choice but to put you in a facility where you would get around-the-clock care."

"I could have gotten that in my own house," she argues.

"Believe me, Ma, we tried that. Every day, something seemed to come up missing. It was to the point that I was afraid to leave you alone in your house."

"Answer me, what rat-invested dump do you have me living in?"

"I resent you thinking I would do such a thing to you. Actually, it's the most expensive convalescent home around."

"So what about my house? Or did you get rid of that too?"

"Ma, why would you say such a thing?"

"Why? Just look at me; I'm out in public with no purse or lipstick. Why else would I not trust you?"

"You still own it. I've been paying all the bills and keeping the property up."

"Oh, Son, I knew you would never let me down," she says, changing her attitude.

When they get back to Buffo's, Scotty asks to use the phone. He dials his home and wonders why his mother isn't answering. Then he remembers that she is probably at the ceremony for the job coaches.

"Is everything alright?" Buffo asks while walking into the room.

Scotty hangs up and explains the entire situation to Tony. "I wish I could be at that ceremony to thank Stanley for all he's done for me."

"When and where is this ceremony taking place?" Buffo asks. When Scotty tells him, he leaves the room again to make some phone calls inquiring about the situation.

Chapter 47

Meanwhile, the awards ceremony is about to take place. It's set up outside in a large field. Lucky for all who attended, it turned out to be a beautiful, sunny day, not too hot and not too windy. As the job coaches begin to walk on stage, the audience applauds. As soon as the coaches take their seats, Paul Janson walks up to the microphone.

"As the owner of the company, I want to thank all of you in the audience who have enrolled in the program. And I want to give a big shout out to the great job coaches for the fine job they've done."

He explains that the company's main goal is to find employment opportunities for people. "These coaches are the life blood of this program. Without them, none of this would be possible. It is customary to award the job coach who has far exceeded expectations. As you all know, this was a very competitive year. Without any further delay, I would like to present the winner of this year's job coach of the year!" Paul reaches to the bottom of the podium and takes out the trophy.

Just then a black Cadillac rolls up as close as possible to the stage area with its horn blowing. Everyone stares as two men, dressed in black suits, exit the vehicle.

Buffo, the ruggedly-handsome gangster, makes his way to the stage with Scotty by his side, still dressed in the expensive suit. Stanley takes one look at Buffo and fears for the worst. When they approach the stage, Buffo asks Scotty to point Stanley out. Sweat begins to pour down Stanley's face.

Buffo walks up to Stanley, and he begs, "Please, whatever you do, let my wife and kids know I love them. Can't you wait until this is over?"

Buffo leans over and whispers, "No." Buffo walks over to Paul, grabs the microphone from him, and says, "Listen up. I did a little checking, and I see that the winner of this competition belongs to one man and one man only.

"Yes, this award goes to Stanton Ryan," Paul Janson states, walking over to Stanton with a smile. Just as he is about to hand Stanton the trophy and bonus check, Buffo grabs it out of his hand.

Paul gets agitated. "Excuse me, Sir, but I am going to ask you to leave, or else I will have security remove you," Paul insists, unaware of Buffo's identity.

"Try to get me off this stage and just see what happens to you," Buffo warns menacingly.

Suddenly, Senator Ryan, Stanton's father, hurries onto the stage. "Everyone needs to calm down. This can be easily taken care of. Let's just hear what Mr. Buffo has to say."

"Senator, long time, no see," Buffo says. "As I see it, Stanley there won this contest fair and square," he says, motioning to Stanley. "Your son's candidate, the one with a million degrees, quit his job yesterday. Sonny Boy here, Stanley's candidate, is still employed. If my math is correct, that makes Stanley the winner," Buffo explains.

FIRED!

"Is there anything I can do?" the senator asks in a low voice.

Buffo talks right in the microphone, "The other day, the senator told me he wants to donate the property he bought to develop into high rise condos. Isn't it right, Senator, that you are going to scrap building condos? Instead, you decided to build a recreation center and a not-for-profit employment agency. The program will be free for those in need! Just think, everyone will be able to enroll in your new venture. Now isn't that correct?" Buffo pressures the senator in front of the whole place.

"You would be right," the senator unwillingly agrees.

Buffo hands Scotty the trophy and prize money.

Scotty walks over to the microphone. "Everyone, listen up. I have a few things to say. Stanley Rogers is the best coach ever. If it wasn't for him, I would never have gotten the job with the Boss. Working for Buffo has made me feel something I never have before. I'm not the guy I used to be. No, now I'm Sonny Boy. Thank you, everyone, for listening to me. It's time I give this to the man who stood by me. A man who told my mother he had no bad feelings toward me. He blamed himself, not me. Thank you, Coach," he says before handing Stanley the trophy and the prize money.

Stanley stands up and shakes Scotty's hand. "I can't even believe you did this for me. You'e a man like no other. I want to thank you for being so thoughtful. God bless you, Scotty J. Fahrenheit," he says, giving him a hug.

There isn't a dry eye in the whole place.

Buffo walks up to Stanley and shakes his hand. "I would like to offer you a job working at the senator's new employment agency. You will be the trainer for all the job coaches. Senator Ryan has agreed to triple the salary you are now receiving.

Stanley, this is an opportunity of a lifetime—one that you have proven yourself worthy of."

"I don't know what to say," Stanley remarks.

Cindy comes on stage and says to her husband, "Say yes, Honey, because we really need the money."

"Senator Ryan, as soon as your employment center is built, I would love to be the trainer for all the job coaches."

Stanton walks up to his father. "Even though Stanley and I are always in competition, I've grown to like him. Dad, if you wouldn't mind, I, too, would like to join Stanley and be employed at your new agency. What do you think?"

Judy, the senator's wife, walks on the stage and whispers in his ear. "I've never been as proud of you as I am today. For all these years, I thought that I made a mistake by marrying you. Today shows me how wrong I was."

"Gee, this is one big happy family," Buffo says. "The senator put me in charge of hiring the construction crew. We should be breaking ground sometime next week. Stanley and Stanton, be ready because I don't mess around. Bing, bang, boom, and before you know it, the place will be built," Buffo adds as the senator looks on in utter disbelief.

Just as Paul is wrapping things up, the news media arrives. A pretty newscaster comes rushing to the stage with the crew chasing behind her with their cameras. "Excuse me, is there a Scotty Fahrenheit here?" She yells.

"Buffo points to Scotty and asks, "What seems to be the problem?"

"Scotty, we're here to ask you how you took down Woodson, one of the most notorious serial killers?"

FIRED!

Scotty puffs out his chest proudly and says, "I have my irritable bowel to thank for that. If it weren't for that weightlifter dude coming into that gas station bathroom, I wouldn't be here today," Scotty says, giving the weightlifter most of the credit.

"Is it true you went to Woodson's house unarmed?" the pretty news anchor asks.

"Boss told me never go unarmed," Scotty says as Buffo tries to hide from the cameras.

"I broke the door down and chased him around with a bat. I was able to keep him down until the cops showed up and cuffed the scum bag."

"I can't believe you weren't afraid," she continues with the interview.

"Lady, with all due respect, if you knew what I've been through, you would understand."

"Feel free to tell us," she pries.

"I really don't know where to start. Maybe I'll start with working for Spinelli," he says before he notices Stanley vigorously shaking his head no.

"Actually, better yet, I got a job as a scab at the pesticide company. So the felon I worked with screwed with the hose, and I got a face and mouthful of chemicals. I almost died. Then I escaped from the hospital and wound up in the front seat of the serial killer's car.

"Well, Scotty, we just want to tell you that you are considered a hero. If it weren't for you, this man may still be out abducting people and taking lives," she says, ending the interview.

The Outrageously Ridiculous Adventures of Scotty J. Fahrenheit

People from the audience begin to come on stage and ask Scotty for his autograph. Scotty is amazed as the camera men make sure to keep the cameras rolling.

Buffo waits until Scotty is finished signing autographs before they head back to his mansion. In the limo, Scotty asks Buffo, "You must be good friends with the senator?"

"I did some favors for him, and now it's payback time. I guess you could say that I came to collect."

"You must have done something really outstanding for him to do what he promised."

"It's all about tying up loose ends," he chuckles.

Scotty asks him to explain.

"You see, Sonny Boy, in this world, you do things. Sometimes it's for yourself. Well, actually, most of the time, that's the case. Today I was in a generous mood, so I did it for someone else," Buffo explains.

"I have to admit that you are such a religious man," Scotty compliments.

"I try to live according to the Bible. I especially follow the part where it talks about an eye for an eye. Sometimes we go further, but I believe God understands."

"So you go after the bad guys?"

"There's a part in the Bible that I am really fond of," Buffo says before Scotty interrupts.

"What part is that?"

"It's where God tells anyone who hurts a child to tie a millstone around his neck and jump into the sea."

FIRED!

"Wow, that's pretty harsh," Scotty admits

"No, really it isn't. I had to deal with a few of them, and trust me, tying a millstone around their neck and throwing them into the sea would have been a better fate for them than mine."

When the limo pulls up to the gate, Buffo advises Scotty to close his eyes. "Keep um shut," Buffo says, helping him out of the limo. When Scotty is out and standing in the driveway he says, "Okay, you can open your eyes now."

In front of him is his green Valiant. But it looks a thousand times better than the last time he saw it.

"Wow, Boss! Whose car is that?"

"Don't you recognize your own car?" Tony laughs.

"That's *my* car? I thought I was never gonna get her back. How did you do it?" Scotty wonders.

"Does that really matter? Just tell me what you think?"

"She's out of this world! I can't wait to take her for a spin."

"What are you waiting for?" Buffo says, tossing him the keys.

"This must have cost you a fortune. I don't know how I can ever repay you!" Scotty says, trying to give him a hug.

"Hey, none of that emotional stuff," Buffo gently pushes him away. "Remember, we're supposed to be tough guys. You don't owe me nothing. It's me who owes you," Buffo says, patting him on the back.

"You owe me nothing, either," Scotty says. "I just can't believe you got my car back."

The Outrageously Ridiculous Adventures of Scotty J. Fahrenheit

"When I walked in the body shop, the owner was more than happy to tell me, 'no charge.' Anyway, enough about that. Get in the car and take her for a drive."

The car has been restored as a high-performance vehicle. Scotty gets in and starts it up. The car has open pipes and it sounds like a race car. As soon as he gives it a little gas, the car takes off.

After a few minutes, he comes back and tells Buffo that his life is complete, all except for one thing.

"What's missing?" Buffo asks.

"That would be Charlotte. I can't seem to get her off my mind."

"Remember what I said about loose ends?"

"Yeah."

Then go get her," Buffo orders.

"How am I supposed to do that?"

"You get in that souped-up car and find her. Don't let her say no. Do whatever it takes. Understand?"

"Yeah, I think so."

"Then what are you waiting for."

Scotty thanks Buffo and heads out. The only problem is that he has no idea where Chalotte lives. That's the only question he forgot to ask her.

***

Meanwhile, it's just about six o'clock and Charlotte's family has just finished Sunday dinner. Her father turns on the television and summons the family to the living room. "What's going on honey?" his wife asks.

FIRED!

"Sometime during the six o'clock local news, my new commercial for the firm will air. I just hope it's worth all the money I shelled out," he mumbles.

The news anchor starts with the story about Woodson. "We met the man responsible for taking down one of the most prolific serial killers of our time," she says, rolling the footage of the interview with Scotty from earlier in the day.

Both Charlotte and her sister immediately realize who it is.

"Daddy, that's Scotty!" Charlotte exclaims excitedly as her father tells everyone to be quiet so he can hear the interview.

After the footage, the news anchors agree that Scotty is a hero who just saved the life of Donny Junior and potentially other victims.

Charlotte's father is in complete shock.

"Daddy, isn't that proof that he's employed?" Charlotte cries.

"Dear, look at the suit he is wearing. I am with Charlotte, he must have a well-paying job," his wife agrees.

"I would say he might be working for the FBI," Charlotte offers.

"I must admit, that suit is a dead giveaway that spells success," her father adds.

"What's the verdict, Lawyer? Will you allow your daughter to date Scotty?"

Before he gives an answer, there is a news flash. "We are at Jamesville correctional facility with one of the guards."

The guard, just about to speak, is no other than the one Scotty gave Buffo's three hundred dollars to.

The Outrageously Ridiculous Adventures of Scotty J. Fahrenheit

"Serial Killer Woodson was found unresponsive in his jail cell with a homemade shank stuck in the back of his head. We have no reason to believe this was anything other than a suicide. My deepest condolences to all the lives this man destroyed. May everyone affected by this animal rest a little better, knowing that he will never hurt another person," he says before the network goes to a commercial.

***

Meanwhile, Scotty is busy trying to locate Charlotte. The manager of the store she works at tells him he just missed her. Scotty begs the guy to give him her address. "I would never give out any employee's information, especially after what just happened," the manager explains.

"What just happened?" Scotty says, forgetting all about Woodson.

"Haven't you been up to speed lately?"

"Let's talk about that. How can you ask that to a man whose car can practically break the speed of sound?" Scotty says before the manager walks away shaking his head.

Scotty spends hours trying to locate the love of his life. Having no luck, he makes his way home. His mother meets him as he walks in the door.

"My son, the hero. I had no idea what you did."

"What did I do?"

"Are you kidding? I watched it on the news. I had to take the phone off the hook because it won't stop ringing. Everyone is congratulating me for having such a heroic son. My only regret is that your father didn't live long enough to see his son accomplish something," her voice grows thick with emotion.

FIRED!

"Ma, my only regret is that I don't have Charlotte."

"When you go to bed at night, get on your knees and tell God all the reasons you and Charlotte should be together. Remember what you learned in Sunday School—" she asks before being interrupted.

"Do you really expect me to remember something I learned like a thousand years ago?"

"It's about God answering all our prayers. Just know God is always looking out for our best interests. Have faith that if Charlotte is the one, she will someday walk with you."

"Ma, I don't just want her to walk with me. I want her to marry me!" he says before giving his mom a hug and going to his room.

He changes into his pajamas gets down on his knees to pray.

"Dear God, thank you for all the great things you've done for me. You know how much I want Charlotte, so I won't pressure you by going on and on about it. Just one thing, God. Would it be too much to ask what you have in store for me next?"

About the Author

Carolanne Porto will be the first to tell you that she enjoys writing thrillers—novels that leave the reader shocked and perplexed.

Now she feels that it's her time to carry out her mission and uncover a highly transmittable contagion that seems to have become eradicated, one she hopes will make a comeback and become the biggest plague of all time! This particular contagion is better known as laughter, and anyone who reads the hysterical novel *Fired!* is guaranteed to become infected.

Carolanne lives in Central New York with her husband, Charles, and has owned the hometown restaurant Café 119 in Manlius, New York, since 2001. She can be contacted at sonnyp119@aol.com.

Follow Author Carolanne Porto on Facebook!

Look for the next books in the series:
Book 2: Hired!
Book 3: Wired!

CPSIA information can be obtained
at www.ICGtesting.com
Printed in the USA
BVHW042329090323
659872BV00001B/3